Red Clark o' Tulluco

Center Point
Large Print

Also by Gordon Young and available from Center Point Large Print:

Fighting Blood

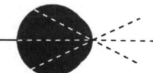

This Large Print Book carries the Seal of Approval of N.A.V.H.

Red Clark o' Tulluco

GORDON YOUNG

CENTER POINT LARGE PRINT
THORNDIKE, MAINE

First US edition: Doubleday, Doran
First UK edition: Methuen.

The text of this Large Print edition is unabridged.
In other aspects, this book may vary
from the original edition.
Printed in the United States of America
on permanent paper.
Set in 16-point Times New Roman type.

ISBN: 978-1-68324-557-5 (hardcover)
ISBN: 978-1-68324-561-2 (paperback)

Library of Congress Cataloging-in-Publication Data

Names: Young, Gordon, 1886-1948 author.
Title: Red Clark o' Tulluco / Gordon Young.
Description: Center Point Large Print edition. | Thorndike, Maine :
    Center Point Large Print, 2017.
Identifiers: LCCN 2017031116 | ISBN 9781683245575
    (hardcover : alk. paper) | ISBN 9781683245612 (pbk. : alk. paper)
Subjects: LCSH: Large type books. | GSAFD: Western stories.
Classification: LCC PS3547.O4756 R43 2017 | DDC 813/.52—dc23
LC record available at https://lccn.loc.gov/2017031116

CONTENTS

CHAPTER I

A Poke on the Nose

Three young cowboys swung from their horses in front of the marshal's office, dropped the reins, shook themselves and straightened their belts, looking up and down the dusty street as strangers do when for the first time they have come to a town that is much talked about.

"Nice peac'ble place," one murmured with an air of content, and the others grinned slyly.

As they marched into the pine-fronted little office the marshal took his booted feet off the desk and straightened himself. He eyed them quickly, noticing that they were young, dusty, and had the earmarks of range-bred boys. All wore two guns, which was not quite befitting for young punchers, but they all took off their hats in polite awkwardness and grinned with the friendliness of young pups that wanted to frolic.

The marshal cleared his throat. "What c'n I do f'r you fellers?"

"How d' do?" said the lanky red-headed boy who had walked in first.

"Umm. Howdy," said the marshal, stiff and doubtful.

"Me, I'm Red Clark of Tulluco."

7

"Umm." The marshal squinted a little the better to take a close look at Mr. Red Clark.

"An' this here is Tom Jones of Tahzo."

Tom Jones was slender, loose jointed, looked shy, and squirmed as he bobbed his tow-colored head at the marshal.

"Oh, yes. Umm," said the marshal softly, nodding. He wasn't quite sure that he liked these boys. They looked full of the devil.

"An' this here," Red Clark continued, jabbing out with a forefinger, "is Billy Haynes from Lelardo."

"Hmm-umm," said the marshal eying the short tubby boy, who had a cheery moon-shaped face and legs like a moon, too—like two new moons. Mr. Billy Haynes was plump and bow-legged.

He grinned and twitched at his hat brim, jangled his spurs in shifting from one foot to the other, and looked happy but uncomfortable.

"Well, what c'n I do f'r you-all?" the marshal asked, important and not quite favorable. The marshal was proud of his star, careful of his dignity, and suspicious that these youngsters were up to some joke.

"Well, sir," said Red, "we're strangers. We heard tell this was quite some cow country you-all have got down here."

"That there is right," said the marshal, aloofly agreeing.

"We've come to town for to have some fun. An' you know how 'tis. Folks with a bad sense o' humor sometimes put whisky in yore lemonade an' soda pop, so—"

Billy Haynes snickered, and Tom Jones grimaced as if trying to pretend that he didn't have a toothache.

The marshal cleared his throat and looked severe, but Red went on:

"My dad, he used to be sheriff of Tulluco, an' he sort o' got me in the habit of takin' off my guns an' leavin' 'em with some responsible party like the marshal or barkeep when I went into a town where I wasn't well knowed. That is, when, like now, I was just wantin' to have some fun. So me an' Billy an' Tom here, we was wonderin' if—" Red's fingers began to work at the buckles of his belts.

"Boys," said the marshal, warming up a little and sounding paternal, "you are doin' wise. Yes'ir. 'Cause this here is shore a tough town, an' them as looks for trouble don't live long. Two guns is all right for them as is on old Jake Dunham's special payroll. You-all know about Mr. Dunham, I reckon?"

He spoke with pride as if mentioning favorably the country's leading citizen.

"Yeah, you bet!"—"Shore!"—"He's well knowed about," said the boys.

The marshal nodded, approving their respectful tones. "You just leave yore guns here with me, don't get drunk, don't make no noise, behave

9

yoreselves, and nobody won't bother you." Then, impressive and paternal, "But I gotta warn you. Speak low an' step soft. They's bad men workin' f'r Mr. Dunham, an' they don't like no back talk. So speak low an' step soft."

"Huh," said moon-faced Billy Haynes, "sounds like we was goin' to church!" Then Billy looked more embarrassed than ever and blushed under his leathery tan.

"Me," said Tom Jones mildly, as if a little awed, "I've always wanted to see a real tough town."

"You'll shore as hell see 'er here!" said the marshal, impressive. "Why, even with me settin' on it, tight, the lid blows up near ever' night. Some o' Mr. Dunham's men, they take liberties. Yes'ir. Till I call 'em down."

The marshal squinted as if to show how he intimidated bad men.

"Well, as you see," Red replied, swinging his guns onto the marshal's desk, "we're quite peac'ble boys. We come to eat some, set in corners of saloons, an' read o' newspapers, an' maybe whittle a little on the hotel front porch!"

They stood by, attentive and interested, while the marshal hung their guns on pegs along the wall; then marched out.

As Red picked up the reins of his horse he said, "Now, then, you wall-eyed hombres, you, behave yoreselves. Ol' Pop in there will spank! Now f'r the corral!"

They rode at a reckless gallop right into the wide doorway of the Stage and Livery Company's barn, and a large, broad, bulky man with a big red face flung himself to one side to escape being knocked over. As it was, he stumbled over a bucket, fell, and arose swearing. He kicked the bucket to pieces, then strode back along the stalls to where the boys were swinging out of their saddles.

"Why the hell," roared the bulky man, "don't you look where you're goin'! You almost run over me!"

"Look where we're goin'?" said round-faced Billy Haynes, looking carefully at the wrathful man, noticing his ponderous belly, fat cheeks, red nose. "Huh. Maybe we did!"

"What's that? What's that?" The angered man grew redder and waved a fist. "You sawed-off measly little runt! Why, damn your soul—talk back to *me!*"

"Oh, I've sassed handsomer men 'an you," said Billy. "They couldn't help bein'!"

The angered man fairly stuttered in blurting oaths and shook both fists.

"If it's agin the law to talk to you, I'll 'pologize," said Billy, with casual toss of chubby hand. "But if 'tain't, then git to hell away from here. I don't 'sociate with folks that use bad language. Ner I don't like yore nose. It ain't purty. The color ain't what I call becomin'. Go on, git!"

11

The big man stood speechless, glared, and seemed to swell. The muscles of his thick bull-like neck tightened; the veins stood out on his wide full reddish face. He opened and closed his fists as if the fingers twitched to grasp Billy's neck and break it.

At last, as if coming to himself, he said, "Damn your soul! You ornery louse-packin' smart aleck, you! I'll skin you alive!" The big man drew back his foot and swung it; but instead of standing still to be kicked, fat little Billy Haynes jumped high in the air and drove a fist squarely to the nose that he had criticized. The big man, losing his balance more from the swing of his own foot than from the blow, went down and bumped the back of his head against the stall post. He lay there, half knocked out, peering vaguely with blank glazed eyes.

Billy pulled at his leather cuffs and waggled his fists, excited and eager to fight some more.

Tom Jones took him by the nape of the neck and pulled him back. "Pick on fellers yore size!" said Tom reproachfully. "Just s'posin' he'd fell on you—you'd be all squashed. Shamed of you! Come into a nice quiet town an' start a ruckus!"

Red Clark, standing watchfully, saw the big man's hand move up with fumbling reach toward his holster as he arose to a knee. Red spoke with menace:

"Put yore hand down, feller! You touch that gun

an' I'll plant both my heels right in yore belly. We ain't got no guns. We're peac'ble boys. Just rode in from over Tahzo way. You tryin' for to spoil our good time?"

The big man got up slowly. He seemed dazed and rubbed at his eyes with a forearm, blinking as he looked from one to another of the boys. He brushed the straw and dirt from his legs with a sort of absent-minded slaps. Then he straightened, scowled, and said slowly, deep in his throat, with many oaths:

"Just one thing about it! You goddamned whelps don't know who I am! If you want to be alive this time tomorrow—there's your hosses! Hit the leather an' go! Keep goin'! Me, I'm Jake Dunham!"

The three boys stood as if struck dumb. Billy Haynes's mouth hung wide as if trying to breathe and couldn't. Tom Jones looked as though he had got a couple of walnuts between his jaws and couldn't close them. Red Clark swayed back on his heels and said softly, "My good gosh A'mighty!"

Jake Dunham swelled up some more, glowered in a sort of pompous satisfied rage at their frank, half apologetic astonishment. He didn't have the least shadow of humor. A punch on the nose was a serious thing to the cattle king. He probably had not in forty years had one before. He cursed, warning them out of the town, out of the country, slapped his holster, gave each a full-faced glare, then swung about on his heel and strode off, breathing noisily, puffing.

Red whistled softly between his teeth, gazing after Mr. Dunham's broad back and shaking his head.

"I reckon," said Tom Jones, poking a thumb at Billy Haynes, "as how you an' me, Red, had better strangle this here little bump off a log! Why, you quarrelsome, ornery, lop-eared, turnip-faced piece o' last year's sausage, you! When bad luck it was bein' handed out, you took along yore Maw's washtub, didn't you?"

"How'd I know!" said Billy plaintively.

"Spite o' me an' Red's good manners f'r an example, you still got to go an'—"

"Yeah," said Red, "of all the folks in this here town an' country for to pick on, you got to poke Jake Dunham's nose! Why couldn't you have hit yoreself in the face an' so improved yore looks an' satisfied yore terrible fightin' instinks?"

Fat little Billy swallowed a time or two, then grinned. "I reckon I'd better go find me a rat hole an' crawl in 'er!"

"Shucks," said Red. "It's all his own fault f'r not lookin' like a proper cowman ought! So that's Jake Dunham!"

Red gazed out of the barn's wide doorway. Dunham was not in sight, but for a time Red stared as if looking at him.

Dunham was the biggest cowman in ten counties. In the loose, exaggerated gossip of the cow country it was said that Dunham held a thousand square miles of range, that a hundred punchers drew his pay, and that a good deal of it was for rooting out nesters and little outfits that tried to settle down on good grass and water. Being range-bred boys, Red and his friends did not disapprove of Dunham's reputation. They did feel disappointment in his appearance and at such a luckless meeting. It was said that he paid big wages and stood by his men, who were often reckless, lawless, fighting buckaroos.

The boys had ridden into Martinez, expecting to blow their wages joyously, then ride out and go to work for Jake Dunham. Good hands could always get a job with some one of his outfits. They had even sort of hoped to get work at the home ranch, because among other interesting things said of Dunham, it was reported that he had the prettiest daughter ever seen on the range; that rich men and big folks in the affairs of the nation came out to his ranch to vacation and go hunting; that he bossed all the politics in his part of the state, picking assessors, sheriffs, and, being president of the Cattle Men's Association, ran things with a high and heavy hand. So the feelings of the three young punchers for a few minutes were just about as if they had been old-time cloak-and-sword soldiers of fortune who in a street brawl had unknowingly kicked the King of Spain on the shins.

"Y'know," said Red reflectively, "the only thing that's really wrong with this here happenin' is that folks back home is goin' to call us a liar when we tell 'em!"

"Oh, well," said Tom Jones, taking off his hat and rumpling his hair to relieve his feelings, "it ain't our fault. Ner Billy's. If he wants to go round lookin' like a big fat slob, he's gotta expect to be mistook f'r one. An' was. Served 'im right. I bet his daughter takes after 'im, too."

"I bet he shore has got that nose up close to a lookin' glass for to see if it looks like it feels," Red suggested.

"Gosh, don't le's stand an' talk no more." Tom Jones pushed at them. "Me, I'm hungry. Le's get to the hotel an' eat."

They finished unsaddling and routed out the barn boss, who was dozing under an open shed in the corral, and gave him a talking to for letting Jake Dunham go wandering about alone and almost get run over in the barn.

When the barn boss, after the manner of barn bosses, began to talk back, they sassed him so fast and pointedly that for some moments he stood rubbing his numbed ears and looking with a sort of mystified helplessness as the three punchers walked off with the swaying, stiff-legged, spur-scraping stride of saddle-raised men.

CHAPTER II

Wanted, Dead or Alive

The boys paused in the hotel barroom for a round of drinks: that is, round and round and round—three apiece. Then, much refreshed, they went to the washroom, where tin basins stood on benches with a barrel of water near by. They sloshed water on their sunburned faces, combed their wet hair, one after another, on a horn-toothed comb fastened to a chain before a cracked, wrinkled little mirror, refolded their neckerchiefs, slapped the dust off their legs and shirts with their hats and, feeling quite spruced up, started for the dining room.

Tom Jones, thin as a rail and always hungry, impatiently led the way. It was Billy Haynes's opinion that "if Tom he went to work like he goes to eat, he'd 'a' been made foreman long ago!" Fat little Billy hobbled along after him on short bowlegs as if walking on limber stilts, and Red came last. In the hall just outside the dining room they passed a big square new mirror, and Red paused to have a good look at himself. He had seldom seen such a nice mirror. It was interesting to have a good look at himself. The other boys having hurried on, there was nobody

17

around to make fun of him. He was standing there, half furtively pawing at a cowlick of brick-red hair, when he heard a low, soft "Ss-s-s-s!"

Red jumped as if caught doing something unmanly, as a fellow usually does when found peering at himself in a looking glass, and looked up.

High overhead on the stairs stood a young woman, dark as a gypsy and pretty as a picture. She had wide brown eyes that were a little moist, as if near to tears, and her red lips were parted as if holding her breath. After a moment's staring, she smiled in a hurried sort of way, and when Red opened his mouth to say, "My good gosh!" she raised a slender finger to her lips and, bending over the banister, peered hard at him.

"Will you do something for me?" she whispered.

"Gosh A'mighty, you bet!"

"*Shh-h!* Not so loud! What is your name?"

"Me, m'am? I'm Red Clark o' Tulluco!" His tone, his look, his earnestness, seemed trying to tell her that Red Clark of Tulluco was a fellow that would take the world by the tail and whip it about his head to please a pretty girl with dark moist eyes.

She smiled as if the name pleased her, but that may have been just the way of a woman when she wants a favor, for she had perhaps never heard the name before, though it was a name pretty well known for rash devilment on some ranges.

The girl hesitated with her hand at her breast, then, anxiously, as if taking a risk, drew an envelope from her waist and looked quickly all about.

"Will you take this?" She held up the letter. "Never tell anyone? Give it to—find and give it to—" she stopped, again looking about nervously—"to Mister Walter Rodman?"

"I shore will!" said Red instantly, reaching upward.

She leaned forward, peered down at him, studying his upturned face.

"And never let my father know?"

"No, 'am!" he promised readily.

She still hesitated; then, whether or not she knew anything of the men of the range and how to tell what sort they were by the way they looked, she seemed pleased by Red's bright blue eyes, his long nose, wide mouth that seemed shaped for grins, and a kind of homely good-natured radiance that glowed on his face.

"I'll trust you!" she said softly. "And, please, oh, please, don't let anyone know!"

The letter fluttered down. Red's fingers clutched at it, pawing the air, but missed, so that it fell to the floor. As he stooped he looked up and saw her draw back with a noiseless gasp, frightened. At that moment he heard the clatter of a spurred foot coming through the swinging door.

Red slipped the letter inside of his shirt as he straightened and turned.

The newcomer was tall, dark, handsome, young, and looked like somebody of importance, with a nice new corduroy suit and the trouser legs down over tight tan boots. But the fellow looked proud and mean, and his glance at once jumped from Red's face toward the top of the stairs suspiciously.

"What are you doing here?" he demanded.

"Huh. Do you by any happenchance own this here hotel?" Red asked with bland impudence.

The fellow's glance lifted to the top of the stairs, then, "Don't act smart! Tell me, what are you doing here?"

"Me? Why, right now I'm standin' in my boots!"

The man in corduroy took a long impatient step and stood closer, frowned. "Now, listen here! I won't have any of your sass. Who were you talking to?"

"Did you hear me?"

"Yes!"

The tall dark man glanced up the stairs, then demandingly stared at Red, who jabbed a thumb across his shoulder toward the mirror and retorted amiably:

"I talk to myself like that whenever I feel like it!"

"But you were stooping over. Did you pick up something?"

"Good gosh, feller!" Red poked out a boot. "Can't a man buckle a spur strap without bein' talked to like a cow thief? An' who the hell are you, anyhow? An' if you don't own the hotel I reckon I'll make myself as much to home as I want." Red slapped a trouser pocket, making gold pieces clink. "I c'n pay!"

The man in corduroy eyed him with chill disfavor. "Smart aleck, eh?"

"Yeah?" The brick-colored hair of Red's cowlick seemed to bristle.

"You're a stranger in this town," said the fellow in corduroy, as if giving a warning as to why Red shouldn't show bad manners. "Wha's your name?"

Red grinned. "Show me yore badge first!"

The man smiled in a grim, mean, pleased way, slowly moved his hand and turned the edge of his vest. There, bright as a new star, was *Deputy Sheriff.*

Red's grin widened. He bobbed his head. "My bluff she has been called! You win. Me, I'm Red Clark of Tulluco."

"How long have you been in Martinez?"

" 'Bout an hour. An' f'r a stranger, I'm gettin' acquainted plumb fast. My horse near run over Mister Jake Dunham down to the stage barn, an' he give me a cussin' that I hope I don't f'rget

21

soon, 'cause it'll come in handy when I got feelin's to express."

"I know your kind," said the man in corduroy with a sneer. "We take the starch out of them on this range!"

"Yes'r. I'm already a lot humble. Don't I look 'er?" Red looked about as humble as a chipmunk that has been licking spilled whisky.

The man in corduroy smiled in his slow, mean, satisfied way, spread his shoulders a little, and said, "And my name is Wallace Dunham. I'm the Old Man's nephew. So, if you've stepped on his toes, I'll give you some friendly warning. Get out of town. Get out of the country. Get off the earth!"

Wally Dunham laughed. There was a kind of wicked good-nature about him. He thought that Red was a good deal more impressed and flabbergasted than Red perhaps was.

"Now, tell me, Red," he asked condescendingly, "were you talking to the Old Man's daughter just now?" Wally Dunham gestured toward the top of the stairs.

"Not that I knowed of, I wasn't!" Red was trickily trying not to be untruthful. Red was curiously honest, hated to lie. His tone was very sincere in meaning that he hadn't *known* he was talking to Jake Dunham's daughter.

"That's good," said Wally Dunham. "You meddle in the Old Man's affairs and you'll find yourself barefoot in hell! I caught a glimpse of her up there. I know she's up to tricks. But I've got a piece of news that'll take the starch out of her too!"

Wally Dunham looked pleased and sure of himself. He seemed ready to talk some more, but just then Billy Haynes poked his moon face through the swinging door and gasped with friendly excitement:

"Hey, Red, what you doin'? Come on! Tom Jones he's turned rustler. Et his steak an' drug yourn over to his plate!"

"Billy, come here an' meet a new 'quaintance o' mine," said Red. "He's dep'ty sher'ff, close relation of Jake Dunham an' ever'thing! He says f'r me to shrivel up an' blow away like I was some tumbleweed!"

Moon-faced Billy said, "Huh. They is a fam'ly likeness about the nose, ain't they?"

Wally Dunham now realized that Red had not been in the least impressed by who he was, who his uncle was, or by the bright star pinned inside of his vest. "You goddamned smart alecks'll change your tune if you stop long in this town!" said Wally, trying to be impressive and being merely angry. "Out of my way! And keep out o' my way! D'you hear?"

Billy clapped a palm behind an ear. "Hey? Speak a little louder, won't yuh?"

Wally Dunham glared, said, "Goddamned

fools!" and strode past Red and up the stairs without looking back.

Red watched him and half hoped he might hear a girl's cry for help. He would have been glad to go a-jumping. Red hazily felt that old Jake Dunham must after all be purt-near all right if a girl like that was his daughter.

Billy pulled at his sleeve. "Aw, don't take it so to heart. Folks'll like us fine when they get to know us better. Yore sort o' beauty is new an' strange to 'em, Red. Makes 'em skittish. Come on!"

After supper they went into the hotel barroom for another round of drinks. It being the supper hour, not many people were there. Red edged up to where the bartender was wiping glasses and asked, "Join us?"

The bartender grinned. "I'd git fired if I ever discouraged folks in spendin'." He poured himself a drink out of a special bottle. "Here's how, boys!"

"Have another 'n," said Red. "An' I wonder could you tell me where I c'n find a feller named Walt Rodman?"

The bartender said in a mild paternal way, "Yo'-all are nice boys, but I got to be drunker'n I ever git to laugh."

Red said earnestly, "Wha's the matter? I ain't tryin' f'r to be funny. I'm askin' serious."

"Yeah?" The bartender studied Red's face. "He a friend o' yourn, maybe?"

"Nope. He ain't. But a party asked me for to look 'im up an' sort o' say howdy."

"Umm-hmm," said the bartender, putting a bottle on the bar. "Have one on the house. If I knowed where I c'd find Walt Rodman, I'd be tellin' it to the sheriff. Look over there behind you. She ain't been up more'n half an hour."

Red twisted his head across his shoulder, then turned about, stopped short, sort of gasped. With swinging stride he crossed to the wall and stood before the big poster, still glistening with undried ink.

$5000 REWARD
For
Walt Rodman
Wanted
Dead or Alive!

In smaller type it was stated that Walt Rodman was wanted for the murder of Jim Cummings, Charley Poe, and Lou Wain.

Red whistled in surprise. "Gosh A'mighty!"

A description was printed below. Walt Rodman weighed about 150 pounds, stood 5 ft. 9 in., was aged 26, had blue eyes, brown hair, was well educated, knew the country as well as any man in it. The warning was given that he would shoot on sight. Persons knowing or hearing about him were advised to communicate at once with the sheriff or with Jake Dunham.

Red peered in astonishment, shook his head, remembering the dark moist-eyed girl. Jake Dunham's daughter. Could she have gone and somehow taken up with a plumb bad fellow? He called Tom Jones and Billy Haynes over to have a look.

"Five thousand dollars," said Tom. "I'd buy me a hotel an' marry the cook!"

"Shucks," said Billy. "I'd buy the world an' put me a fence around it!"

"Maybe Dunham would forgive us some o' our sins if we caught 'im?" Tom suggested, not very sincerely.

Red led the way back to the bar and planked down a gold piece. "I reckon he's purt-near what folks call a killer!"

"Nope," said the bartender, making glasses and bottle slide into place. "He ain't. Not what you call naturally. But he's been right smart riled. I reckon you boys are strangers, huh?"

"We was a couple o' hours ago."

"Walt, he's well knowed in these parts. Yes'r. 'Cept f'r the time he was back East gittin' edycated, he growed up in this here country. An' if you ask me, I'd say he's goin' be mighty hard to catch." The bartender waved an arm toward the poster. "He sprinkled some lead in a couple more fellers this afternoon that ain't dead yet, so they didn't get their names printed."

" 'S afternoon!"

"You boys must 'a' kep' yore ears in yore pockets!"

"We just rode in 'fore supper!"

"Tell us about it," said Red, leaning forward on the bar.

"They's a lot to tell, an' us barkeeps ain't surposed to—"

"Have another drink," Red urged.

"Thanks. Y'see Walt, he's been round town here for about ten days, lookin' sort o' glum an' unsoc'ble. Long about noon he lit out with some folks a-chasin' 'im. 'Cordin' to what I hear, they split the party to head 'im off, but he doubled back an' got clean away. So them posters has been printed an'll be plastered all over the country."

"What'd he done?"

"You-all are strangers," said the bartender tolerantly. He pushed out the bottle. "On the house. Walt knows the country like I know the bumps in my bed. An' he's got friends." The bartender again waved a hand toward the poster. "Jim Cummings, Poe, an' Lou Wain—they was thought to be pretty good men with a gun. Walt, he knocked 'em over this afternoon, the which has made old Jake some fretful."

"Humm," said Red, eying the poster and putting

his hand to his shirt where something rustled faintly under his fingers. " 'Tain't manners to be cur'us, but I'm just itchin' all over f'r to know what the ruckus was about."

The bartender picked up the glasses, wiping the bar. He shook his head like a wise man who is going to keep his mouth shut; then, with confidential hunch of shoulder and twist of mouth:

"Fact is, Son, nobody 'pears to know just *what* percipitated the little doin's"—a hand waggled at the poster—"you've just read about. But they is an old quarrel 'tween Walt and Jake Dunham."

The bartender dropped his voice and looked warily about.

"You-all bein' strangers, you really ought maybe to know. Ever'body else in the country does! Y'see, the Double X outfit, an' near all the other Dunham brands, used to b'long to the Dunham and Rodman Cattle Company. Dunham and Old Man Rodman, they was pardners from the time they was kids. An' unlike most pardners, they was mighty good friends an' never had no fusses. Well, sir, they made 'em a will, each leavin' the other near all of his holdin's. It's done lots o' times, y'know, 'cause if one pardner dies an' the heirs grab off their share, sellin' out—why it just naturally busts things all up. O' course, each expected the other for to take good care

28

o' his relations, an' all that. It was just like one fam'ly, so to speak."

The bartender glanced about and dropped his voice still lower. He looked furtively from side to side as he hurried his words, trying to tell it all in one breath:

"Then one day old Rodman's body, it was found on the road with some forty-fives in him, an' young Walt having had a quarrel with his dad over losin' some beef money at poker, folks sort o' thought things, though he wasn't what you call downright suspicioned.

"But folks begun to say that Walt he said old Jake Dunham hisself had done it, which wasn't no way for to talk. Jake's got his faults, but shooting folks in the dark or when they ain't lookin' ain't one of 'em! Naturally, old Jake then wouldn't give Walt a dime. Jake, he's got some purty high-handed notions, but sure as hell's knee deep, he's honest—'cordin' to his notions of what honesty is!—an' you c'n just better bet he never wanted old Rodman to die. They was old-timers together, an' just like a right hand and a left hand to a feller's body.

"That was about three 'r four year ago. Young Rodman he went away. Not much was heard o' him till about two weeks ago when he come to town. Late yesterday, Jake an' some o' his folks come. I don't know the ins an' outs o' what happened, but the first thing anybody knowed,

Walt Rodman was leavin', and Tig Burns an' some other boys was out after 'im. Them there"— again a hand waggled at the poster—"had the bad luck to catch up with Walt! So jus' you keep yore mouths shut an' don't let on I've told you."

"Tig Burns?" said Red. "That feller!"

"Yeah!" said Tom Jones. "I shore have heard o' him!"

"Gee gosh!" Billy murmured, and left his mouth hanging open.

The bartender looked at them with half closed eyes and nodded significantly. "Maybe ain't the greatest man with a gun that ever lived, but none has lived so far that ever drawed agin 'im!"

Red looked moodily at the bartender and was tempted to ask about certain stories he had heard of this Tig Burns, but his fingers absently felt of the letter inside his shirt and brought his attention to another subject.

"How long ago did you say it was knowed about this Walt killin' them fellers?" he asked.

"Not more'n an hour 'r a little more ago, I reckon."

Red grunted meditatively. The dark gypsy-like girl must have given him the letter without knowing that Walt Rodman was a fugitive.

Men from the dining room were now crowding in for their drinks and talking in low, quiet, tense tones, eying the poster. The bartender moved along the bar, scattering glasses.

"My gosh, Red," said Tom Jones, "you look like this here Rodman's doin's was some o' yore concern!"

"Maybe that's how I feel."

"Was the feller that asked you to look him up an' say howdy a good friend o' yourn?" little Billy inquired.

Red eyed the bland moon-face. "Yes'r, in a way. I'd do most anything f'r to have that party be a friend o' mine!"

"Aw, come on, Red." Billy pulled at his arm. "Don't look so like you was gettin' the bellyache. Le's go somewhere an' have some fun. Me, I feel lucky. I'd like some poker."

CHAPTER III

With His Own Gun!

It was dark when they came out of the hotel barroom, but the street was lighted by the blazing doorways of saloons and gambling houses.

Martinez was a pretty good-sized town for the cow country and felt important because it sat at the end of a railroad's feeder. The enterprising merchants had built board sidewalks to keep mud from the winter rains out of their stores. Hitching rails lined the street.

Right at the dead center of the main cross streets a windmill pumped water into a trough that was always overflowing.

Now and then a party of men galloped in, returning from the hunt for Walt Rodman, got off their horses, and went clattering into saloons or restaurants, where they whistled in amazement at the new posters.

Five thousand dollars was sure some money. Though the reward notice was signed by the sheriff, everyone knew that Jake Dunham was putting up the money. Anyhow, Dunham owned the county; some said the state, too.

Red and his friends poked their heads into one gambling place after another, until they came to the Silver Dollar. It was wide and roomy and looked like a nice place, with rows of bottles behind the long bar, and every kind of a gambling layout from a crap table to the Old Army Game, with the roulette wheel clicking amid the rattle of chips; and a fat, squint-eyed man frowned down from the faro lookout.

The Silver Dollar was not crowded. Its barn-like space was intended to take care of the swarming punchers that rode in after the spring, and especially the fall, round-up. Punchers didn't like cramped quarters where they were taking their fun any more than where they did their work. So now the Silver Dollar looked almost lonely with only some fifteen or twenty men scattered about.

Red and his friends had a drink, leisurely looked about, sized things up, and strolled toward the roulette wheel. They dribbled a little money on the layout by way of experimenting with their luck. It was bad. They dropped a dollar or two on the crap table, and lost.

Red wasn't in a mood for gambling. Tom Jones, not being lucky, didn't care much about it; but Billy Haynes had a great weakness for poker. His moon-mask of a face was just as unreadable as any card shark's expressionless stare, and Billy had the nerve of a ring-tail baboon which, at least on the range, is said to look particularly innocent when it "ain't."

Billy walked over to a table where five men sat with hat brims pulled low, rather tensely playing poker and betting tall stacks of chips. Three of them were punchers, one a townsman, and the other had the neat clothes, the long white fingers, the washed-out, lean, half-sneering face of the professional tin-horn. As this fellow raked in a good-sized pot he raised his eyes, giving Billy a careful look; and, like nearly everyone else who gazed into Billy's round bland face, misjudged him.

"Want a hand?" asked the tin-horn.

"Don't mind 'f I do," said Billy, poking a hand into his pocket.

With shift and scrape of chairs a place was made, and Billy edged up to the round table, sitting next to the tin-horn, who had his back to the wall. Billy bought himself twenty dollars' worth of chips, pushed up his hat instead of pulling it forward like the others, grinned sociably, and seemed innocent. After a half-dozen hands the men began to eye him with slow, studied, and not wholly favorable glances. He was a hard one to figure. He was pretty sure to hold good cards when they thought he didn't; and if he didn't have them, his round, plump, good-natured face had a way of looking as though he did. And just as sure as somebody thought he was bluffing, he wasn't.

"Say, yo're so lucky," said one of the cowboys

with a sort of friendly irritation, "that if folks was to dig you a grave I bet they'd find a gold mine!"

"Anybody try to dig me a grave," Billy answered smiling, "I hope they find 'emselves some lead!"

Tom Jones, finding Red sort of moody and not like himself, moseyed about like he was lost, and finally hovered about the roulette table, playing zeros.

Red had his mind full of thoughts about the gypsy-like girl and Walt Rodman. She had given him her secret, so he couldn't talk to anybody, not even his friends. Next to a crazy rashness when angered, Red had a very stern sense of dependability. When he thought something ought to be done, he was pretty likely to do it; and even if he had no idea of ever finding Walt Rodman, he had no idea at all of ever telling anybody about Jake Dunham's daughter. He edged over to near the end of the long bar and stood with his back to it and rested on his elbows. Instead of looking about, most of the time he stared absentmindedly at a knot hole.

A lean, slope-shouldered, weary-looking old-timer came along, eyed Red for a moment, then started by with a backward look about the room. He stumbled on the toe of Red's boot.

Red, as if awakened, said quickly, " 'Xcuse me, mister. My feet is some troublesome, even when I'm sober—like now!"

The old-timer paused and looked Red over again, quite as if he hadn't seen him before; then in a quiet weary hopeless sort of tone asked, "You ain't one o' Dunham's new men?"

"Nozir. An' what's more—" Red grinned, half hesitating, not quite sure whether or not to mention the little unpleasant meeting with old Jake Dunham—"I reckon it ain't likely I'll ever be ridin' for the Double X. 'Pears like I ain't lucky."

"So?" asked the old-timer.

"Have a drink?" Red suggested. "I just need me one more, an' maybe two, for to get up courage enough to tell the truth."

"Sure," said the weary-looking man, glancing at Red's waist and hips and noticing that he was without a gun, but seeing that the marks of belts and guns were on his cow-leather chaps.

They had the drink. Red, with much good-nature, told the truth about having nearly run over Mister Dunham and how Mister Dunham cussed, and how little Billy Haynes—"that there baby-faced shrimp settin' 'cross over there in the poker game"—jumped up like a rubber ball on the bounce and poked Mister Dunham on the nose.

But the old-timer didn't smile. He looked with sad-eyed calmness at Red, then gazed at Billy and nodded.

"I knowed you was a stranger. Nobody as ain't

'd never say ' 'Xcuse me' to ol' Frank Hollar."

"Yeah? What'd Mister Hollar ever do?" Red asked sympathetically.

Old Hollar looked about; then, with a kind of hopeless tone, like that of a man whose spirit was broken, said, "Me, I had a homestead with good water back up agin the hills. With some cows. Ol' Jake Dunham, he offered me the choice between sellin' at his figger or fightin'. Me, I said I'd fight."

"Then Tig Burns come—him an' some men. He set there cool an' easy. He talked. He said Dunham had give orders that I wasn't to be hurt if I showed reason. I wouldn't budge an inch. He drawed. I wore two guns them days. But he broke my right arm. I whipped out the other gun. He smashed my left shoulder. Then, when I picked myself up, he laughed in his col' mean way, an' he said his orders was not to hurt me more'n could be helped on account o' me havin' been good friends with ol' Rodman onct. So now would I sell at the figger Mr. Rodman offered, or did I want my knees busted too? Me, I sold. I been laughed at ever since. My arms, they is all stiff an' crooked."

Hollar waggled his arms at his side, peering hard at Red as if expecting to see him smile.

Plainly, the old fellow had had his head turned a bit by his troubles, was just the least little bit loco in a sad sort of way. Red rather doubted the story. He didn't doubt the meanness of Tig Burns, and so said, "Umm. I hear this Tig Burns is good with a—"

"Good? *Good?* He's plumb bad! They ain't a drop o' blood in his veins that ain't as bad pisen as a rattler carries in its fangs! He couldn't never a-worked f'r the Double X when ol' Rodman was alive. Nosir."

"Me, I've heard about this feller Burns from the time I was big enough to have ears. They say he c'n outshoot anything or anybody that wears guns."

"Son," said Hollar, "that there is so. He can shoot. Why, I've seen him hang a whisky bottle by a string five feet from the floor, back off ten yards 'r a little more, cut the string with the first shot, an' smash the fallin' bottle before it hit the floor! What chanct has an hones' man got agin that sort o' shootin'?"

"Yeah, so I've heard tell," said Red, unimpressed. "But, y'know, he knows that bottle ain't shootin' back. Now, you take, f'r instance, that kid over there playin' poker— with the baby face. He ain't no great shakes of a shot—not at bottles 'r old cans. Out campin', if we want meat, we don't send Billy to look f'r a deer. But he shows up mighty well when anybody starts shootin' at him, like now an' then some hoss thieves has done. He's calm but inter-rested an' cheerful. I wonder, does this

Burns feller do so good if somebody shoots first?"

Old Hollar shook his head regretfully. "Nobody can. He's watchful, an' quicker 'n chain lightnin'. Ever'body's scairt o' him. I don't blame 'em none. I'm scairt myself. He shows off sometimes when he's been drinkin'. Jus' wants to keep folks good an' scairt. An' they are!"

Red said nothing but let his hands drift to his hips. From the time he could toddle he had been gun-trained by the grim and deadly sheriff of Tulluco, who figured that being able to shoot quick and straight was the only way to command respect among desperadoes. Desperadoes had eventually killed the sheriff. But they had done it from behind.

Red was a lot better hand with a gun than a wild, reckless young fellow had any business to be. It gave him a rather exuberant overconfidence; and if he kept out of bad messes it was only because he was downright honest and had a strong sense of justice. All of his instincts and sympathies were, no doubt owing to his father's training, on the side of the law.

Young as he was, Red had learned that he had to be angry before he was at his best with a gun; and the madder he got, the faster and straighter he could shoot. He seldom got mad, which was a good thing, because he didn't have a lick of sense when he was. His sun-tanned hide was packed full of impudence, but of the good-natured kind.

"Well," said Red, lifting a hand toward the new reward poster, "young Rodman, if you b'lieve what you read, must be plumb good, too. Maybe *some* folks took pains not to be where they'd have to try an' stop 'im. Hmm?"

Hollar gazed at the poster. "He ain't a bad boy, Walt ain't. I've knowed him since he was a little bit of a shaver. They say he come down on them fellers Injun fashion. Shootin' from under the neck of his hoss. He c'n ride an' he c'n shoot. They killed his boss, but he rode off on one o' theirs."

"Quite some reward, that there."

Old Hollar snorted. "Make it fifty thousand, an' they'd never catch Walt. He's got friends!" The bright glow in the old man's eyes made it clear that he, too, was one of them. "An' he knows this here country—knows places back up in the mount'ins these valley punchers never heard of."

"Think Burns could go up again 'im?"

Old Hollar nodded slowly and waggled his arms again. "The way Tig c'n shoot ain't human. Uh—here he comes now!"

Tiger Burns, with a pair of Double X killers at his heels, paused at the door, looking through, seeing who was there, sizing them up, before he came in.

It was just the instinctive precaution of long habit. According to the stories that were told, there was quite a time in Burns's life when he could not walk the streets of a town. He had been an outlaw. Now he was under the protective employment of Jake Dunham, but a killer still. So always he paused warily before passing through a doorway, and glanced to the right and left with darting black eyes.

Burns was not quite as tall as the average man, but chunky, muscular, with a kind of gliding, cat-like smoothness in his movements. His hands were oddly small for a man of his weight, and they were as black as his sunburned face, for he never wore gloves. Good reason why. He didn't earn his pay by letting a rope burn through his hands, and gloves slow up a man's gun play. He was a half-breed of some sort, about forty or a little more. The name Burns was supposed to have been one he had taken when his own got too well and unfavorably known. He liked range finery, which some people said had not always been come by honestly. He might wear bright silk shirts, and a tall broad hat weighted down with a band that was heavy with silver, a buckskin vest embroidered with colored beads, and long silver spurs that trailed rowels as big as dollars. His chaps were fancy-stitched with long rows of silver conchas, for he never did any cow work. But his guns were old long-barreled single-action forty-fives. And though he did not wear gloves, he did wear long stamped-leather cuffs.

He was black as the Jack of Spades, with a bony square face and lank straight black hair that hung down over his ears but was evenly trimmed. His eyes were small, deep-set, with the look in them of a black-eyed weasel's, and his thin lips twisted nervously, now as if about to grin, now as if tasting something bitter. And like all killers, he was vain, cruel, with a curious mixture of audacity and timidity—such as dangerous wild beasts have.

Tiger Burns and the two men with him turned to the bar and had a drink; then the Tiger, with his eyes fixed on Red, came along back toward him and Hollar.

"Me," said Red half to himself, "I guess this is where I get word to git outa town, the same bein' sent by the Dunhams, old Jake, an' young Wally. An' do I go? Maybe so."

But as Burns came up he stopped short and turned his dark hard eyes on old Hollar, spoke with a sour sneer, contemptuously:

"Bellyachin' some more, hunh?"

Old Hollar, completely intimidated and bluffed, spoke humbly:

"Jus' havin' a drink with this here young feller."

Burns moved his head as if a look at Red weren't worth the trouble of making his whole body turn, gave him a sidelong glance, staringly. "New kid, hunh? You workin' for the Old Man?"

"Nope."

"Oh," said Tig Burns between his teeth, "you give short answers, hunh? Know who I am?"

"Yep."

"You know who I am? You don't act like it!"

"What you want me to do? Fall down in a fit?"

Burns's head moved with a little backward jerk, and he said ominously: "I'm used to bein' spoke to respectful!" He frowned in a way that he knew had frightened any number of men older than this boy, tough men, bad men.

"Me, too!" said Red.

"F'r less 'an your snippiness," said Tig Burns, who evidently had had many drinks that evening, "I've nicked men's ears!" Burns was in an ugly mood. Walt Rodman had got away from him and left some dead men to show the way he had gone. "If you ain't workin' f'r the Double X, what the hell you doin' in town here, anyhow?"

"Spendin' some wages an' mindin' my own business."

"Yes, an' it's my business to ask strangers theirs, see? Where's your gun?" Burns flipped a hand toward Red's hip. "Somebody take it away from you, heh?"

"Where I come from," said Red, flushing a little, "folks that are just out to have some fun take off their guns when they come to town."

Burns sneered. "Huh. Safer, hunh? Where the hell did you come from?"

"Me, I'm Red Clark o' Tulluco."

"Oh-ho-ho. Tulluco, huh. So you are Red Clark o' Tulluco. Huh-huh." Tig Burns stepped back and spit on the floor. Then he smiled, showing his teeth. They were bright white small teeth, more like a cat's than a man's. He spoke with a drawling sneer. "I've heard o' Tulluco. Un-hunh. Used to be a wall-eyed lousy sheriff o' Tulluco by the name o' Clark, Red Clark too. Some relation o' yourn, maybe, huh?"

Red did not answer, being instantly infuriated. The sort of anger that made a wild fighting fool of him was beating at his heart. He knew that the next time anybody ever pried his guns off him in this man's town would be with a crowbar, after he was dead. When Red was thoroughly angered he was likely to do any crazy thing. He swallowed hard, feeling choked.

Burns saw and was amused. "Whatever become o' that old devil, anyhow, hunh?" He spoke with the long-drawn sneer of one who isn't asking for information, but to be disagreeable.

"You're talkin' about my Dad!" Red's voice was low and husky. He pushed the words through a tight throat, and they were scarcely above a whisper.

"Well, now, ain't that just too bad!" said Burns, pleased. "Why you s'pose I give a damn whose Dad he was? Or who your mother was? Or whether 'r not you had a mother?"

Red growled, "Goddamn yore soul!"

44

"Huh-huh-huh!" Burns lifted his head, grinning. "If you're just honin' to make any corrections on my remarks, maybe ol' Hollar here'll loan you his gun. His arms bein' sort o' crooked an' stiff, he only uses a gun these days for to crack hisself walnuts!"

The two men who had come in with Burns now passed by on their way to the roulette table, but paused for a moment, grinning. They saw that Burns was trying to have a little of his sort of fun.

"What's the matter, Tig?" one asked. "Gettin' yoreself a little raw meat for to chaw on?"

"Tig, he don't never even take the trouble for to spit out the bones," said the other, halfway addressing Red. "He jus' chews 'em up an' swallers 'em!"

"Nothin' here but a cripple an' a shypoke!" Burns's tone seemed to invite his friends to go on and leave him alone to insult the cripple and shypoke as he pleased, without any help from them. And they went on, grinning.

"Now, 'f I remember right," said Burns, sarcastic, "this here Sher'ff Clark o' Tulluco had sort o' got hisself the repytation o' bein' sudden lightnin' on the draw, hunh?"

Every word and intonation indicated Burns's contemptuous disbelief in Sheriff Clark's reputation. Red's neck settled down on his shoulders. He looked straight into the black eyes of Tiger Burns. Red's hot blood seemed fairly to

45

froth through his veins and hum in his ears. It was the insult, the sneer, the studied offensiveness of this dark, murderous bully that made him furious—these, and the feeling of being unarmed and helpless.

"Yore Dad, eh?" Burns grinned, prodding Red, tormenting him. "I was down in that there bum country o' Tulluco 'long about the time some fellers held up the Tulluco bank, shot up the town, an' walked off. 'Pears like I sort o' remember this here Dad o' yourn kep' hisself hid under a bed till after they was gone. Then he struts out an' says as how they was lucky he wasn't in town at the time. 'Pears like he makes the bluff o' straddlin' a hoss an' strikin' out after 'em. Must've found 'em, 'cause he never come back! Found somebody as was a little quicker'n him, hunh?"

"He was shot in the back!" said Red tensely, with no more sound than a whisper.

"You're a liar!" Burns snarled. "Jus' tryin' to cover over the ol' four-flusher's repytation. He'd go out an' shoot men from some hidin' place, then come back an' say he drawed first, fair an' square! Him an' yore mother too was dirty, ornery, sneakin' ol' thievin'—"

Red went through the air as if thrown. Tiger Burns, with startled jerk of swift hands, reached toward his guns, slung low on his hips with the holsters tied down. Before he touched them,

46

Red's uplifted knee caught him in the belly. Burns's gulping groan was loud as a shout, and doubled up with pain he lurched forward. His outthrust face met Red's knotted knuckles in an uppercut that fairly straightened Burns's body. Dizzy, with the breath knocked out of him and his head swimming, yet the gunman still instinctively groped toward the heavy wooden handles of his forty-fives. But Red was all over him like a wildcat on a dog. Burns knew nothing of fighting except with guns. Perhaps in his whole life had never used a fist. And Red was just as much of a madman as if he had broken out of a lunatic asylum. He smashed right and left, with fists, with elbows, with knees; he butted and kicked and gouged. He blinded Burns's eye, cut his mouth on the catlike teeth, drove a knee into his groin, knocked his head this way and that, all in a whirlwind flurry—expecting to be shot and not caring.

Burns outweighed the puncher by fifty pounds, was chunky, solid on his feet, and though he had probably never in his life been struck in the face before, he would not go down. He reeled and staggered, dizzily; spit blood and curses, scarcely struck back at all, but fumbled desperately for his guns.

Men all over the barroom leaped up, staringly, and stood in their tracks. It was hard to believe their eyes. Deep down in their hearts they were a little glad to see Burns get a thrashing, but not for a moment could they feel that the fight would have any other ending than the sound of a gun and the spraddling fall of the young red-headed stranger.

Burns's right hand, with the instinct of twenty and more years' practice, whipped up a gun, pulling high to clear the long barrel; but one of Red's fists smashed him on the ear, and the other hand, with a twisting wrench, fastened on the gun, jerking it from Burns's fingers. Almost simultaneously, Burns's left gun cleared its holster and was fired blindly, burning the inside of Red's chaps. Red had torn the gun from Burns's fingers with a hold that was upside-down for shooting, but he whaled Burns over the bare head, striking as if with a hammer. Tiger Burns went down with a bleeding gash on his head and lay as quiet as if lead had been poured into his heart.

Most people thought of Red as a mild, peaceable, good-natured boy; others knew that he was the next thing to a lunatic when he got going. He did not have the least notion that the fight was over simply because he had dropped Burns. With a lurching pounce he grabbed Burns's other gun off the floor, gave both a pinwheel spin to try their balance that was just as fast and neat as any man had ever seen; then he jumped aside, backing up to the bar, and faced the crowd over leveled cocked guns.

Now it happened that, at the very moment Red had jumped Burns, another commotion had started over at the card table, where the tin-horn gambler, having dropped a few chips to the floor, had—in leaning over to pick them up—taken the opportunity to slip the end of an ace between Billy Haynes's chap-covered leg and the seat of the chair.

Just as Red was bracing himself to jump at Tiger Burns the tin-horn, drawing a derringer, had declared Billy a thief and stood up, pointing at the card under Billy's leg; and the innocent Billy gaped, looking down at it, and was as much astonished as if he had found a rattlesnake in his lap.

Then Billy slowly arose with his hands up, facing the gambler.

Fights were common in Martinez. It was the way of the town to let each man kill his own snakes, and bystanders were supposed to get out of the way however they could.

Young as Red was, he had had to look through smoke lots of times to see what was going on, and though he might act the fool, or worse, he wasn't easily rattled. He saw Billy with his hands up. He saw the gambler with a derringer in his hand, half absently pointed at Billy, while the gambler's startled face was turned toward Red.

"Drop that pepper-shaker!" Red called at him.

The derringer fell from the gambler's hand.

"An' you, all you!" Red called, moving the guns. "Outa yore chairs! On yore toes! Come a-climbin' with hands up!"

Now it happened that Tom Jones had spun about at the roulette table and started across the barn-like room to help Red climb the fellow, whoever he was, that had started a fight with Red. Then Burns dropped, and Red, over leveled guns, was putting the hands of the crowd in the air.

Tom Jones didn't hesitate. He didn't know what the row was over and didn't care. If Red had started something, it was for him to chip in and see it through. Tom grabbed a gun from the holster of the man nearest him, backed off, stepping backwards toward the bar to get alongside Red, and yelled, "That goes! Everybody up! All the way! This here's ser'us!"

Explosive shouts of "Hold up!" broke out, half affirmingly, but with a kind of questioning.

"No, 'tain't!" Red called. "But they's goin' to be some funerals if anybody tries to stop us! We come in here an', bein' peac'ble, left our guns with the marshal. Tig Burns, he wanted a row an' he got it. An' any more o' you hellbenders as wants it—speak up!"

"That goes!" Tom Jones echoed. "Come on, Billy!"

"Not till I get what's comin' to me!" said the imperturbable Billy.

The tin-horn, known as Nifty Steve—whether from his clothes or because of his nimble fingers—had promptly dropped the derringer at Red's command and put his hands as near toward heaven as he was ever likely to get them.

And Billy said to him, "You're bankin' this here game! You cash me my chips before I go a step!"

"I can't! This here is hands up!"

"Cash me my chips, doggone you!"

"He'll shoot!" Nifty Steve shouted. Perhaps he was using an excuse not to pay up, perhaps he was really afraid of the look in Red's eyes.

Red crouched slightly with elbows out and almost shoulder high, and he seemed to be watching in every direction at once. His muscles were tense. His wide mouth had a down-drooping twist on one side that was like the snarl of a terrier ready to bite.

"Hey, Red!" Billy called with plaintive insistence. "Make this here feller put down his hands so he can cash me my chips!"

"Settle that game!" Red ordered.

"Come on," said Billy. "Hurry up. An' I don't go till I get me ever' dime!"

Red edged back a step at a time toward the door. Tom Jones moved along with him but kept a sharp lookout behind Red, where two or three men were standing peaceably with hands half up. The bartender was half over his own bar, leaning forward, looking down, scarcely able to believe his own eyes, for there lay Tiger Burns, just the same as dead, knocked out cold by a young and unarmed puncher.

Then old Hollar lifted up his voice in a shrill, gleeful shout. "Me," he said, addressing the men there, all of whom knew his story, "Me, I've lived to see Tig Burns get it! With his own gun—after he shot an' missed."

He ended his little speech with a shrill yell, as if half drunk. He was a simple, slightly crazed old fellow. Burns had broken his spirit, made him crawl, and take the bantering and bullying of other men.

Nobody there liked Burns well enough to take up his fight, not after the way he had been licked. They couldn't help but admire Red, who now, very plainly, was not trying to do anything but hold the Tiger's friends in check until he and his friends could get away. Burns didn't have the sort of friends who were eager to take up his fight. They knew he was a mean dog of a man, a bully that liked to torment people who were afraid of him. Evidently Red hadn't been much afraid. Most of the men who held their hands up, none of them very unwillingly, felt more like praising Red than shooting at him.

Billy Haynes, chubby, bow-legged and unhurried, tramped away from the poker table as he rammed gold pieces down into his pockets.

Fat-faced little Billy didn't know how to get excited. He called toward the men, "I didn't take nothin' 'cept what was mine, won fair an' square. An' don't none o' you believe I stole that card!"

As they neared the door, Tom Jones, with a wary look all about to make sure the gun he held would not longer be needed, laid it on the bar and shouted vaguely toward the man from whom he had taken it:

"Thanks f'r the loan of 'er, mister!"

The next moment Tom whipped it up again. Two men with hurrying stride came through the doorway and stopped short, astounded, looking over the room wide-eyed. One was Wally Dunham, sort of fine-looking in his new corduroy; the other was old Jake Dunham, big and broad and powerful. He opened his mouth to shout, and his mouth stayed open, silent in a wide gasp, utterly dumbfounded, for he was looking squarely into Tom Jones's gun.

"Don't look round, Red!" said Tom. "I got 'em! March right along in here, you fellers. With your food-grabbers up—like you was askin' for more! The which you'll shore as hell get if you don't ac' peac'ble!"

"What the hell!" said Wallace Dunham, lifting his arms reluctantly.

"Good guess you made!" Billy shouted at him.

"Hold up?" old Jake asked. No doubt about it,

he was more astonished than afraid. He didn't look afraid at all; but slowly, like a fellow who knows what is best, half lifted his arms with palms out.

Red sidled off toward a corner, in that way getting into line with the Dunhams without turning his back to the men clustered about the tables out in the big room.

"Hold up nothin'!" said Red. "Ask the barkeep f'r perticulars. We're just sayin' good-bye to some folks as was rude. An' it oughta inter-rest you, both o' you, to know that these here two guns I'm holdin' come off yore pet killer, Tig Burns. Took barehanded!"

"Yeah!" said Billy, more earnest of tone than his words sounded. "We been a lot misunderstood, Dunham. Honest, I didn't know it was your nose I poked down there in the barn, 'r I wouldn't 've done it!"

"You've killed Tig Burns!" said Jake Dunham.

"Hope so!" Red answered promptly. "An' if, when he comes to, he still wants to live, you tell 'im to put a piece in the paper 'pologizin' for them remarks he made about my Dad, an' Maw, too! That goes. 'R I'll make him bite hisself to death. That's how I feel! An' nearly always I do like I feel I ought. Out o' the door, boys." Then, to the room at large, "We ain't stealin' no horses, fellers. We're just tradin'. Ourn's in the corral— good ones. But 'pears like we're goin' to have to

54

hurry some. An' if anybody wants to try to stop us, now's the time!"

Red stood in the doorway. Tom and Billy went through it on the run to pick out the best-looking horses they could in the starlight.

Men shifted about uneasily. They were under the glowering eyes of old Jake. It made some difference that Jake, too, had his hands up respectfully. Also, if these fellows were going to take horses—that made a difference. But nobody risked the draw. Red looked like a man who knew how to handle guns, and the fact that they were Tig Burns's guns, scored with notches undercut along the barrels, had something to do with the willingness of the men to stand quiet.

From outside, Billy called, "Come along, Red. Here you are. Rifles 'n' ever'thing!"

He and Tom Jones had mounted and held a horse for Red right up at the edge of the sidewalk.

Red backed out of the door, going slow, with no sign of haste. Men could see him vanishing backwards through the oblong blob of light that fell through the doorway. He, turned, ramming onc gun into his waistband, made a jump and landed in the saddle.

"To the marshal's office!" he said, driving in the spurs. "I don't leave no town without my guns. Might look as though somebody had took 'em off me an' said, 'Git out!' "

As their horses bounded off, old Jake Dunham

threw up his arms still higher, but his hands were knotted into fists, and he shook them wildly.

"A fine lot o' yeller dogs, you fellers!" he roared. He was remembering the punch on the nose little Billy had given him. "Get 'em! A thousand dollars—two thousand f'r each one you drop!"

Men made sounds of astonishment and stirred, touched with excitement. Two thousand was a lot of money. A man-chase is always fun on the range.

In the wildness of his suspicious anger, Dunham added, "They're in with Walt Rodman! Friends o' his'n! Part o' his outlaw gang he's got together to rustle our cows! An' you're lettin' 'em steal your horses!"

Men with hasty strides and clicking rattle of spurs pressed into a close circle about the unconscious body of Tig Burns, some stooping down, bending close, looking hard, and running their hands vaguely across his breast.

Some said, "Dead as a door knob!" and others, "He ain't!"

Old Jake pushed at them. "Tig'll be all right—'r won't. You can't help him none, an'—"

Wally Dunham strutted dramatically. "Come along, boys! Follow me!"

"Go foller 'em yerself, if you want!" an unidentified voice squawked.

"Ever' man on my payroll that don't hit the

saddle is fired, here an' now!" old Jake bawled, simply blazing with fury. Nearly every man there was on his payroll.

Old Jake was crazy mad, anyhow. He felt that he had never had such a bad-luck day in his life. Everything had gone wrong.

What he had learned of how Walt Rodman had escaped—about twenty minutes after his unpleasant meeting with the three punchers in the barn—had made him forget all about them for the time being. He had other troubles, too; lots of them.

Now he and his nephew Wally had come to the Silver Dollar to find Tig Burns. They had found him, half scalped and wholly unconscious. Old Jake simply wouldn't believe that Red, unarmed, barehanded, had taken a gun away from Tig and cracked him over the head. He didn't call anybody a liar, but he just naturally felt there must have been some trickery in it, somewhere.

He and Wally had thought of a place where Walt Rodman might be hiding out, and they had wanted Tig and some men to go see. They had just put Clara Dunham on a train, with her aunt for a guard, and were sending her out of the country, clear off to Chicago—which, according to range notions, was off at the other end of the world—because the girl in tears and anger had refused to marry Wally. They knew, too, that she had meant to run off and marry Walt Rodman. That was why Rodman had been loafing around town for almost two weeks—just waiting for a chance to elope with Clara. When he learned that, old Jake had been so riled that he was perfectly willing to believe all the scandalous and evil stories anybody in the countryside cared to tell about Walt Rodman, and he meant to corner him.

He was guessing wildly, even if honestly, that these three strange young punchers were perhaps Walt Rodman's friends. People had told Jake that most likely Walt would organize a band of rustlers and try to take by force what he believed, or at least claimed, was his by inheritance.

Of all the men there, Wally Dunham was Tiger Burns's best friend. Those two understood each other, had some liking for each other, though Burns was a little contemptuous of Wally, and Wally had a lot of secret uneasiness about Burns, who was not an easy fellow to manage.

Wally had been made a deputy sheriff because he was the sort that liked carrying a star, and it helped him in bullying some folks; but he kept it pretty well out of sight, because the hard, tough punchers had a way of making sarcastic remarks; and old Jake wouldn't fire a good man simply because he said things that hurt Wally's feelings. Jake liked his nephew all right, but he also liked the rough, tough, hard-riding, plain-spoken men of the range. They were his kind of people. He had lived with them from boyhood, knew them, wanted them about him.

Wally, wanting to shine and being excited, raised his voice loudly in stirring the men up to chase the boys.

"They've stole your horses!" he yelled.

"I bet they took that roan o' yourn!" said someone.

"They've held you up! Made you look like hicks!"

"You sort o' hiked yore arms up a little too, didn't you?" a voice inquired.

"They're in with Walt Rodman, who's killed your friends!"

"Tig, he is yore friend, ain't he?"

"Yes, and I want to catch an' hang 'em! Two thousand dollars—Uncle Jake here'll make it three! Won't you, Uncle Jake?"

"Since when," old Jake bellowed, almost pleading, "won't my men chase hoss thieves?"

That stung the men. They liked old Jake. After all, those wild-headed kids were hoss thieves! Some cursed, and with lurching swing of bodies started for the door. Others surged after them. Excitement grew. They ran about the street, mounting. With yells and clatter, with shooting overhead to rouse the town, they brought men running from other saloons. Hasty words of explanation were flung. There was more running to saddled horses, and horses reared, pressing against one another. Men who had just heard the news swore loudly. Incredulous voices called, "Ol' Tig is dead?" and were answered with "Yeah!" or "Knocked cuckoo," or "Head smashed with one o' his own guns!"

Shouts went up, yelling the size of the reward. Men said, as if the facts were known, that the strangers were rustlers. With yips and whoops, horsemen streaked off through the town.

CHAPTER IV

The Slide Down
the Mountain Side

As Red had scrambled into the saddle, giving
the order to make for the marshal's office, and
settled himself in the seat, he found a rifle under
his leg. Baby-faced Billy, born and raised in
the bad lands of Lelargo, and being naturally
inexcitable, had picked good horses, giving first
choice to those that carried rifle scabbards; but
if there was no rifle on the saddle, as with the
mount he had chosen for himself, he simply took
a rifle into his hands. So they started off well
armed.

In two jumps Red knew that he was on a fine
horse. Later he was to learn, and be pleased, that
chance had put him on Tig Burns's long-legged,
deep-chested hammerhead, a powerful brute,
not overly gentle, but about as good as any man
could want.

They bounded down the dusty street, and
with a pull that set their horses to plowing the
dust with rigid forelegs and high toss of head,
stopped before the marshal's office. It was dark
within. The marshal was about town, loitering
with friends at some bar, pretending that he

was sitting on the lid to keep law and order.

Red jumped off, tossing the reins to Tom Jones, and with scrambling rush tried the door. It was locked. His shoulder hit the door, and the door vibrated with a slight sway.

"You're goin' open 'f I have to butt with my head!" he said, and plunged at it again and again until, with protesting squeak and splintering, the box latch came away from the wood, and the door flew open.

Red landed knees-down inside the doorway. With hasty scratch of match he looked up toward the wall. There were the three pair of guns on pegs. He grabbed his own first, guns that he was proud of, having once won them in a little shooting contest from horseback. In the language of the old cowman judge who had awarded them, "Son, yo' don't need to have to take no back talk from nobody, suh!"

Now, as Red was buckling them on, shots rang out up the street where the men had taken to their horses to give chase.

"Come along outa there, Red!" Tom Jones yelled. "They're after us!"

"I bet they ain't goin' to be so eager to catch us as they pertend," said Billy, trying to roll a cigarette and still make sure that he wouldn't drop the rifle he was carrying.

Red jumped through the doorway, handing up the heavy belts, studded with shells.

"We shore are weighted down with shootin' irons, like first-class bad men!" he said.

"Wait a minute, Red, till I find a match," said Billy.

"Be plenty a fire in hell, you rummy!" Tom Jones told him.

"I ain't goin' there," said Billy, with a lighted match near his nose. He shook out the match, then reached for his belt and guns.

"To the hills!" said Red, and he jumped into the saddle and set his horse into a bounding gallop.

"Be like goin' home!" Billy tried to say, but the cigarette was in his mouth, and both his hands were occupied. He liked hilly country.

Red had stuffed Tig Burns's guns into the saddlebags. He could not help being pretty pleased with himself at having taken them off the notorious killer, and he meant to keep them. The remembrance of how Burns had spoken of his father, the sheriff, made Red as hot as if his clothes were on fire.

The pursuers caught hazy sight of them. Yells and shots came through the starlight. The fugitives turned in the saddle and shot, each a time or two, just by way of letting the fellows who were giving chase know that it was not going to be wise to get too close. Rifles whanged at them, and there was the rapid *pop pop pop* of the forty-fives.

The three boys knew no more about the lay of

this country than they knew of China, except that riding in that afternoon they had seen that beyond the town some four or five miles the sandhills rose up and broke themselves into bluffs, and far behind lay the wooded hogbacks of the Santee Mountains. So they made for this rough country as instinctively as prairie dogs make for their holes.

"Just goes f'r to show," said Red to himself, "how folks can't sometimes allus tell about fellers. Four hours ago we was nice peac'ble honest boys, wantin' for to spend our wages sociable. Now, without doin' a thing wrong, we're desperadoes on the dodge! I don't know how she's ever goin' to come out. I know one thing: I ain't goin' to be hung for no hoss thief if I can help it. We maybe'll have to get old Jake up in a corner some'eres by hisself an' coax him for to listen to our explanations. I'm shore willin' to 'polergize f'r Billy's poke on the nose. But, outside o' that, we stand pat!"

Then his hand went inquiringly toward the letter inside his shirt. It was still there, and also he still had a pleasing picture in his mind of the dark, gypsy-like girl who had smiled and trusted him.

"Ol' Jake *can't* be such a bad feller!" Red decided, arguing with himself.

On they went, riding recklessly, cutting across country, with the horses taking sudden jumps in the dark that jolted them half out of the saddles.

All the horses were strong and fast. Billy Haynes, even in the dimness of the street lighted only by saloon doorways, had a keen eye; and, like the generous little chubby devil that he was, he had turned over to Red the one that he thought was better than the one he kept for himself. Red soon found that he was having to pull on the reins to keep from getting ahead of his friends. Tom Jones had sentiments similar to Red's and so checked in his horse, letting Billy lead; and Billy had an instinct for picking the roughest way. Over in Lelargo it was all desert and rocky country, and that to Billy was home. He had a way of patting his plump belly and declaring that it took a good man to grow fat over where he came from.

The swarm of galloping punchers who had followed them out of Martinez, and who knew this Santee country, swore in amazement at these wild-headed fools who left the road and went scrambling up steep hillsides where they were, if not overtaken, at least slowed down so as to come within rifle shot; but they swore louder at the breakneck speed with which they took off down other hillsides in the dark where even good horsemen in the daylight went slow.

"Damn crazy fools!" fellows said half admiringly, one to another.

Red and his friends, even to escape being shot

at, would not flail their horses up a steep hill, but gave them their heads to make the climb, and repeatedly were almost overtaken by eager men who with spurs and quirt beat every ounce of strength from their horses. But the fellows who did that soon had to lag behind, and the pursuers straggled out in a long line. Many, finding their horses tired, and others, seeing the chase was not soon to end, stopped, talked it over, and turned back. But plenty kept coming.

At last they cut into a road, and Red, riding alongside little Billy, leaned over almost close enough to bite his ear and yelled, "Now, don't you get off this road till I tell you! We got better horses than them—an' can outrun 'em!"

They went on and on, climbing gradually. The road curved like a crippled snake's track up a shale butte; and the men of Martinez who had stayed with the chase thought they now surely had the three punchers. With hasty flogging, much yipping, and hasty popping of guns, they came, pressing hard.

"Holy Judas!" Billy yelled as he pulled up at the top of the butte and saw in the dim light that the road, having come to the top of the hill, turned right around and started down in an almost straight line, with a high bank on one side and a sheer drop-off on the other. "We go down there," said Billy, pointing at the road. "We have to keep our backs to 'em and get picked off easy!"

The situation was even worse than Billy thought. The pursuers, knowing the road and the lay of the country, had no sooner seen that the boys were sticking to the road and climbing the shale butte than they split their party, some following as fast as they could, while others cut up over and around the butte to get to the other side and head off the young punchers when they started down the straight steep grade.

"What we goin' do?" asked Tom Jones. "Pile off an' make it a fight?"

"Shucks," said Red. "If we can't escape in the dark we shore wouldn't come daylight!"

"I wish I'd been a good enough boy for to have some wings!" said Tom, peering over the side of the butte that seemed to drop down into bottomless darkness.

"You'll get wings all right," Billy told him with comforting assurance. "Bat wings!"

"You bump off a log," said Red. "You're leadin' this here party. Do somethin'!"

"Can I leave the road—now?" asked Billy.

The pursuers were coming up the road and, having the numbers that made them bold, rounded the bend with guns flaring. Tom Jones's revolver spit fire-flashes back at them, warningly.

"You-all are cornered!" someone called. "Give over!"

"Give over hell!" Billy yelped. "All right, pards. Set tight an' foller me! Here goes!"

Billy drove his spurs deep, and his horse took off down the steep, straight grade of the descending road; then, going at full gallop, Billy yanked his horse to one side, left the road, and plunged into the darkness on the almost up-and-down shale side of the butte where, probably in the whole history of the Santee country, no horse ever before had left its tracks.

Red gasped, "The crazy fool!" but ploughed his spurs into his horse and, with the feeling that he was simply jumping off the edge of the earth, followed—with Tom Jones at his heels.

Red afterwards said that it was just like a drunken man being in a snow slide. There was simply nothing for the horses' feet to hold to. The shale was soft, a little greasy, and loose. And this particular butte seemed to have no bottom. If hell didn't have that sort of a chute to dump souls down, then the devil, he had overlooked a nice improvement. The horses, back on their hocks, with heads held high by tight reins, and forelegs out like rigid poles, went skittering dizzily. The men reeled and bobbed and swayed, for this was not like being on horseback at all: it was like sliding down the steep roof of a barn on greased shoes.

Nobody followed them. Nobody would have followed them on a hundred-dollar bet. They wouldn't have done it again themselves on a hundred-dollar bet, but not knowing exactly what they were in for, and not caring much—Billy never much cared what he did—they did it.

Overhead, men on foot with reins in hand leaned forward, peering, and swore in a kind of humbled astonishment at the flashing black blobs of shadows that coasted down. The pursuers had a half unwilling admiration for the crazy kids. Nobody fired. The watchers stood in a kind of thrilled suspense. They thought, too, as Wallace Dunham said, "Deader than door knobs!"

Billy's horse was the first to go over, falling headlong and pitching Billy in a long dive. But he held to the reins and didn't land on his head. He struck with catlike clawing of feet and hands at the loose shale that gave way under his touch—just about as though he were swimming in lumpy water or a pot of warm grease. He on the seat of his trousers, and the horse on its side, slid on and on.

Tom Jones was the next to topple. His horse simply lost its balance and swayed over, with Tom getting his leg from under but keeping a hand on the mane as he coasted belly-down, like a kid on a cellar door.

Red, who had the idea that a good horse knew more than any two men, loosened the reins, jerked his feet free of the stirrups—for with the horse down on its tail, now one, then the other, stirrup was scraping deep in the shale—and grabbing the horn with one hand, made his body as loose as he could, so there would be less rigid weight to pull against the horse as it scrambled this way and that to keep its footing. As he went skittering the thought danced through Red's head that this was the nearest thing to having a hold on a piece of lightning that had ever happened to him.

The horse seemed now to be half standing, or trying to stand, on its head; now coasting with hind feet first and lying over on its side; but still the animal didn't quite lose control of its balance.

And when they brought up at the foot of the hill in a heavy drift of the shale, deep as a snow bank and slick as ice, the horse, with scrambling clatter of feet and grunting heave, arose readily. Red let go of the saddle, keeping the reins in hand. When he tried to walk he skittered about like a man, half drunk, on loose ice.

Tom Jones and Billy were also scrambling through the shale drift, and also on foot. They knew very well that nobody would come down that shale slide after them. Besides, if anybody did come down he would be all spraddled out and helpless, so they would have no trouble at all in explaining that they were nice honest boys who'd been misjudged.

They were concealed in the deep night shadows of the bluff; and, as they did not call out one to another, the watchers high overhead thought, of course, that these three lunatics had broken their necks, or at least some bones, and so could be picked up the next morning. If the listeners at the top of the butte heard the rattle of the shale they concluded that it was merely the horses, also probably with legs broken, scrambling about.

"Them crazy damn fools!" was the respectful, half commendatory comment of the baffled men at the butte crest who presently mounted and rode wearily back toward town.

The three boys, all limping and feeling pretty badly knocked about, led their horses down into the hard, sandy bed of a deep arroyo, and came together, peering at one another in the darkness, each a little afraid the others had a broken leg or something.

"Anybody hurt?" Red asked in a low voice.

"Depends on what you call hurt," said Tom Jones. "No, me, I ain't hurt! Jus' skinned alive. A couple inches knocked off both elbows. Half my hair wore off from slidin' on it. My nose, it is peeled. There ain't a spot on me big as a dime that ain't complainin'. Both my knees has been broke off short—r' feels like it. But otherwise, me, I feel fine!"

"The settin' place on my britches, it is gone!" said Billy wistfully. "An' my belly, it is scraped like somebody had used spurs on it. Next time I come down there it'll be on a feather bed!"

"Nex' time you come down there," said Red,

"it'll be clear plumb alone. You ain't goin' to have no comp'ny. At least, none o' mine."

"Ner of mine!" said Tom Jones.

"Nobody but a Lelargo lizard'd ever 'a' tried it!" Red insisted.

"I don't much mind bein' shot an' hung," Tom went on, "but I'd shore hate to ever be scairt again like that. I tried to pray some, but couldn't even cuss!"

"Yes'r," said Red, bending down, running his hands over the horse's legs and knees. "Neither o' you is nice boys f'r a feller to keep comp'ny with. Billy in per-tickular. Poke ol' Jake Dunham on the nose. Set on aces in a friendly poker game. Try for to break yore friends' necks by leadin' 'em down a pres'pice. Then complain 'cause chaps ain't made to cover settin' places! Look at us skinny fellers, like me an' Tom. We ain't got no bunches o' fat, like you, for to take the wear off our bones!"

"That there is right," Tom insisted. "Ain't enough meat left on me for to give a buzzard a flavor o' what I taste like!"

"You are alive, the which you wouldn't 'a' been if you hadn't follered me," said Billy. "An' in yore old age you c'n take yore gran'chilern by the hand an' show 'em where you onct come down!"

"Mine, bein' sens'ble kids," Red told him, "would say, 'Gran'pa, you're a liar!' "

"Well, you ornery, ungrateful galoots," said Billy, loosening the cinches, making ready to straighten blankets and saddle, "had better not find nothin' wrong with yore hosses. 'Cause mine is just a little skinned—an' he ain't goin' to carry double. Respect'ble fellers, I wouldn't mind givin' 'em some help. But no danged outlaws as beat men over the head with guns an' hold up saloons. No, sir! Me, I come of a respect'ble fam'ly!"

"I got a couple pounds o' rock down the back o' my neck," said Tom Jones. "I feel like I been buried an' was wearin' my own tombstone!"

"You ain't ever goin' be buried. You're goin' be hung f'r crow meat," said Billy cheerfully. "You got a neck as was just born in the shape for to have a rope fitted to it!"

"You little human dumplin', you!" said Tom, swinging his saddle back on his horse and reaching for the cinch. "You're a wall-eyed devil in the shape of an egg with legs on 'er! I'm goin' home an' tell my Maw what you've done to her on'y child!"

"Ow!" Billy exclaimed as he scrambled into the saddle. "I ain't got no britches where britches oughta be! An' as f'r yore Maw—you changed so since you left home, you'd have to write yore name on yerself f'r her to reckernize you! As 'tis, anyhow, ol' Satan, he's got his brand on you! My youth, it has been misguided

73

f'r ever to think you was a friend, 'cause—"

"Oh, shut up," said Red. "You two are worse'n magpies." He climbed into the saddle and, looking about in the darkness, asked, "Where do we go now?"

"Come on," Billy chirruped. "I'll show you."

"You've showed me enough!" said Red. "From now on, feller, you foller!"

"Huh, over in Lelargo," Billy assured him, "we wouldn't think that was nothin'! Chilern do that f'r to exercise 'emselves!"

"Over in Lelargo," said Tom Jones, "they hatch a peculiar breed o' liars. Little fat uns!"

"Nothin' for it but to keep goin' on up toward the hills," Red advised. "Come along. We'll take it slow f'r a spell. Maybe we can sneak out an' get off while our friends up yonder is discussin' our funeral arrangements!"

The horses moved along almost noiselessly through the hard sand.

CHAPTER V

Walt Rodman

The next morning sunup found the three friends in the chill shadows of the wooded hogbacks.

They were stiff and cold and hungry. Their horses were stiff and tired. The boys were lost, or the same as lost, for they didn't know where they were or where they were going, or how near enemies might be behind or ahead of them. It was a pretty cheerless fix to be in. There was not even the excitement of being chased to warm them up. They had nothing to eat and did not know where to get anything. In the morning light they looked one another over and made sarcastic comments on their personal appearance.

"You look like you'd been took apart an' put together in the dark by somebody as didn't quite know how!" said Tom Jones to Billy.

"You sort o' look scrambled yerself!"

"How I look an' how I feel is similer!"

"I'm hung-ger-ee!" said Billy, amusing himself by imitating a baby's whine.

"An' somewhere somebody is a-eatin' flapjacks with 'lasses an' coffee!" Tom Jones remarked. "Hot coffee—umm-mm-m!"

"If you fellers don't shut up, I'll fry some

steaks from a couple o' punchers. One fat. One lean," Red told them. "Keep a-comin'!"

So they went on, pushing their way through the brush, downhill, and at last came to a tiny stream that ran along through a deep rocky bed. They got off and let their horses drink, then half stripped to wash themselves, splashing and shivering, pausing now and then to drink deep and so ease the hunger-ache of their stomachs.

Good cold clear mountain water is a fine appetizer, and Tom Jones said he was all ready to eat a couple of nice live wolves.

Billy pointed out some trout in a pool and talked about how good crisp-fried trout would taste, until Tom couldn't stand it any longer and threw rocks in the pool. "What a feller can't see he don't want so bad," said Tom.

Red, still more proud than he was willing to admit about carrying off Tig Burns's guns, was examining them. He prodded out one loaded shell after another.

"Would you jus' look!" he called, holding out his hand to show the cartridges. "The half-breed snake! The nose of ever' bullet is split!"

Red drew back his hand and with a kind of dazed blank stare looked fixedly at nothing. Tom and Billy twisted their heads to see if Red was looking toward anything, and, seeing nothing in particular, looked at him again, looked questioningly at each other. It wasn't like Red to act that way. "Matter?" Billy asked, mild and coaxing. Red did not hear. "Gosh," Tom murmured.

Then Red gave a little start as if waking up. He opened his hand and peered hard at the bullets, nodded grimly, fixed his eyes steadily on nothing, and a moment later in a low queer tone, thinking aloud, said:

"He 'peared to know a lot about how my Dad died. An' in my Dad's back there was two—" Red looked down at his trembling hand where lay the split-nosed bullets—"dumdum forty-fives! So the doctor said."

"But, Red," little Billy urged, "other men c'n split—"

"Can but don't! Would you 'r me? Would any man as expects to have to throw a bullet a couple o' hundred yards? No. But a killer like Tig Burns, who usual ain't more'n a few feet off—an' it ain't just that! It's the way he talked about my Dad! Called me a liar when I said my Dad was shot in the back—an' he was! Why, damn his black, half-breed, yaller-bellied soul! He thinks hisself fast on the draw—an' I got a feelin' he sneaked up an' shot my Dad in the back 'cause he was scairt to draw agin 'im face to face!"

"You shore walloped him plenty!" said Tom Jones.

"I hope I didn't smash his head! Good God, how I hope it! I want him to live! I'll draw agin

77

'im, face to face, an' kill 'im with his own guns—an' split-nosed lead! So help me, God, I will!"

"I know how you feel, Red," Tom Jones urged, "but—"

"Don't be no fool, Red," said Billy anxiously. "A man like him—you'd be nothin' but what bird bones is to a coyote!"

"Shut up! I've took my oath. You heard it. I'll show him, and all as cares to look on, that an honest man c'n draw as fast as any killer—an' shoot as straight! Shot Dad—in the back! An' if he didn't do it he's the sort as would—an' that's enough f'r me!"

"You are gone plumb loco!" said Tom Jones, made uneasy by the low rasping sound of Red's voice, which was not at all as he had heard Red ever speak before.

"All right. What 'f I am? When I say I'll do somethin', I'll do it 'r get killed tryin'. That's all bein' alive is good for—to do what you ought. You boys c'n go back to where we got friends, but me, I ain't goin' to leave this goddamned country till Tig Burns is buried!"

"He hurt you, an' I'll kill 'im myself," said Billy, " 'f I have to sneak up an' do it while he's asleep. Me, I ain't got no scruples about givin' a rattlesnake the first bite."

"Now," Tom Jones announced, "I know you're crazy—to talk 'bout us goin' off an' leavin' you."

"Then come a-risin' an' a-ridin', you fellows,"

said Red. "We're on our way. I don't know where the hell to—but from now on, me, I wear Tig Burns's guns so as to have 'em handy when we meet!"

Red went on, leading the way, going slow, sitting sour and glum. His friends dropped back and talked uneasily, with Tom Jones saying:

"I never seen 'im act this away before. Does he have crazy spells?"

"Yeah," Billy answered softly. "I reckon. He had a couple over in Lelargo before we drifted down into Tahzo an' picked you up. By the time he was cured o' them spells, like this here, the remains o' fellers was scattered all over the landscape. An' Lelargo, it is full o' hellbenders. Men on the dodge come in there for to rest, an' some of 'em made the mistake of thinkin' Red was just a fool kid. When he's good an' riled— well, you seen 'im climb Tig Burns barehanded!"

"My gosh," Tom Jones replied, "ever' little dust-up we've had, he's been plumb half good-natured, free an' easy, like he was havin' fun. Now he sort o' looks mean an' talks it. 'Tain't like 'im."

" 'Tis too. Red, he's naturally ser'us minded when he thinks they's somethin' he oughta do. He'd fight a rattlesnake an' give it first bite! No foolin'."

They went on, following downstream in the river bed, taking it easy over the slippery boulders, and much of the time on loose gravel, for the water was very low.

In a couple of hours they came to where a trail crossed. They drew up, looking from left to right, wondering which way to turn.

"Me," said Red, more like himself again, "I'm allus lucky. We'll toss." He fished down into his trousers pocket for a dollar, and saying, "Heads is to the right," tossed the coin, catching it in his palm. It was tails.

He glanced to the left a little reluctantly, having been slightly in favor of taking the trail that seemed to lead back to the open country in the general direction of the town.

He nodded. "All right. Better to be lucky 'n handsome," said Red. "Now, me, I'm both! This here coin—an' money talks!—says f'r us to turn left. So off we go!"

Off they went, toiling up the narrow, rocky path, not thinking of anything much more than where they were to get something to eat, when, without the slightest warning, from behind a rock at the turn of the trail some fifty yards ahead a forty-five barked at them.

Red, being in the lead, felt the bullet pass his cheek. Then it splattered, knocking up a dash of rocky dust, against the high bank within an arm's reach of his saddle. A puff of smoke arose from where the bullet had come. Red, with a sort of instinctive fall, went out of the saddle, simply sliding from the horse as he made a grab at a holster and, jerking his head in a way that shook off his hat, was ready for trouble. He landed feet down and from the side of his horse peered across the saddle, forty-five in hand.

Tom Jones and fat little Billy Haynes went out of their saddles in much the same way, reins in one hand, a gun in the other. But as Billy was not tall enough to see easily across the saddle, he half squatted, peering up under the horse's neck and grinning like an eager child about to start an exciting game.

"Can they be them fellers that chased us?" asked Tom.

"How'd they get away up here ahead of us, then?" said Billy. "They're jus' some other misguided ignerent folks. World's full of 'em!"

One shot, then silence, and no sign of the marksman during the long minute or two that they stood there, surprised, ready for trouble, listening, watching intently.

It seemed very strange. If an enemy lay ahead, scrouged down in such an advantageous place as that, having them at short range and more or less in the open, why only one shot?

"I bet he run," Billy suggested. "He caught sight o' my deadly eye, an' it scairt 'im out!"

"Hey, you up there!" Red sang out, seeing no one. "What's the matter with you? Go on an' fight—'r apolergize, damn yuh!"

81

Then they heard a voice, loud with a kind of surprise and almost half reproachful. "Why, hell, you ain't Tig Burns!"

"That," said Red, indignant, "is worse'n bein' shot at!"

A tall, angular, hard-looking man of about forty rose up from behind a rock. He frowned from under the upraised brim of his hat, peering as if very much puzzled.

"Yo'-all Tig's men?" he asked.

" 'Course we ain't!" Red yelped. "Gosh A'mighty, feller, don't be insultin' that away!"

"Then what you doin' on his hoss?"

"Me, I traded with 'im, all in a sort of a hurry, down there to town last night!"

"Yeah?" the man asked incredulously.

"You got ears! That's what I said."

"Liars got tongues, too!" the man shouted back, unimpressed.

"Listen, feller!" Red proclaimed. "I don't mind a-tall bein' bushwhacked by somebody as is full of the laud'ble intentions to knock that Tig Burns off his hoss—but now you've seen yore mistake, be sociable!"

"Where yo'-all goin'?" the man demanded.

"On up to the hills!"

"Oh, naw, you ain't! You c'n jus' turn tail an' hike back down to where you come from!" Then, a little hastily, "An' don't go gettin' no finger-itch an' be a-scratchin' on them triggers. This

82

here trail is guarded. Other fellers clost behind me. An' you'd get a skimpy sort o' funeral!"

"We go back down where we come from, we'll get lynched, too!" said Red.

The man eyed them suspiciously. "An' deserve it, I reckon! Yo'-all don't pull no wool over my eyes. Yo'-all are either hoss thiefs 'r liars. Maybe both!"

"What's the matter with you, anyhow?" Red demanded peevishly.

" 'Tain't me. I'm all right. You fellers is all wrong! An' jus' so you'll be enlightened some, get-a hell out o' here. Light back down there to ol' Jake Dunham an' tell 'im yore little flim-flam didn't work!"

"Feller," Red protested, "you are barkin' up the wrong tree! If Jake Dunham don't like you half so much as he don't like us, you oughta curl up an' cry 'cause you're so bad hated!"

"That," said the grim man, unimpressed, "is smooth talk f'r to fool me. An' it don't. Not a mite. Let me see yore backs—movin' fast!"

A voice or two from unseen men called to the sentinel of the trail, and he answered something across his shoulder, but with wary alertness kept his eyes on Red.

In a moment two other men appeared, or rather their heads, looking out cautiously.

"Say, feller," Red called earnestly, "you're tangled all up in some mistaken notions. If you're agin that Dunham crowd, we oughta be friends!"

"Bush-wah!" said the tall fellow calmly.

"Who are you-all?" one of the newcomers asked, rising up.

"We're just some stray punchers as rode into town yesterday and got misunderstood, bad. We rode out with a lot of dust under our feet, an' bein' strangers, got lost. We sort o' hiked for the high country so as to make it harder to get found. An' here we are!"

"Yo'-all cooked up that story to come up here, nosin', an' try to catch Walt Rodman," said the grim tall man. "Yo'-all took Tig Burns's hoss, an' Wally Dunham's hoss, just to pull the wool down over our eyes so we'll maybe take you in. Now 'f 'twas *me*," he went on calmly, "I'd jus' load you down with lead an' let you stay. But other folks has other notions, so I'm sayin', 'Git!' "

Red's voice rose with sudden interest and much assurance:

"Hey, if Walt Rodman's up here, let me talk to 'im! He'll be glad, I bet you, for to see *me!*"

"He ain't here!" said the man quickly. "He's gone. Rode off." He waved a long arm, indicating a vast distance. "No use lookin' for 'im. Left the country."

"Yeah," Red answered. "Folks guard the trails an' shoot at other folks to keep 'em from follerin'

friends as has left the country, got clean away—
don't they!"

"Maybe as how they do," said the fellow,
nodding.

"Now, listen. You poke out yore ears an' catch
these here words. You go tell Walt Rodman a
feller is here as he'll be mighty glad to see. A
red-headed feller, just my size. I got somethin'
for 'im, an'—"

"A piece o' lead!"

"You can't guess worth a damn!"

"Does Walt know you?" asked the second man
encouragingly.

"No, he don't. But a good friend o' his does. I
want to talk to 'im!"

"Then drop yore guns an' come, hands up!"

"I don't drop no guns for no man! But you let
Walt Rodman speak, an' we'll come—hands up.
I'll jus' bet you my horse here—"

" 'Tain't yore hoss!"

"Maybe not, but I got rights to it. An' I'll bet
'em agin yore hat as how Mr. Rodman pulls
down my hands to shake 'em!"

The strangers eyed him critically, a little
impressed even if very skeptical. They were
wary men, cautious. It didn't seem quite reasonable that strangers would be on Tig Burns's
and Wally Dunham's horses without permission.
Yet, since Red was willing to meet Rodman, the
offer did not seem wholly unreasonable.

"I don't believe you," said the grim man, not with finality.

"I'm tellin' truth," Red urged persuasively. "I ain't no good at lyin'. Look us over careful. We're nice fellers. Stick yore head out more, Billy. Let 'em see yore angel face! An' you, Tom, do the same.

"See them faces? They look like a picture of inner-cence havin' a pleasant dream. Gosh A'mighty, 'f I wasn't sure Mr. Rodman'd be glad to see us, would I be standin' here arguin'? Use yore judgment some!"

Red's half-bantering insistence mystified the watchers. They were ready to distrust any carefully made-up story, but this bantering impudence was puzzling. If Red had begged to be believed and tried to be earnest, they very likely would have sneered scornfully.

The sentinel and his two companions studied the punchers and talked together in low voices. After quite a while they seemed to come to an agreement. Their spokesman called:

"If yo'-all are up to any shu-nan-e-gann, you'd better hit yore leather and make some dust. This here ain't just a little fracas. It is war, an' Jake Dunham is goin' to learn hisself a lesson. Yo'all *are* strangers. But o' course he wouldn't be sendin' anybody up here as was well knowed. So now yo'-all c'n either make yourselfs some haste in gettin' off, 'r come out in the open an' set quiet till Walt gits here. What do you say?"

"We'll set," said Red, and began unsaddling.

"See here," Tom Jones spoke up. "Are you plumb sure that there party that asked you to look up Rodman is somebody as will make you welcome to 'im?"

"Huh. 'F I was Walt Rodman an' that there party sent me to 'im, I'd be the gladdest to see myself of anybody in the world—nex' to the party her—hisself!"

"Gee gosh, Red! Was it a girl?"

"Shh-hh-h! I ain't goin' to tell no lie, an' in a way of speakin', I don't persackly know. But she wore skirts!"

Little Billy eyed Red reproachfully. "You are damn near a liar, Red. F'r three months I've slept by you, et with you, rode with you, an' you ain't seen no girls 'cept them wall-eyed hookers over in the San Arnez dance halls. Tell me, Red, er you runnin' a blazer? I don't much care, on'y I'd sorta like f'r to know."

"'Tain't manners to talk disrespectful about a woman, 'specially one you never seen!"

"Ner one you never seen neither, I suspect," said Billy.

But Tom and Billy loosened the cinches of their saddles and squatted about on the rocks, waiting with what patience they could, when they were hungry, sore, ragged, and uncomfortable, under the guns of the men who watched them, still suspicious.

The boys were a little suspicious that Red was up to some trick with Walt Rodman, and nagged him with uneasy questions about what he meant to say, and was there really a girl? Red grinned mysteriously and invited them to set tight and look on—learn something, maybe!

It was an hour or more before a young man, tall and quiet, with a rather tense, fine-looking face, stepped up on the rocks where his friends stood guard.

He looked down at the three strange punchers with suspicious scrutiny.

"Who are you boys?" he asked.

Red introduced himself, then Tom and Billy; adding, "We got orders f'r to get outa the country owin' to some misunderstan's."

"What happened there in town?" asked Rodman, who had a steady voice and steady eyes.

"Well, sir," said Red, "maybe you'll think I'm a liar, the which ain't no reason a feller oughtn't tell the truth. It was this hereaway. First off, down there to the stage barn, a big feller that we almost run over, he got sassy, an' Billy here, he poked 'im on the nose. Then the feller he told us his nose was Jake Dunham's! An' us, we'd come ridin' in expectin' for to go to work on the Double X.

"Then, next, 'r purt-near next, Wally Dunham,

88

he took a dislike to me an' said I was to hit leather an' make some dust. He showed me his d'p'ty sher'ff's badge an' looked like I oughta faint 'r somethin'.

"Then, next, we went to the Silver Dollar, an' Tig Burns he come a-walkin' in. He asked me my name, an' I told him. Then he made some remarks about my Dad. When the doin's was over, Burns laid on the floor with his head busted, an' me—I'm still a-wearin' Tig Burns's guns!"

Rodman shook his head, cool and unconvinced.

"That's right, Walt. Don't b'lieve 'im. She's a trick. An' he's a liar. No man 'ud poke Tig Burns!"

"Yeah," said Red, "you know a lot, don't you? Maybe Tig Burns give me his saddle and his horse for to come up here an' lie to you fellers. But would he give me his guns—any more'n he'd cut off his arms an' let me have 'em? Well, sir, I've got 'em. Maybe I stole 'em while he was 'sleep! Maybe he *was* 'sleep! Leastwise, he laid plumb stiff—but didn't snore none while I took 'em. They are in my bags. You watch me clost to see I don't start no monkeyshines, an' I'll fish 'em out."

They watched him closely. He opened the saddlebags, pulled out the guns, and holding them by the barrels walked slowly over to where Rodman stood, and held them out, butts first.

"I don't know Tig Burns's guns well enough to tell," said Rodman. "But you, Harry?"

The tall grim man eyed Red with alert suspicion, moved closer, bent his long neck. Plainly, he did not intend to be convinced; but he was. "My good gosh, these is them!" He straightened up, looking at Red now in another sort of way, incredulously. "I seen them handles 'nough times—pokin' up over his holsters like snake heads! Feller," he demanded, still thinking there was something shady about the facts, since no gunman, while he lived, would give over his guns, "how did you get 'em?"

"Took 'em," said Red.

Harry bent low again to make doubly sure of no mistake. "An' would you look at them undercut notches! Sights filed off. Tig'd give up his head sooner'n them guns. Somethin' queer!"

"Yeah, I reckon," Red agreed. "F'r the full an' complete details, so you won't keep on thinkin' me a liar, you jus' send down to town an' ask questions!"

"We'll have word from town this afternoon," Rodman answered warningly. "If what you tell ain't so, it is going to be mighty bad luck—for you boys!"

"Suits me," said Red. "An' till you get that there word, maybe this other thing I got here'll help you feel sort o' nice an' peaceful toward us. Can I put my hand inside my shirt?"

90

"Yes."

Red drew out the letter the girl had given him but retained it in his hand while he spoke:

"A mighty pretty girl who's a lot smarter'n you fellers—since she knows an honest boy, like me! when she sees 'im—asked me on the quiet for to give this to Mister Walt Rodman. You're him, ain't you?"

Rodman hesitated, eying Red. Then he grabbed the letter without a word and tore open the envelope. He read the note quickly and at once reread it.

Rodman thrust out his hand. "Red, you *are* welcome!"

"See? What'd I tell you 'spicious bozos?" he demanded of Tom and Billy.

"I'll take a chance on you boys," said Rodman. "This letter—come along!"

"If you are thinkin' about takin' us where they's somethin' to eat," said Tom Jones, "why, me—I'm in a gosh-awful hurry!"

CHAPTER VI

Walt Rodman's Story

Rodman took them off the trail some distance to where horses were tied, and, mounting, led the way some miles to where a log cabin stood in a small clearing right at the edge of a cliff; and below this cliff lay a sunken valley, walled in on all sides by sheer rocks.

The floor of the valley was practically level, and even now, in the late summer, green and lush, indicating that springs flowed there. A few cattle and horses, looking about as small in the distance as flies, grazed knee-deep in the grass.

It was a sort of great nature-made corral. One of the boys asked how in the world it was possible to get horses and cows down in there or to get them out? Rodman said there was a rough trail or two, hard to find, and harder to follow, leading out.

When little Billy noticed that it was not more than two good jumps from the back door of the cabin to the rocky edge of the sunken valley, he said, "My holy gosh! If a feller stumped his toe goin' out o' the door, he'd land on his nose a long way from here, wouldn't he?"

"Yes," said Rodman quietly, "he would."

"How'd anybody ever find this here place?"

"Eight or ten years ago," Rodman told them, "a bunch of outlaws roosted up here. Take a good look at this cabin and notice how it is built. With loopholes. If you look closely, you can see that the logs are speckled with bullets.

"The outlaws used to gather horses and cows—horses mostly—out on the range and run them into the valley down there. They weren't exactly rustlers, because there was no chance to get the stock to market from there. But they were horse and cow thieves, and a bad lot.

"They got mighty troublesome, so my father began to lay for them. Nobody ever came up here in the mountains, those days. Too rough for cattle. Nobody ever comes now, except once in a great while a hunting party or an old miner. My father found out where the horse thieves were and how to get here. So he brought up a bunch of the boys. I came along. Was pretty much of a kid at the time. Thought it great fun!

"Well, it wasn't a fight—it was a siege! We had them cornered, or thought so. They were surrounded with their backs up against the edge of this precipice. And they couldn't break through, and—so we thought—couldn't run!

"Two days and two nights of it—then no more shooting from the cabin. We thought they were all killed off. Our boys crept up cautiously and found—well, we had dropped three or four out of the half dozen, but the others were gone.

"Then we knew why they had built right here at the edge of the canyon-like valley. There is a trail right off the back door, leading down along the wall of rock. It's so steep even a goat would have to watch carefully in going down.

"That morning, just before daylight, the two who weren't hurt had started down. Later we saw them far below, down there in the valley. Catching horses. Some of our boys tried to go down there after them but couldn't make it. Nearly broke their necks and had a hard time climbing back. They didn't know then that you have to crawl down the trail backwards and barefooted! Try it with boots and you are just out of luck.

"But as a fellow goes down he is pretty safe—if he doesn't fall. Nobody can shoot at him from up here because he is flat up against the rocks, and there is a slight overhang to the rocks. You boys take care of your horses, and I'll stir up something to eat."

"Me, I shore like the sound of your voice!" said Tom Jones.

They watered and turned their horses into a small corral and went into the cabin, which was a curious building of peculiar shape, not square but three-cornered, with the sharpest angle facing thc clcaring, and the base of the triangle right up against the rock wall of the valley which lay far below. This arrangement put any attacking party at a disadvantage.

The walls of the cabin were not high, but seemed lower than they were because roughly split boards lay on the rafters, making a sort of platform overhead, a kind of garret where in the old days the outlaws had stored provisions and truck that was packed in.

The cabin doors were very heavy, opened in, and could be barred by crossbars as thick as beams. The windows were narrow and unglassed. They were, in fact, small doors and could be barred the same way. High up on the walls were the loopholes for which a man would need to stand on a stool or bunk or table to shoot. They were built that way so that shots which came through them would not strike low enough to hit men who were walking or sitting in the room.

The fellows who had built this cabin knew what they were about, probably having learned from experience what arrangement was best for standing off a posse.

Rodman brought out provisions. Billy and Tom Jones eagerly were turned loose as cooks in the corner that served as a kitchen. They soon had a fire roaring in the home-made stove and were slicing steaks from the deer that hung in the shade just outside. An onlooker might have thought they were preparing to feed a dozen men instead of merely three. They recklessly cut into the bacon, mixed nearly a dishpan full of flapjack dough, and put the half-gallon coffee pot on to boil. Also they quarreled like regular camp cooks, who are known to be vain of their reputation for bad tempers; but paused now and then to say, "Umm-mm-m!" as they sniffed hungrily.

Rodman and Red sat on the doorstep and talked. Red listened encouragingly, but Rodman was not a man who told everything to strangers, even under favorable circumstances; and Red was not one to ask questions on short acquaintance, though he had a restless and eager curiosity.

"After my father died—was killed—you've heard how?" Rodman looked at him intently.

Red nodded and answered guardedly: "I hear tell he was bushwhacked."

"Murdered!" said Rodman. "Well, after his death, three or four of the old hands who couldn't get on with Jake Dunham came back up here in the hills. They raised a few cows and horses down there in the sunken valley. They prospected a little, hunted and fished. All in all, they've been taking life pretty easy. Rarely go to town. Jake Dunham suspects them of rustling, or so he says.

"I don't know what has come over Jake in late years. He was always a rather overbearing man, in a way. But I liked him. Called him Uncle Jake from the time I was that high." Rodman measured with his palm. "Nobody ever thought he wasn't honest until just a couple of years back. Now most people think he isn't.

"Well, all these men up here were friends of my father's. And are friends of mine. Every last one of them believes that Jake Dunham killed my father—to get the ranches they owned together. But I try to be honest about what I ought to think, even if I am hot-tempered. Sometimes I almost think maybe Jake did kill him. And sometimes I think he just couldn't have done a thing like that! Jake's changed a lot since then. God knows I've got reasons enough to hate him, yet—"

Rodman broke off moodily. Red nodded, almost grinning a little. He felt that he knew about one good reason why Rodman didn't want to hate Dunham: that reason was dark eyed and just about as pretty as a girl could be.

"Of course," Rodman went on, "I knew all about the wills they had left. It's a common sort of thing among the old-timers, and Jake's folks and mine seemed almost like one big family, except—" He hesitated, then he touched the pocket where he had put the letter Red brought to him. "Only *she* wasn't like a sister! From the time we could toddle—I'm a little the older, quite a little—we said that we were going to get married. We still say so! That's what all this trouble is over now. That and something else!"

Red cocked his ears expectantly and kept still, but Rodman did not go on and explain about the "something else." Red, with assurance, guessed that it was the fact that Dunham accused Rodman of having killed his own father.

"You see," Rodman continued, "I've known for a long, long time that I would most likely have some trouble with Jake. I didn't want it. But if he made it, I couldn't take it laying down. As I said, these men up here were all friends of mine. So before I showed up in town there a couple weeks ago, I had already come up here and asked them what if I should run into some trouble down there at Martinez and have to take a short cut to some place that was safe—could I come up here? They said I could. They said more than that. Lots more. Made the invitation real strong. So here I am."

Rodman might have told something more, but Billy and Tom Jones sang out that everything was ready for the feast.

The punchers ate prodigiously. Billy and Tom Jones, in a kind of rivalry, as if wanting to show how much they approved of their own cooking, stayed at the table until everything was cleaned. Then, being stuffed, warm, tired, they did not need two invitations from Rodman before they took off their boots and chaps, rolled into the bunks, and slept as if they were never to awaken again.

It was dark when Red woke up. He lay still a moment, listening suspiciously to a voice that seemed a little familiar. Then he grinned, satisfied. The voice he heard was that of the old fellow, Frank Hollar, who had stood by and seen everything happen in the Silver Dollar; and now he was singing Red's praise in a high key.

He sounded a little hysterical, because the men he was talking to appeared to think that he was exaggerating the story of what the boys had done.

"I tell you, it can't be 'zaggerated!" Hollar squawked. "He jumped Tig Burns barehanded an' took away his gun an' whaled 'im over the head with it! Then them boys stuck up the saloon an' was backin' out when in come the Dunhams—an' had f'r to put their hands in the air! I see it all, I tell you."

He described everything, how the boys had been chased, and how they had got away by riding lickety-split down Shale Butte, where no man before them had ever walked and carried a bridle—much less "set a saddle."

Red grunted and stirred, sat up rubbing his head, and pretended that he had not been listening to the talk that went on about the lighted lantern on the table of rough-hewn planks.

Hollar, looking a little more daft than ever, pumped his hand, saying, "They was sure a lot o' disappointed coyotes went down to the feet o' the Butte, come daylight, an' didn't find no cark-ess-ez!" He cackled loudly. "Ol' Jake, he swears he's goin' f'r to have you hung for hoss-stealin'. Young Wally, he done an Injun war dance on his ears—he was that overhet! When I left town, Tig Burns he was settin' up talkin' to hisself sort o' fuddled-like, wantin' to know which hoss it was as kicked 'im, an' feelin' about f'r his guns."

After a time Rodman asked Red to take a little walk, so they went out in the darkness and perched themselves on the corral fence.

"Hmm," said Rodman, just a little embarrassed for a beginning. "I wonder, can I ask something an' you won't get offended?"

"Shore."

"Well, now, listen. Are you boys on the dodge? 'Cause, if so, I'll see as how you have a guide clear across the mountains and get away. I'll be plain and truthful. I like you fine. But I can't let outlaws throw in with me—though I am near to being one, it seems, myself."

"All we ever done that's wrong is what Hollar told you about—'cept poking Jake accidental on the nose! We come bustin' into town with pockets full of wages, ready for to be sociable. Things got all messed up. Does a feller on the dodge walk into a marshal's office an' leave his guns?"

"Never," said Rodman.

"When Tig Burns passed them remarks about my Dad—nothin' but some paralysis could have kept me from climbin' him. An' since we're talkin' facts sort o' confidential-like, I'll tell *you* something. I'm not going to leave this country till I've killed Tig Burns. Face to face. With his own guns. With one of his own split-nosed slugs. I got me a suspicion from the way he talked that he knows too much about the way my Dad died—shot twict in the back with split-nosed forty-fives!"

"Good Lord! Can that be?"

"The only way," Red went on, "I'll ever think Tig Burns didn't do it is for the Angel Gabr'el to toot his horn real loud, then shout down the name of the man who done it! Even then I'll think maybe Gabr'el wasn't watchin' very clost when it was done. I got my mind made up. I think even if I knowed he didn't do it, I'd kill Burns anyhow, just 'cause he needs killin'! My Dad, he sort o' tried to teach me that I allus oughta do what needed doin'. An' for twenty years Tig Burns has needed killin'."

"Your father was murdered, Red," Rodman replied. "Well, so was mine. But I—I have been accused of having killed mine!"

"You know," said Red promptly, "my Dad, bein' sheriff, he had notions about things. An' one of them notions was that the first thing a guilty man does is to accuse somebody else o' doin' his crime. Now, who accuses you?"

Walt Rodman was silent for a moment. "I'll tell you the whole story, Red. Tell it quick. I did have a quarrel with my father just before he was killed. Over a poker game where I lost some money. But it was my money. My father never liked gamblers, so he said I was a fool—the same being truth.

"Well, sir, after my father was found dead, everybody wondered. Folks said that Jake Dunham said that maybe I had done it. I don't know now whether Jake really said such a thing or not, but I imagine there are some who said it first to him. It made me mad. I said, 'If old Jake didn't kill my father himself, I guess he knows who really did!' I oughtn't ever to have said that.

"Somebody told Clara—Jake's daughter, you know—what I'd said. She said she would never speak to me again. So I went away. I went off to California. And I made some money. I made a lot of money. Then, when I sort of looked around as to how I was going to enjoy myself, I knew that I had not forgot, and never would forget, Clara. So I wrote her a letter. She wrote me. She said that if I wanted her to come and get her! So I came. She was willing to run away with me, but I wouldn't have that. I wanted her fair and square. Then, if I couldn't get her, after I'd tried honest, it would be time to elope.

"I came up here to my friends and made arrangements. Then I went to town and wrote Jake a letter. A long one. Told him all about myself, how I was rich now, and how I was sorry if I had ever said anything that hurt his feelings. Well, Jake, he was away from the ranch. He's nearly always away. So I waited.

"The next thing I knew, Jake and some men, with Clara and her aunt, come to town. That was night before last. I wasn't there. I'd rode off to visit a man who used to be a good friend of mine, and nobody knew just where I was except old Hollar, who everybody thinks is a little off. And he is. But only a little.

"Well, sir, old Hollar, he hung about town there listening, and he heard things that made him excited. He started out to find me. Met me on the road. He said Jake had come to town to send his daughter East, clear away. He said that two of Tig Burns's close friends was saying that they had heard me tell there in town, when I was drinking, that I had killed my father, but that nobody could prove it, so I was all right now. I was going to be arrested just as soon as I hit town. That is what old Hollar told me. You know how old Hollar is. He *is* a little cracked, and he hates Jake.

"I didn't know how far to believe him. He had come out on the best horse he could get, and he had a good one. So we switched saddles. He went back to town one way, and I went on the other. I was troubled, but I couldn't quite believe him.

"I rode right into town, and some good friends of mine saw me first and said, 'Get out, quick! They are after you! Jake's killers are laying for you.'

"They told me much the same thing Hollar had told. So I turned around and started. About ten minutes later Tig Burns and his men were kicking up the dust. I know this country like a rabbit knows a piece of sagebrush. For the same reason, too. I run all over it when I was a kid. I started one way, then, when they split up to head me off, I doubled back. I meant to dodge them. To hide down in a gully till they rode by. But when I saw them coming, I saw that two of them were the fellows who were going to swear that they had heard me say I had killed my father. So I felt something like you did about Tig Burns when he passed remarks about your father.

"I headed my horse toward them, gave him the spurs, took the reins in my teeth, a gun in each hand, and I didn't care whether or not I was killed. I downed two of them, then the other fellow cut and run. My horse was down, but I jumped another horse and followed till I could get him.

"Then I jumped my horse into an arroyo and worked along—walking some of the time so as not to be seen. I got up here late last night.

"This letter you brought me is from Clara. She thought I was still there in town and that her father wouldn't let me see her. She wrote to say that she was being watched every minute, so I must help her get away because she was going to be sent back East on the night train—if she did not marry Wally Dunham. She said she wouldn't marry Wallace Dunham to save her life. She has never liked Wally. Never did, even as kids. Jake used not to like him so very much himself, but of late he sort of seems to have changed his feelings.

"Old Hollar just told me that Clara went last night. Told me too that there are some posters out for you boys. One thousand dollars each for being horse thieves—and friends of mine! Hollar says that everybody there in town thinks that you boys are outlaws. Too desperate to be honest men. The way you held up the Silver Dollar—as if used to that kind of thing. And rode down Shale Butte!"

"We don't deserve no more credit for ridin' down that shale," said Red, "than a feller does for fallin' downstairs. We just started an' couldn't stop goin'. We tried to stop! Yeah, we shore did. And me, I reckon it ain't hard to figger what kind of a deal you've got. Cards plumb stacked agin you. Old Jake, young Walt, Tig Burns and his sidekicks, have just naturally put their heads together an' run in a cold deck on you. An' will they, do you think, come up here after you?"

"Yes," said Rodman, "if they find out I am up here."

"Any way in partickular to keep 'em from findin' out?"

"Not that I know of. They may not think of looking up here. They know I have friends aplenty close to Martinez. They'll look there first."

Red rolled a cigarette thoughtfully. "Do you want some advice?" he asked at length.

"Sure do, Red."

"An' she's sure good advice. It's my Dad's, and he was some experienced."

"Let's hear it."

"Well, sir, it's my Dad's notion that whenever you wanted to have an understandin' with a feller as has got wrong notions and is some stubborn, catch 'im alone, carry 'im off to where you won't be interrupted, an' talk. I've tried 'er a time 'r two, an' it worked fine."

"I doubt it in this case."

"Umm-m. Maybe. Now, me, personal, I've got to sort o' poke the notion out o' Jake Dunham's head that me an' Billy an' Tom is outlaws. We ain't. We couldn't be, 'cause we just ain't made that way. An' I think maybe Jake Dunham would talk some reasonable if we three got 'im alone. If us boys go catch 'im, can we bring him off up here for some private conversation?"

"I'd rather not, Red."

"Sometimes it does take several days before a stubborn feller'll loosen up an' absorb some reason. But we could try."

"You really mean you would carry off Jake Dunham—bring him up here?"

"Shore."

"Keep him till—"

"You just better bet! When a feller's got wrong notions, it's yore Christian duty for to help 'im get rid of 'em. I try to be a mighty good Christian that away. 'Specially when somebody gets the notion I'm a horse thief! I didn't steal no horse. I borrowed 'im. We left plumb good horses in town. 'Twas a sort of trade-like. Ain't my fault if Tig Burns ain't satisfied with the horse he got. Few fellers ever is in a hoss trade. Me, myself, now, even I ain't. My Blackie's a lot better'n Burns's hammerhead. Got more sense—prob'ly from associatin' with a better man. But do I complain? No, sir. Jake Dunham, he ought to be made to understand things."

Rodman laughed a little. "Do you realize that Jake Dunham is the biggest man in this county? In the state, even?"

"Yeah. An' that's jus' why I'd use my eloquence on him. Persuade him you are an' honest hard-workin' boy, and he'll tell other folks to b'lieve like he does."

"But how could you do it?"

"Easy. I don't know just how—yet. But I allus do what I think oughta be done—providin' there ain't too gosh many people makin' objections. An' me, I'm a powerful persuader when some-body suspects I ain't honest. What you say? You'll have a chance to talk to 'im too, after I get done!"

Rodman reflected, then shook his head. "I

didn't quite think you were serious at first. I don't know yet whether or not you really are, but—"

"I never was seriouser!"

"No, I couldn't agree to that. May sound weak-kneed. Probably will to you. But I don't want to make Jake any more angry at me than he is."

"My good gosh, man, you couldn't—'less he'd offer ten thousand dollars f'r your head instead of five!"

"I know. But you can't understand, Red."

"But I know how to make ol' Jake understand, I bet!"

"In spite of all this trouble, I can't really hate Jake Dunham. Why, I almost grew up under his arms. He's bullheaded and blind—would never in the world have made a success except for my father. But I've always believed old Jake was honest. Sometimes I do have doubts. But down in my heart I'm sure that he has just been lied to, fooled, worked on. There's Wally Dunham, you know. I wouldn't mind having a private talk with *him!*"

"Say, maybe *he* shot your father!"

"I've often wished that I could think so. He had more than anybody to gain by it. My father never liked him, wouldn't let him have any authority over the men. Now, if anything happened to old Jake, Wally would get every-thing—or nearly everything. Half to Clara, perhaps. I don't know."

"Then why don't you suspicion him? I shore would!"

"Best reason in the world, Red. Wally Dunham was back East at the time."

"Sure?"

"You're right I'm sure. I took particular trouble to find out. I wanted to suspect Wally Dunham. Even though Clara didn't like him, I was always more or less jealous of him. Knew that he wanted to marry her. Knew why—or at least, I think so. He wants to own the Double X."

"I'd like for to suspicion him too," said Red. "I don't like the clothes he wears. I don't like his manner toward strangers. He's too inquisitive."

"Well, Red, the only thing we can do is to sit up here a few days and rest. Old Hollar tells me that my friends there in Martinez are arranging to start the report that I've been seen making my way off south toward the Mexican settlement. That'll push the hunt off down that way."

"I don't like bein' in hidin'," said Red. "Makes me restless. Allus to-fore, I been able to walk into any man's town an' give my right name."

"I'll have Hollar tell my friends to get the report started that you boys were also seen down there. Hollar's not as big a fool as he looks—though he does act it, sometimes. But you can trust him. You especially! He's going to slip back to town and keep his ears open. We'll just sit tight and rest a while."

"That there is plumb suitable," Red agreed. "I got an ache in all my bones an' the skin knocked off o' some mighty big private places. Billy's britches is all wore out where he needs 'em most. Tom Jones, he looks faded, bad. That there shale slide is no place for to wear yore Sunday clothes. We're all willin' to rest some."

CHAPTER VII

The Double-Cross

Two or three days later Hollar came back from town, slipping up through the darkness, and was challenged on the trail by Red and Billy, who were standing guard.

Hollar was laughing to himself as he came along, and he slapped his leg, almost doubling over in the saddle, and almost doubled over with a silly kind of laughter in front of Red and Billy when he got off his horse and came up to them.

"You found yoreself a new brand o' whisky?" Red suggested.

"Bet he's got some fleas on his ribs," Billy offered.

"Hu-hi-hu-hi-he-hehe!" said Hollar, pawing the air. *"Ho-ho-ho!"*

"Go on an' laugh!" Red urged. "Good f'r the liver, I've heard folks say. Makes you fat, all the same as something to eat!"

"Gosh darn," said Billy, laughing. "I caught a whiff o' his breath an' it sent me off too. Somebody tell you somepin funny?"

"I played—*he-he-he!*—the damn'est joke—*he-he-he!* Yezir, the damn'est joke on Tig Burns—"

"Bet he was 'preciative!" Red murmured.

"I been—*he-he!* laughin' ever since f'r to think of how he'll look, nex' man he tries to shoot!"

"Bet he'll look inter-rested if the same is you!" said Billy.

Hollar had been drinking and was joyous. "*He-he-he!* He'll feel a fool."

"Won't that be nice!" said Billy. "But did you bring me some britches, like I told you? An' Red an' Tom's shirts?"

"Listen to what I done!" Hollar begged, laughing.

"I reckon," said Red helplessly, "we got to. Go ahead."

In a rambling, drunken, disconnected way, to which the boys listened without much interest or understanding, Hollar said that by mistake he went into a room at the hotel that he thought was his own; but it wasn't. The lamp was still burning, and Tig Burns, dead drunk or sound asleep—maybe a little of both—was lying there, dressed down to his spurs, but his guns were hanging on a bedpost.

Tig must have been in a bad way to forget to put a chair against the door. Such killers as he were afraid of bad dreams unless the door was blocked when they slept.

"Did you bite 'im?" Billy guessed.

"No," said Red. "He slapped 'im good an' hard right square on the wrist! Least, that's what I'd have done."

"I played him a joke!" Hollar explained, laughing drunkenly. "I soaped his guns—new guns—sights off—*he-he-he!*"

"Aw, now," said Red reproachfully, "why didn't you wash his face too? From what I remember of how his face looked, it needed some soap!"

"I bet Tig is sure scairt o' soap!" Billy affirmed in mock approval.

"When he goes to shoot—" Hollar again almost doubled over, he was so tickled. "I was careful. Took the soap away, so he wouldn't know!"

"Plumb cuckoo! All right, Hollar. Ride along up to the cabin. Tom Jones is goin' f'r to eat you alive if you didn't bring him no shirt."

"An' if you didn't bring me britches, I'll take yourn off you!" said Billy. "I need 'em, man!"

Hollar had not brought anything but the strong smell of whisky and a vague joke, so he went on, feeling aggrieved and discouraged that his little trick on Tig Burns was not appreciated.

"What you reckon he done?" Billy inquired.

"Yeah," said Red, after Hollar had ridden on. "I reckon it took Tig Burns three minutes, maybe not so many, for to know there was something slick on his guns. Maybe he don't shoot a man ever' day, but he draws f'r practice. Aw, hell, Billy. There you see the in-jur-'us effects o' drinkin' bad whisky."

"He'll sure see the in-jur-'us effect o' forgettin'

113

my britches," said Billy. "An' 'twas my money—poker money, too—he got drunk on.'"

"Well, he's goin' see some more injur'us effects, too! Me, I ain't goin' have a feller like him loafin' around town there, playin' his kind o' jokes—not when he knows where we are and how much money is on our heads. You stick here, Billy. Me, I'm goin' up an' join the council o' war. As a scout, Hollar is done. The moral to this here tale is, don't drink no bad whisky. Drink the kind I do!"

Red went off up toward the cabin, and the nearer he got to it the more slowly he went. His mind was made up to see to it that Hollar was not trusted any more; still, he felt a little sorry for the old man.

When he got there and paused at the doorway, listening, he found Hollar sitting in repentant dejection, taking a good hard drubbing from the tongues of his friends. Red's sympathies sort of switched about, for, after all, Hollar was not quite right in his mind.

The three old-timers who had taken Walt Rodman under their wings because they had known him from the time he was a little shaver, and had known his father, laid into Hollar without mercy. For one thing, they had asked him to bring shells for their revolvers and rifles. Hollar had forgotten them. For another thing, they had wanted him to bring some flour. Having to feed the three young punchers had very much disrupted their commissary layout. Hollar had forgotten the flour too.

They had also warned him, emphatically, not to drink. Now he was drunk.

Also something had gone wrong about the report that was to be started about somebody having seen Walt heading south. Hollar had to admit that Tig Burns and his men were right there in town now, and old Jake Dunham, too.

Everything appeared to have gone wrong, and Hollar had to take the blame. Probably deserved most of it, too.

"An' we gotta have them carte'ges!" said one.

"Ain't enough to last more 'n a couple o' hours if we have to start usin' 'em fast," another agreed.

"An' some flour!" The man who spoke eyed Tom Jones, who as maker—and eater—of flapjacks would have won a prize anywhere on the range.

"An' poke him away some'eres." The man pointed at Hollar. "He ain't dependable. Drunk as a biled owl. Jus' when he orta be sober as a judge!"

"As a judge is supposed f'r to be an' often ain't!"

"Awso," said another, "we-all have gotta know what's goin' on there in town! Ain't none o' us dare f'r to go, neither!"

So they swore at Hollar and repeated all they

had said about having to have cartridges, flour, and information.

At last Rodman spoke up. "Boys, there's Dod Wilson, you know. Lives there about six miles from town. If I start now I can get over there about sunup. Dod will go into town, buy supplies, bring them out to his place, then I can bring them on over here."

"But don't you let him know where we have holed up!" said one. "He'll get drunk an' blab shore!"

"That there Wilson place is mighty clost to town," another objected.

"An' if you bring all we want, be too much to carry. Hollar here c'd have brought a pack hoss!"

"Didn't need 'er, bein' an ass hisself!"

"But Walt, he can't be bothered with no pack hoss. He may have to cut an' run. An' I don't like Walt's goin' alone. He's plenty able f'r to take care o' hisself, usual—but the onusual is mighty likely to happen!"

"An' if any o' us showed up there along with Walt, Dod Wilson, he'd know right off where Walt was a-hidin' out. An' Dod's mighty loose-tongued when he's had a drink 'r two!"

After much powwowing, during which Hollar dozed and finally went into a drunken sleep, it was decided that Rodman, Red, Tom, and Billy would start at once and ride for Dod Wilson's place. They could do their traveling in the dark;

and being four of them, could put up a pretty good fight if crowded.

"You make Dod think you're heading south, 'mong the Mexicans," Walt was advised.

Dod Wilson had an adobe house, a water hole, mostly mud, and a couple hundred cows that ran with the Double X. He had once done Walt Rodman's father, and Jake Dunham too, a big favor; and they had given him a water hole that he could call his own. He felt proud of himself, being about the only little rancher in the country that never had any trouble with the Double X. Wilson was shiftless and easy-going and not likely to have trouble with anybody.

"I had been out visiting him that day you boys came to town—the day I rode off in such a hurry," Walt Rodman explained. "He told me then any time he could do something, to let him know. He hasn't any hard feelings against Jake, except as nearly everybody has changed some the last few years owing to the way Jake himself has changed. Like most of the old-timers hereabouts, he knows Jake hasn't done right by me."

They reached Wilson's place before sunup, and a couple of lank dogs made a racket that brought Wilson to the doorway in his stocking feet with a rifle on his arm.

Rodman called out, "Hi, Dod!"

"Oh, you!" said Wilson, in surprise. "An' who's with you?"

"Friends!"

"What you want?"

"To have a little talk."

"All right. Come along up to the house, I reckon."

They rode up and went in. Dod Wilson, by lamplight, looked Red and his friends over carefully with an air of distrust while he listened to what Walt Rodman wanted. The dogs sniffed at the young punchers' heels and seemed doubtful.

"I reckon," said Wilson reluctantly. "But 'f old Jake ever found out! He's throwin' conniption fits now, right there in town, I hear. I guess he was plumb right in sayin' you boys was friends o' Walt's."

"Yeah. We shore are!" Red affirmed.

"Where you boys hidin' out?"

"Closer by then maybe folks think," Red answered promptly. "An' we don't think it best to tell nobody, 'cause we like for folks to be truthful in sayin' to Jake's men that they ain't got no notion of where we are!"

Dod Wilson looked at him from under drooping lids and nodded. "That there is right. Yeah. I don't wanta know. Jus' asked. Jake, he is worse riled 'n I ever seen him before."

"You'll go to town for us?" Rodman asked.

"Shore. O' course, Walt. Yeah."

"An' hurry back," said Red.

"What's the hurry, huh?"

"Well, Dod," Rodman explained, "we would like to get away early this afternoon."

"Shore. I see. All right. I'll jus' hustle. You boys make yoreselves to home. I'll be back along a little after noon, shore."

Wilson stirred up a greasy breakfast, took the money they offered him, saddled, and rode off, leading a packhorse, followed by the two dogs.

"Queer old codger," said Walt Rodman. "But he's all right, Dod is. He once ran down and killed a pack o' rustlers all by himself!"

"Umm," said Red, unimpressed and mighty full of doubt.

Dod Wilson's house and corral were down in a little hollow between low sandhills.

The boys took care of their horses, then drew lots as to who was to stand guard for the first two hours. Rodman and Red drew the short straws.

"Them sleepy heads is allus lucky," said Red, as Billy and Tom spread out blankets in the shade and, with their forearms for a pillow, prepared to doze. "They ain't got no heads, much. They jus' got some big bumps on the end o' their necks!"

"Yore sarcasm can't disturb my slumbers none," said Billy.

" 'F I had me a face like Red's," Tom Jones explained, "I'd go around makin' folks pay me not to scare their womin an' chilern!"

"You shypokes had better snooze," Red

advised. "Two hours ain't a long time. An' I wanta rest my ears."

Red and Rodman filled up on hot coffee, strong as lye, and went up a sandhill. Red watched vigilantly, but Rodman nodded.

"Go on, curl up yore toes an' take it easy," Red urged; but Rodman, wanting to do his part, squatted cross-legged and tried to keep his eyes open.

Red was particularly alert. He did not feel quite at ease. But he had a good view of the surrounding country. Hills billowed gently toward the town, and nobody could come within two miles without being seen.

The long, hot day passed. The middle of the afternoon wore away with no sign of Dod Wilson, and Red impatiently guessed that he was drunk.

"My gosh," he complained. "Some folks never do learn that the right time for to drink is when they ain't got nothin' else to do. Even then they ain't no sense in takin' more'n you want!"

Along late in the afternoon Billy saw a wisp of dust over beyond the hills that lay toward town. He called attention to it, and all of them watched and waited.

After a long time Dod Wilson came in sight.

"He most sure ain't hurryin'—like he was told to do," said Red.

"But he's comin'. That's somethin'. I thought maybe he'd died o' age on the way," Tom Jones remarked. "That packhorse has gone lame," said Billy.

"Yeah. Sure has."

"That'd slow him down some."

"Yeah, but wouldn't have kept him in town all day!"

Dod Wilson came up slowly, at a crawl. "I'd been here sooner, boys, but my pack hoss went lame just outside o' town there."

They felt somewhat reassured by seeing that Dod wasn't drunk.

"Well, come on down to the house," he said. "I shore got good news. Ever'body's rode off south today. They figger you fellers, none o' you, is up in this country now."

"An' we sure ain't goin' to be long!" said Red. "That early start is all shot to hell."

"But night travel, it is cooler," Billy suggested. "An' even if you can't see nothin' much, other folks is in the same pickle about seein' you."

It was just beginning to get dark as they went down the hill to the house. With hasty grabs they began to unload the packhorse and make ready to divide the supplies on their own saddles.

Billy was interested in the trousers that had been brought, and Tom Jones was making away with all the shirts for his own saddlebags. But Red, who had been through more smoke than any of them, promptly laid hold on the ammunition and rammed some boxes of forty-fives into his saddlebags.

Dod Wilson had a bottle of whisky and was urging them to come into the house for a few little drinks before starting off.

"Come on, Walt," said Wilson, pulling at his arm. "We may not meet agin f'r a long time. An' I shore wish you luck."

Then Red, just because it was his nature to see what was wrong with a hurt dog or a horse that limped, ran his hand down over the foreleg of the packhorse. He knelt, feeling carefully. On his knees, through the beginning of twilight, he peered up toward Dod Wilson, who had his back turned, very earnestly telling Rodman what a good friend he was.

Red felt all about the horse's ankle, then stood up. He looked down at the horse's foot, then at Wilson's back.

The next moment he went into action with a long stride that rattled his spurs as he crossed to Wilson. Without a word he caught Wilson by the shoulder, jerked him about, and smacked an open palm squarely in his face.

Rodman exclaimed in protest. Billy and Tom stared, open-mouthed. Wilson settled back on his heels with hands half up in astonishment.

"Damn yore soul!" said Red. "Start to reachin' 'cause I gotta kill you! You need killin'!"

"Hey, Red, what—"

"Shut up!" said Red, pushing Rodman aside. "Wilson's goin' do the talkin'. Why you got a piece o' wire twisted 'tween that horse's fetlock an' hoof? Made yore horse go lame!"

"I never knowed—I wonder who could've done that?" said "Wilson, confused.

"Yo're a liar! You knowed it! When a hoss goes lame, the first thing you do—anybody does—is to take a look! You done it yoreself!"

"What you mean? Why'd I do that? After I done you fellers a favor. I don't know what yo're talkin' about!"

"Yo're more'n a liar!" Red told him. "Hit yore saddle, boys! This lousy shypoke's sold us out! Too much money on our heads. He couldn't think of a better excuse for bein' late than to have his horse go lame! An' he had to be late—wait till dark so fellows could ride in unseen an' surround us! We're cornered, I tell you!"

"Dod Wilson!" Rodman was stern. "Is that the truth?"

"Naw—naw—naw—I didn't. There ain't—not as I know of—no wire!"

"Like hell there ain't!" said Red. "Listen! I hear—be quiet a minute—*hoofs!* They're comin'!"

"That's his game!" cried Billy. "He timed it for sundown—we're shore surrounded!"

Wilson made a wild, scrambling leap for the

doorway, drawing his gun and, without warning, shooting backwards as he jumped.

Almost simultaneously four guns flashed flame at him. Who may have hit him or missed him, they never knew; but Wilson pitched forward with outsprawled arms, half in, half out of the doorway. The heavy rewards on these men's heads had been too much for him.

The shots they fired at him were heard in the distance and brought yells. Men who had come out to take them by surprise guessed that some of their party had come close enough to open on the "outlaws."

"They've got in behind us! Light out for town—then turn!" said Rodman.

"You lead the way, Walt! You know this here country!"

"I'm dang soon goin' to learn it good," said little Billy, "if they keep runnin' me around over it like they been doin'. I allus sort o' never sympathized before with jack rabbits dogs chased."

Rodman made a flying jump for his horse. All of them were only half in the saddles as their horses, with rapid clatter of hoofs, took off up the low sandhill in front of the house.

Red had rammed his revolver deep into its holster and with cocked rifle upflung in one hand drove the spurs deep. He expected that this would be pretty serious work; and his mind was made up that he was not going to be hanged for horse stealing.

As the boys rode out of the shadows and came into a silhouette on the crest, a dozen rifles seemed to blaze at them from all sides. But the house had not been entirely surrounded. Red's discovery of the wire and his quick suspicions had given them a precious few minutes' start before their pursuers could establish a circle. Moreover, the boys bolted in the very direction that nobody expected they would take, since it was straight toward town. The pursuers had carefully got in back of Wilson's so as to cut them off from the rough hilly country. Had the boys tried to head in that direction they would have been knocked out of their saddles in five minutes.

Now the firing was at long range, too far for accuracy with revolvers or very much with rifles, because the enemies were shooting at galloping shadows, shadows strung out in a line. Red, being the last in the line, had the most bullets sent at him, and some whined like peevish insects close by his head. He returned snap shots, just by way of showing that he would shoot rather than in much hope of hitting anybody. Though he was fast and deadly with revolvers, he never had had much practice with a rifle.

The haze of twilight was deepening. Red tried to keep one eye on Walt Rodman, who was way ahead, leading and flinging futile shots from his revolver.

Rodman knew the country, every hill and arroyo in it, and he might turn off suddenly, vanishing down some arroyo, either to the right or left. Billy followed behind him. In pulling the rifle from its scabbard it had slipped from his chubby hand, so Billy was not shooting. Red thought it was just as well. Billy couldn't hit anything with a rifle anyhow. The distance was too far for a forty-five. Besides, reloading on a galloping horse was chancy work, the next thing to impossible. Billy sat tight and rode hard, saving his shots for close range.

But Tom Jones had his rifle out and, being a pretty good shot, was trying to let the pursuers know it. His lanky body was twisted about in the saddle, and the reins hung loose. His horse swerved, not slackening speed, but leaving the direction that Rodman was going. Red yelled at him, but a yell in that clatter and excitement meant nothing.

Red swerved too, following Tom, meaning to overtake him and set him right. But before he could get anywhere near alongside a long chance bullet caught Tom's horse squarely in the head. The horse plunged high and fell hard, carrying Tom with it.

"Squashed like a bug!" Red gasped, spurring up, then with rough jerks brought his tough-mouthed horse into wild bouncing stiff-legged bounds beside the dead horse.

Red looked hastily about him. It was too dark to see clearly in the distance, but he could see the black bobbing shapes of riders not more than half a mile away and coming fast. He could hear them yelling too, like Indians on a charge, and firing as they came.

Red leaped off, tugging frantically, calling Tom's name. Tom was unconscious, and his leg had been caught under the dead weight of the horse.

"Gosh, he ain't dead—I know he ain't!" said Red in anguish. "But if they catch me they'll hang us both—but while I live they won't hang him—'r wish most gosh awful hard they hadn't! Jake Dunham's to blame f'r all this!"

He straightened up and yelled, just a wild, wordless yell of defiance and anger. Never before in his life had he ridden off and left a friend. It was hard now. For all he knew, Tom was dead, but he did not believe it. Rangemen were hard to kill. Tom was tough and hardy. Red felt like a coward in feeling that it was wisest to ride on. But when his mind was made up there was nothing indecisive about him.

Red returned to his own horse with a headlong jump that carried him into the saddle. Guns flashed at him rapidly, and yelling went up. Men called vaguely one to another, half gleefully. They thought they had him.

He lay low, ramming the spurs deep in the horse's flanks and holding them there, gouging, pressing the last flicker of speed from Tig Burns's long-legged hammerhead, riding blindly, though with quick, staring glances he searched the darkness for the fleeing shadows of Rodman and Billy. But there was no flash of guns in the distance. Perhaps they were tearing down the slope of some low hill, out of sight.

Some of the men stopped where Tom Jones had fallen, but others came on. Red knew how to get speed out of a horse, and the hammerhead knew how to give it. He knew that this horse was one to be trusted recklessly, and so let him go, pushed him, chancing anything that might happen.

The hammerhead did not once stumble, but sure-footed as a goat pounded through the darkness with neck straight and nose out. He took arroyos as if he had wings, sailing across, landing with a scrambling thud, and going on.

"Boy, I love you!" said Red as the horse flashed across a dark streak in the ground, scarcely breaking stride.

Darkness had come, starlit, with heavy shadows in low ground and on hillsides. In so far as he could, without making too wide a circle, Red began avoiding the crests of hills; but he did not begin to guide his horse until there was no longer the pulsing thump of pursuing hoofs beating on his ears.

At last he pulled down in the shadows of a low hillside and twisted about in his saddle, listening. He could hear, or thought he could, vague far-off shouts and an echoing flutter of hoofs that diminished. There was no shooting now.

Men had lost his trail, were riding blindly, hoping luck would help them cut him off. So Red figured. He wondered if they had overhauled Rodman and Billy, but felt pretty sure they hadn't. Rodman would be about as hard to catch as a flea in a blanket.

Red dismounted and loosened the cinch. He hesitated, listening, then said to hammerhead, "Old son, you've done noble! I'll give you a chanct to get some real breath!" He pulled the saddle off.

"An' now, old top, if we have to skin outa here bareback, don't you dump me! They've lost my trail, and me, I'm lost myself. Don't know where the hell I am, 'cept that I can't be far from town an' she over that-away."

He listened intently, peering all about, but saw nothing, and only the vaguest of far-off sounds drifted through the night stillness.

"I'm lucky. I'm allus lucky. An' you—you ain't lucky, hoss! You must have some plumb bad notions about men. Tig Burns first, now me! But usual, me, honest, I don't knock hell out of a horse. No more'n some men knock it outa their wives. If I could find me a woman half as purty an' reli'ble as a dozen hosses I've owned, I wouldn't be single no more!"

He stroked the horse's cheek and put his own against it. Red had much the same love of horses as of puppies. Some men might treat horses as though they weren't human, but he had a feeling that they were a lot better than just "brutes."

He reloaded his rifle and put a fresh shell in his revolver, then rolled a cigarette, lit it inside the crown of his hat, and covered the glow with his palm as he smoked.

"I bet they're cussin' your long legs," he said, whispering. "Some of 'em stopped to have a look at Tom. That give us the jump. An' we done some fancy twistin' back there a piece. I bet they think we turned an' made f'r the tall timber. Well, we ain't! My Dad, havin' been sheriff, I've learnt a lot of cussedness from fellows he's had to catch. The main thing as makes a man hard to catch is for him to have a fresh horse—when you ain't. How about it, Son? Do you feel freshed up? Are you ready for some more o' the same? Me, I hope to the Lord we don't have none, though!"

Red refolded the blankets and saddled up, put the reins over the saddle horn, and fastened the rope over the horse's neck with a half hitch about the nose. He took the end of the rope and went cautiously up to the crest, peering across.

There lay the lights of the town not more than a mile away. Red stared all about, a little confused.

"Why, dang it! away over yonder is the hills! We've rode damn near clear all around this desert metrop'lis! They didn't expect us to come thisaway. It shore is plumb wrong to fool folks so bad, now, ain't it? I wonder was Tig Burns anywhere near closc to me tonight? Not expectin' for to have all this pleasure, I left his guns up there to the cabin, hid.

"Come on, Son, let's be moseyin'. This here is big country, an' there's lots of places f'r fellows to go lookin' f'r us. I've learnt from my Dad that them that's hardest to catch don't do what you 'xpect 'em to. And nobody's goin' to bc expectin' us to come ridin' toward town!"

Red talked to his horse just about as he would have talked to a friend, for about the same reason, too: to relieve his own thoughts and feelings.

So, not knowing what he was going to do, or even wanted to do, but having an idea that he was going to do something before sunup that would make certain people wish they had never heard of him, he set out across country toward the town.

He didn't know where the road was, and hc didn't want the road anyhow. He might overtake or meet people on the road.

He knew very well that he was going toward town on account of Tom Jones. Hazily, at the back of his head, was the notion that he might be able to get Tom on horseback and ride off. He and Tom and Billy had been accused of horse stealing; and it would be just like Dunham's men to put Tom on the knotted end of a rope in short order, but there weren't many suitable trees out on the sandhills. There were some on the edge of the town. It would be like Dunham, so Red thought, to want to make the hanging of Tom a kind of show; and the thought ran through his mind, "Any time anybody hangs a friend o' mine there's goin' to be more funerals than just his'n!"

CHAPTER VIII

Town Trouble

Red, on horseback, edged cautiously up near the town. He grinned with satisfaction, feeling pleased because he knew that hereabouts would be about the last place in the country anybody would expect to find him. There ran through his thoughts the sage observations of his father, the sheriff: "What folks don't expect is easy done, allus!" And he added, half aloud: "An' it makes 'em have such funny looks on their face when they see you doin' it!"

Red was really a simple-minded sort of boy, with no self-awareness at all of being crazily reckless. He just had "notions," and to him they seemed perfectly reasonable. When the impulse came to do something, it was very seldom that other and more cautious ideas rose up to oppose it. In a vague way, he had a lot of faith in his "luck," which was perhaps nothing in the world but a headlong self-confidence.

He regretted that he didn't know Martinez better. Though it was "no great shakes of a town," still, it was pretty good-sized for a cow town; and one where he did not have the symptom of a friend or know a soul. He approached the town slowly, keeping off the road, cutting through sage and cactus that lay like dabs of blackness in the shadows, and made for a clump of scrawny cottonwoods that he remembered having noticed vaguely the first time he rode in.

He had to be careful because nearly anybody would recognize Tig Burns's hammerhead "an' start in to make 'emselfs disagree'ble."

As nearly as he could judge, there was no excitement in the town. Nobody was galloping through the streets. He took that to mean that the men who had gone out to Dod Wilson's had not yet begun to come in. Perhaps they had got onto Rodman's and Billy's trail. Perhaps they were just scouring the country.

"I reckon I'm the first one to show up. Now, if I ride up clost, somebody's li'ble for to see this horse. If I don't ride up clost, I'm mighty li'ble for to have to take one that can't run so fast when I leave."

He recalled having noticed that there was a blacksmith shop by the cottonwoods, and a small corral where horses were turned in until the smith could get round to them.

"Won't be nobody there this time o' night." He judged by a long look overhead at the stars, of which he did not know much, and by figuring out the distance he had traveled, that it must be close on nine o'clock. "Just the shank of the evenin'. A lot o' hell c'n pop 'tween now an' midnight."

For some time he sat on his horse in the shadows of the cottonwoods, watching and listening. He was right on the edge of the town, an unfamiliar and hostile town. "I wisht I was some prophet, so I'd know sort o' what to expect!"

Still in the saddle, he took out his pocket knife and, feeling all about, began to cut the thongs, stuffing them into his pocket. He had the hazy notion that he might want to tie up somebody who happened to be acting as guard over Tom Jones. As a usual thing, horse thieves weren't hanged in the dark. Red himself had been among those who sat all night about a smoldering campfire, waiting for sunup, to hang a horse thief. He felt sure that they would be saving Tom for daylight.

He got off the horse, removed his spurs, and stowed them in the saddlebags; then he tied the hammerhead to the corral, putting a slipknot in the rope and laying the end of the rope well away from the horse's feet.

"Now be a good feller, Son, an' don't whinny," Red begged, in a tone quite as if coaxing a woman, and slapping the hammerhead's neck affectionately.

Then he started up into town.

Martinez was unlighted except for such few lamps as showed through windows, and the bright glow that lay outside of the saloon doorways.

Red knew where the hotel was, the marshal's office, the Stage Company's barn, and the Silver

Dollar—all the most important places, but where he must take a lot of pains not to be seen.

When he got to an alleyway behind the main street he turned up.

"Too bad," he thought, "nobody showed me where the calaboose was. If they put Tom there I c'd drop around an' see 'im."

The alley was pretty dark. He stopped, looking up at the high windows of the dimly lit kitchen of a Chinese restaurant. It was a warm night, but the Chinamen had the door shut and the windows down. A group of them were huddled about a table gambling with beans that they poked and counted with a little stick.

"White men's game ain't crooked enough for 'em," Red guessed.

At the back end of a near-by saloon he could hear vague voices, and he was curious to learn the talk of the town. There was no light near the rear. He edged up cautiously, trying to listen, and peered through the back door. Some townsmen lolled at a table, discussing Dod Wilson and what he had done. Red could not hear clearly but understood that they were enviously talking of the reward money that would come to Dod.

Red nodded, feeling satisfied. "They ain't yet learnt that Dod he has been paid, full, complete, an' permanent!"

Then a cold chill jumped up and down Red's back. He knew that someone was standing right there in the darkness beside the door, had been there all the time, and had grown increasingly suspicious at the way Red seemed furtively to hesitate about coming in.

"What the devil are you up to?" demanded the figure. And as he spoke he struck a match, thrusting it close to Red's face.

"Oh, you're *him!*" the figure squawked.

The man, in striking the match to see Red's face, had lit up his own—the white, lean, half-sneering face of the tin-horn Nifty, who had accused Billy Haynes of stealing an ace.

Red jumped back, forgetting that he had been standing on a low step, and he stumbled, falling over flat on his back in the alley, not in any way catching, or trying to catch, himself, for both hands were pulling at his guns as he went down.

The startled gambler, with practised readiness, drew the pocket gun he kept to kill men with if they won too much, and he popped away frantically. And, thinking Red was hit because he had fallen, yelled, "I killed 'im, boys! I killed the—!"

His first shout had brought the men inside of the saloon to their feet as they faced about, peering. But now the gambler's words were cut off by the double roar of man-sized guns, one a second's tick before the other, fired almost from the ground, for Red's shoulders were flat in the dusty alley, and his arms straight out.

A cigarette paper would have covered where both bullets struck, and if a cigarette paper had been laid there it would have been directly over the gambler's heart.

The thought popped into Red's mind, "Me, I got to hustle now!" He rolled over, getting to his feet, and felt a kind of disgusted regret that the thing had happened when he was trying to nose about, quiet as a mouse.

He could hear the heavy tramp of running men in the saloon, and the calls from one to another of "What's happened?"—"Who shot?" From a nearby alley doorway someone looked out into the darkness and yelled, "Hey, what's up?"

Red yelled at him and instantly shot, purposely sending the bullet wide of the doorway, but wanting to discourage impudent questioning. Then he started at a run down the alley in the same direction as he had come.

On ahead of him Red saw a door open and the black shadows of men surge out. He paused, glancing backwards. Men had also come out into the alley behind him.

"Blamed if some wings wouldn't come in handy!" ran through his thoughts as he glanced back and forth at men who were hesitating and calling through the darkness. Red knew that he was in a pretty tight place; but as much as he had anything like a philosophy, it was his theory that a man was never really cornered until he was nailed down in a coffin. Even then, if you weren't good and dead, you might kick away the footboard and crawl out.

All in a flash it came to him with a feeling of satisfaction that they did not know who he was. The gambler had not called his name. "No matter who they think they're a-lookin' for, they won't think it's me!"

Red shot to the right and left, shooting high, wanting to discourage folks. Mostly, these were townsmen, not ranchers and punchers, who would right willingly have returned the shots instantly. His shooting made men scatter, taking cover. Many of them thought he was just some drunk on a rampage. Those who had been in the Silver Dollar figured he was somebody with an old grudge against the tin-horn.

Red knew he had to do something and do it quick. Bartenders had loaned guns, shotguns, to some men, and they were calling on everybody to join in and settle the fellow. From a doorway up the alley a shotgun boomed.

Red bolted at the back door of the Chinese restaurant. It was not locked. The Chinamen, too distrustful of one another to leave their game simply because some white men were shooting, still hovered intently over the table; but as Red came with a rush through the door they rose out of their chairs with startled squeaks.

"Down, you hombres!" Red yelled at them, kicking the door to.

Seven or eight Chinamen were there, all that lived in Martinez. They came together every night to try their luck in taking each other's money. The small kitchen seemed crowded. The Chinamen jabbered shrilly with heads thrown back in wide-eyed stares. They knew these punchers were a wild, mad lot. Some shrieked at Red, protesting; and one, who appeared to have authority among them, rose up, pointing toward the back door.

"Nozir!" said Red, and with drawn gun pointed the other way. "I'm goin' on through. Any o' you yellerbellies try to stop me—yore Maws'll be sorry!"

He started around the table. He had a puncher's contempt for Chinamen. For one thing, they were foreigners and looked queer; also they were physically weak and easy scared, as a usual thing. But as he cast a backward glance toward the door behind him where he expected pursuers from the alley to come, he caught sight of a wiry Chinese arm uplifted in the forward stroke of a long dagger.

Red ducked low with slithering turn of body, throwing up his left arm and gun protectively. The blade came down, slicing through the brim of his hat as the Chinaman's wrist struck his own. With an overhand swing Red brought down the

140

barrel of his other gun on the Chinaman's head.

"Can't waste shots—" he announced, striking to right and left "—on Chinks—" with far-reaching swing he knocked over another—"when white men may need 'em"

The table was overturned in the panicky scramble, scattering beans and money; and two, as if at a signal, jumped at Red from behind, each catching at an arm. If they had got hold of a wildcat they would not have had an easier time. Red kicked their shins, cracked their heads now against each other, now back up against the wall, swaying them all about as easily as if they had been straw dummies tied to his wrist. One dropped, dizzy and weak. Instantly the gun of Red's free hand lashed down on the coiled pigtail of the other. He then reached up and with full arm swing knocked over the bracketed lamp; and darkness, quick as a wink, came upon them.

Men were in the alleyway, shouting, trying to peer through the high windows. On the floor some Chinamen writhed and squealed. Others, in blind haste, bolted out of the back door, bumping wildly against the gathering crowd and shrieking that the devil had come upon them.

Red sucked in his breath. It had been hard, quick work. He felt halfway indignant. The Chinamen had been stupid. He hadn't meant to bother them at all. He merely had wanted to run through the restaurant, get out on the street, climb the first horse he saw, and make a break for the blacksmith's cottonwoods. There he would have switched to the hammerhead and bolted. But they had tried to stop him.

The unventilated hot kitchen and the peculiar smell that Chinamen have about them when they huddle together, together with the odors of stale cookery, made him more than breathless, almost sickened him.

"Never liked Chinks nohow!" he said to himself. "It's all their fault!"

With fumbling reach in the pitch-black room he felt for the partition doorway out of the kitchen, then he ran toward the street door, bumping against the edges of tables, scattering chairs. It seemed to him that he was making as much racket as if he had been tearing down the building.

The front door was not locked. Doors, excepting such as guarded gold or whisky, were never locked in Martinez. Red opened it and looked through, up and down. The street seemed to be clear. Everybody who had heard the shooting had already run across, making their way into the alley.

Red leaned out, looking for horses. At first glance he thought there was not one in sight, but on looking steadily he saw that there were some away up the street.

"Good gosh!" he complained. "Near as far up there as to the cottonwoods!"

Sounds came through from the back of the alley, where he could hear men at the kitchen door. Voices began calling through the darkness for him to come out, that the game was up.

"Is it, now?" he thought mockingly, and grinned. "Me, I'm just gettin' up a nice sweat!"

He realized that the crowd back there would soon think about this front door. If they thought, as they seemed to, that he was still in the restaurant, crouching in the dark to make a stand, men would be coming around from the alley to guard this door and so cut off any chance of escape.

"I sure got to get a wiggle on me!" he said, and closed the door gently, noiselessly, behind him. He jumped to the sidewalk, looked all up and down the street, then broke into a run, making for the shadows on the other side of the street.

He did not know just where he was going, but he had it vaguely in mind somehow to make a wide circle so as to get out to the cottonwoods at the edge of town. Of course, in crossing the street he couldn't tell whether or not he had been seen, but he didn't see anybody until he was huddled down in a dark doorway. Then a bunch of men came running around from the Chinamen's alley. They came with the straggling haste of fellows who have just thought of what should be done. Their heads were twisted this way and that as they looked about, up and down the street, all the while making for the front of the restaurant.

There they raised reassuring shouts one to another, saying, "He ain't nowhere in sight!"—"Must be still in there!" The reassuring shouts took on a tone of certainty as they saw the front door was closed. "He's still in there!"—"But look out! He's drunk an' 'll shoot!"—"Reckon we all know that!"

They guessed that Red, though they didn't know his name or identity, was drunk because he had acted so queerly. From what they could glimpse as he laid about him in the kitchen, rather like a joyous maniac stampeding the Chinks, they were sure that no sober man would have acted so. Moreover, they were greatly puzzled that he had run at all. Nobody but a drunk or crazy man would have run after dropping Nifty, the gambler. Anybody else would have stood up and accepted the congratulations of a rather favorable community, since Nifty was without honor in the country. Plainly enough, he had been killed only after he popped away two or three times with his pocket gun.

By the code and law of Martinez, of the range itself, you had all the right in the world to kill any man, excepting perhaps a popular marshal or sheriff, who took the first crack at you. But this fellow, after killing Nifty in a fair enough fight, had run—run into a kitchen full of Chinamen and tumbled them about like a coyote in a chicken pen. True, he had fired some shots at respectable citizens there in the dark of the alley, but he hadn't hit anybody; so that little hasty insult could be overlooked. The crowd was curious, not wholly unfavorable, but pretty sure that he was drunk and might be dangerous.

Red, huddled down in a doorway on the corner, heard the broken, excited, half-shouted conversation and understood why people were mystified.

"Still there, huh?" Red inquired, much amused. "Well, I ain't! An' if they go in an' smell that Chinese stink in the kitchen they'll know why I couldn't stay. Looks sort o' like I'm in a pickle. But looks they is of'entimes deceptive—as married folks learn!"

He watched curiously, crouching low, being well hidden by the shadows as long as no one came near. He had put his guns away and was down with fingers to the sidewalk and one knee bent, like a sprinter waiting for the signal. He was waiting for his chance to cut across the street, around the windmill that stood in the dead center of the town's main streets, and so get over near a darkened row of stores where there was no saloon or gambling hall casting its lights onto the sidewalk.

The men before the restaurant stood about with guns drawn, hesitating to go in, half expecting him to come out. They shouted within, telling him the game was up. But they seemed a little uneasy lest he might not believe them, and shoot if they started through the door.

They had simply got it into their heads that this man who had kicked up the rumpus was still inside, perhaps hiding with his tail between his legs, as some men do when cornered, or perhaps—as some men do too—silently waiting to shoot it out. This made them respectfully cautious, the more so as their feelings toward the unknown were not greatly prejudiced, and it would sure be bad luck to get shot by a half-drunken man they felt more inclined to commend than to reproach.

Red was amused by their coaxing yells. "You're all right, feller!"—"Come on out!"—"You played fair enough!"—"Nifty had it comin', mister!"

Then a light flickered up inside of the restaurant. Men had at last ventured into the restaurant dining room, coming in through the kitchen, and they called vaguely to the watchers before the street door. These then began to go in, hurriedly, curious to see the wreckage that had been made, and still half expecting to see the supposedly drunken man lying somewhere about, trembling in an attitude of surrender—or dead drunk.

Two or three of the men, more discreetly timid than the others, hesitated. They wanted to make sure that all was safe before they ventured in.

And Red was afraid to make his break before they too were out of sight. He wanted to head in a roundabout way for the cottonwoods.

At last they stepped within the doorway. And Red started on the jump, with legs flying. He knew that in another minute or two, just as soon as they discovered that he was not inside the restaurant, they would be out on the street, looking about, perhaps go nosing up and down.

He ran on his toes, keeping to the far side of the windmill. Then, without warning, his feet hit something soft and slippery as grease, and they went out from under him, straight into the air, and he landed flat in the soft puddle made by the trickling overflow of the watering trough.

This windmill and water trough were Martinez' civic pride, made the town class A. They stood in the dead heart and center of the town to welcome all thirsty broncs that came in off the sandhills or across the dusty valley.

Red flopped down with a jolt that took his breath, and so stifled certain remarks that seemed fitting and which he surely wanted to make.

He rolled over gingerly, lifting himself on hands and toes. His hands were daubed with mud. Cautiously he squatted and dipped his hands into the trough, washing them.

He squirmed about to ease the clinging clasp of the cold, wet, muddy clothes; then, peering over the edge of the trough, he said, "Gosh A'mighty, now what!" He saw the men come hastily from the restaurant door and gaze uncertainly up and down the street. "They sure got me out on a limb," he reflected. "No gettin' across the street without havin' 'em chase me. An' unfortunately, right now I ain't scairt enough to run good. 'Side', my clothes is too wet. I feel like a baby that needed for to have its diapers changed."

Then Red heard the vague drum of hoofs, coming fast, and listened, trying to place the direction. In the excitement of what had been going on for the past twenty minutes or so he had half forgotten the fight just at sundown out on the sandhills. But now here came some of those fellows that had been out there. They were tearing in, lickety-split, as if they brought news.

"What if they stop to water their horses—an' light a cigarette!" Red thought. "Horses'll snort at me layin' here. Cigarette match'll show why the horses snort—an' the best epitaph I c'n hope for is, 'He shore as hell could shoot!' An' I don't want to do no shootin' with my hands all covered with mud an' wet. I don't want no epitaph. Not even a nice one. An' I reckon right now I am too scairt to run good! Me carryin' a handicap o' all this mud—'twouldn't be fair. An' I'm awful strong f'r fair play. At least from other fellers!"

Men had scattered out along the street, some coming nearer the corner, merging into the shadows so that Red could scarcely see them.

And the running horses were nearer, much nearer. Waiting men clustered about at the edge of the sidewalk, eager to hear what the riders would report.

Red hugged the sloppy trough and looked about uncertainly. His hands were fairly clean of the mud, but wet. He absently tried to wipe them on the front of his shirt while he thought what he had better do. But he did not know which way to jump. By chance he looked up. Thirty feet overhead was the windmill's narrow platform, just below the great circular fan. Up there he would be safe, perfectly safe—if he could get up without being seen. He peered against the starlit sky, searching out the ladder.

The horsemen came thundering down the main street, splattering dust, with some three or four of their horses in a neck-to-neck race. Each man wanted to be first to shout the news, and they yip-ee-i-yipped to let it be known that they were coming.

Red knew that he now had no chance to make his way up that ladder, for the horsemen were close, and men on the sidewalk were staring, and he would have been seen creeping up the windmill. So he did the only thing he could think of, which was to squirm down low under the dripping trough, and again got his hands muddy. But he scrouged close up and almost under the trough and wiped his hands on his neckerchief

149

to get them as dry as he could just in case an argument started—in which case he had it in mind to dump some fellow out of a saddle and take his place, at least for long enough to get to the cottonwoods where he had the long-legged, deep-chested horse resting.

But the horsemen did not pause. Two came on neck and neck, and the others flashed by the windmill with head to tail of the leaders. The riders yanked hard on the reins, and the horses threw up their heads on backward curving necks and with skittering stiff-legged hops plowed up dust as thick as smoke.

The horsemen, with babble of shouts, told their news to the men who came clustering about their stirrups.

"Got two of 'em!"—"Leg's busted of one!"—"They scattered!"—"Tom Jones an' that Billy's been caught!"—"Killed ol' Dod, they did!"—"All rifle work—never got clost!"—"Downed two horses—caught that Jones feller an' the one called Billy!"—"The Ol' Man an' sheriff's bringin' 'em!"—"Ow, you ort o' heard Tig Burns cuss! He was ridin' up back o' Dod's place, expectin' 'em to come out that away when they tried to break through—but they broke through the other way! Tig never got more'n a mile of 'em, hardly."—"But he did see that red-head on his own hoss!"—"Boys are out scourin' the range!"—"Yeah, Tig says he ain't never comin'

to town no more till that red-head is caught!"—
"Yeah, he shore does want that red-head's scalp
f'r a watch charm!"

That was the news, and the town's men, having
heard it, began to chatter. They had news of their
own to tell. Nifty had been killed, and the Chink
restaurant had a cyclone strike it.

Red tried to listen, but now he was also trying
to get up the windmill without being seen. He,
being range-born and well schooled by his father
and his father's old friends, many of them Indian
fighters, knew that it is motion—movement—
rather than the object itself that attracts attention,
particularly in shadows. All eyes down there near
the restaurant were fixed intently on the horsemen
who, in turn, searched the faces of their listeners.
Red climbed slowly, with caution, reaching
up with almost imperceptible movement, and
drawing one foot after the other as gingerly as if
on thin ice.

After he was a little more than halfway up, Red
ventured to go a little faster, for the men were
less likely to glance so high overhead, and also
he was overshadowed by the platform and much
less likely to be noticed even if someone did
happen to glance up.

The town's men stirred up quite a discussion
over the possible identity of the man that
had killed Nifty. The story grew with their
telling. It was quite as if they wanted to make

the horsemen feel other people also had done something worth talking about. No doubt of it, Nifty needed killing—especially as he had shot first. But there hadn't been any strangers around town. Who could it have been? Whoever it was, was a proper sort of man and had shown thorough range-land contempt for the Chinks by not shooting 'em. One Chink was likely to die. He, a newcomer, who did not understand that a white man on a rampage was a privileged sort of character, had tried to poke a slim knife into the white man's back and had been whaled over the head with a gun barrel. And after the fracas in the Chink kitchen the fellow had vanished—just disappeared with no trace of hide or hair.

One of the horsemen made the comment that Tig Burns was sure not likely to take it as a favor for to have his friend Nifty killed, since it was said to be Nifty's habit to share winnings with Tig in exchange for the killer's friendship.

"Yeah, Tig, he ain't havin' no luck these days a-tall!"

"Yeah, Tig, he was figgerin' on knockin' 'em out of the saddle mostly by hisself, an' he didn't even get a shot at 'em! Nary a one! Him havin' no use for rifles—he didn't get a shot. Made him right smart peevish."

"The Ol' Man and the sheriff they've promised not to hang them two they've got till all the boys come in, the which'll then be done, legal and prompt, as they was ridin' Double X hosses when caught!"

"Come on, fellers. Let's water, then likker! The Ol' Man and sheriff'll be along soon."

The horsemen rode over to the trough and let their weary horses drink, while the men in the saddles rolled cigarettes and spoke jerkily, halfway satisfied with the night's work.

Red lay ear down on the platform overhead, listening and meditating:

"Caught Billy, too, eh? That means his horse must've flopped. An' Tom's leg got busted. That means he can't do no fast ridin' even if I got 'im off. Gosh! I wish I had me some good fast brains, 'cause I need 'em! But, by God, one thing is shore sure! Nobody ain't goin' to hang friends o' mine—leastwise till after bullets has stopped whizzin'."

CHAPTER IX

Private Conversation!

Pretty soon other horsemen came in, moving slowly. Folks were on the lookout for them and gathered near the watering trough.

The sheriff and Jake Dunham had brought in the prisoners, who rode with hands tied behind them. Red lay above, listening and wishing that he could convey some sort of signal to cheer his friends. He was clever at imitating the yap of a coyote. He had begun in babyhood, mockingly, and practiced more or less ever since; but he thought the folks down there might get a little overcurious if they heard a coyote yap from the top of the windmill.

"Sort o' make 'em inquisitive," he decided. "An' up here I ain't got much room for to run!"

The sheriff spoke a bit loudly and with an air of having caught the two prisoners all by himself. "Yes, sir," he was saying to the town's men, "just as I shot, this here Jones feller's boss dropped dead!" He was leaving no doubt in their minds that it was his shot that had killed the horse. "Couple o' miles, later, after we lost that Red, I was bangin' away, an' this here Billy's hoss went down—shot in the leg!"

"You're a liar!" said Billy's child-like voice, high in indignation. "He stepped in a hole, an' I bumped my head agin a star—went that high. An' come down all spraddled!"

"Comments from you ain't in order!" said the sheriff sourly.

"Go do yore braggin' in front o' womin folks. They like it!" said Billy.

"You are goin' to be hung so damned high," answered the sheriff, riled, "that buzzards'll have to look up for to find you!"

"Feller, where I come from, sheriffs mostly keep their mouths shut!" Tom Jones put in peevishly. "Or do their talkin' before men as ain't tied up!"

"Yeah," Billy chimed in. "You hang us, an' Red Clark'll cut yore nose off f'r a rabbit's foot. Looks sorta like one, anyhow!"

"You men keep quiet!" said Jake Dunham's heavy voice.

"Then make this pot-nosed sher'ff shut up!" said Billy. "He irritates me awful!"

"You," Jake Dunham went on judicially, "are hoss thieves an' outlaws, an' have come to the end of your rope. How you goin' to take care of 'em tonight, Sheriff?"

"Keep 'em up in my office, I reckon. Like the time we kep' that bank robber. Depytize a couple o' men to set over 'em. We gotta watch out careful that some o' the boys here don't get over-

155

anxious an' sneak 'em off an' hang 'em private."

"You shore as hell do," said one of the horsemen. "If Tig an' his bunch come tearin' in afore mornin'! Tig is shore riled!"

"Yeah," said another, "but Tig he swore he wasn't comin' in till he come with Red's scalp an' Rodman's eyebrows!"

"In the which case," shouted the irrepressible Billy, "he'll be out there till his whiskers drag the ground. Red'll kill 'em, an' don't you hombres get no other notions! He thinks Tig Burns is the sneak-killer that dropped his Dad—in the back!"

Men exclaimed a little at that, said, "Shucks!" Others said, "Red's jus' talkin'!" A few, "He jumped Tig that time when Tig wasn't lookin'!"

"You-all are the gosh a'mightiest bunch o' liars I ever seen!" said Billy. "Tig was a-lookin' right at 'im an' makin' personal remarks. You-all may be scairt o' Tig Burns, but Red, he ain't, an'—"

"Shut yore mouth!" said the sheriff. Then to Dunham, "You comin' along up, Jake?"

"No, Sheriff. I think I'll turn in. My rheumatism has sorta come back. One o' you boys take my horse over to the barn an' put him up." Jake Dunham climbed heavily from the saddle. "If any news comes in, I'll be over to the hotel here. Be sure to send me word. I purt-near hope as much they catch that Red as I do they catch Walt Rodman. So 'f they do, let me know."

"Yeah, Jake."—"You bet, Mister Dunham!"— "S'long, Mister Dunham."

"An' if these boys here loosen up an' talk," said the sheriff, "we'll light out an' round up that Red and Rodman. I suspicion from what pore ol' Dod Wilson said about the way they rode in to his place that they've been up yonder in the mountains. Ain't that right, you fellers?"

"Yeah," Billy answered, jeering, mimicking the sheriff's high-pitched nasal tones, "we been up yander in the mountings!"

"An' you," Tom Jones put in, being full of pain and knowing that he would feel a little better if he could make the sheriff mad, "have jus' been wearin' yourself to a shadder huntin' us in them places you knowed you wouldn't find us! That's the kind of sheriff you are!"

The sheriff swore with feeling. He wasn't a coward, but he wasn't brave enough to be contemptuous when men called his courage to question. He liked to strut about with spread of shoulders and to be looked up to. His election depended on the favor of Jake Dunham, and it hurt to be sneered at before old Jake.

"Hoss thieves an' outlaws," he said, "they can talk big. Goin' to get hung anyhow!"

"Feller," said Tom Jones, "go ahead an' hang us. That's the sort o' sheriff you are. Talk big about hangin' fellers other folks have caught!"

"Come on, come on. Bring 'em on," said the

sheriff, trying to pretend that he wasn't paying any attention to Tom Jones's sarcasm.

They rode off slowly. Men followed in a body to loaf about the sheriff's upstairs office and eye the prisoners, then loiter about in saloons, drinking and talking, half aimlessly waiting for more news from the range.

Red, with hat off and face low, peered, watching them go. His was a hopeful nature, and he didn't balk at risks when his temper was up, but he couldn't figure that he had much of a chance to get his partners away from the sheriff. Tom's leg being broken made things bad, even if Red did jump the guards and put them in the air. Moreover, the unlucky way they had sassed the sheriff would make him take special care to see that they were well guarded and made unhappy.

"The soft answer," Red commented critically, "she is a nice thing for to give—but it takes a hypercriter for to do it. Tom an' Billy is good leather from toenails to eartips. But neither'n has got a lick o' sense!"

His glance shifted, and he saw the bulky form of old Jake Dunham going slowly through the shadowed street toward the dimly lighted front of the Martinez House.

"Rheumatism, hunh?" Red commented. "Gosh darn his ornery ol' hide! Poster me up as a hoss thief! I never stole nothin'—not even a purty girl's heart, the which is lawful! Walt Rodman

158

is sure one lucky man f'r all his troubles. Now me, I got pertickular strong sentiments agin bein' thought a hoss thief. Anybody with gumption could see I got the worst o' the bargain when I swapped horses. It's all ol' Dunham's doin's. An' he's goin' to hang my sidekicks just 'cause Billy poked 'im in the nose. Hmm. I need me some bright ideas. I been so danged unlucky the last few hours that things has got to change. Luck allus does, an' now is its time."

As Red meditated, his temper rose. His exasperation became greater. He was unhappy over his trousers and shirt being covered with sloshy mud, and the way they clung to him, sticky and wet, made him fidget. He was angered because he was labeled as a horse thief, enraged that his friends were to be hanged; and so, all in all, in a mood to do any desperate thing that might suggest itself to him. He would not have hesitated twenty seconds in forming a plan but for Tom's broken leg. A man with a broken leg couldn't sit a horse well enough to get away in a hard chase.

An idea began slowly to creep into Red's mind. He entertained it at first merely as something it would be nice and suitable to do, without much thinking about actually trying it. It was such a good idea that he got interested. The more he looked at it, the more it seemed the only thing to do. It would sure shake the country up if it succeeded, and if not—well, there would be a lot of smoke, and folks would have something to talk about! He grinned with teeth clenched, amused, but with rising determination as he stared across toward the dimly lighted doorway of the hotel.

"Hang me for a horse thief, hunh? Well, they won't use no bigger rope if I steal the whole damn Double X! I ain't much good at poker, me havin' such an honest face that folks know when I'm bluffin'—but now I'm so gosh-danged warmed up an' overhet, I don't know myself whether 'r not I'll be bluffin'! Most likely I won't if they hang my friends. I'm goin' to pertend so hard that I mean business, maybe I can hide from myself any weaknesses I might have about doin' what I'm goin' to say I'll do!"

Red, on hands and knees, looked all about cautiously. There were the vague shapes of men in sight far up the street near the Silver Dollar. He gazed off in the other direction, toward the Stage and Livery barn, then looked across toward the Martinez House.

"I'll need a couple 'r three horses more'n mine. Hoss thief! Gosh, I'm goin' to steal so much maybe they'll 'lect me to Congress. All right, here goes! Umm. Must be gettin' along 'bout 'leven o'clock. By fast ridin' that'll put us over in the mountains along a little after tomorrow noon. Rheumatism, hunh? Well, just so I don't pick you a horse that's got it, I don't much care!"

Red scrambled down, feeling nicely warmed

up by excitement. He paused to wash his hands again and poke his nose and lips into the trough. His mouth felt dry, as if he had been chewing cotton. He wiped his face on his neckerchief, then edged off from under the shadow of the windmill, going cautiously until he had crossed the street. He wasn't so uneasy now about being seen, except at close range, because there were a lot of people in town. Anybody might be crossing the street.

Then he went through the darkness around back of the hotel.

There was a lighted lamp in the kitchen. He stepped with cautious tiptoes on to the back porch and peered through. A man with a pasty pale face and long rattail mustache, in his undershirt and with a dirty white apron about his waist, was sitting in a chair with a newspaper propped before him on the table. He was peeling boiled potatoes for the morning's breakfast and reading at the same time.

A cow-town cook's work is never done, particularly when, as most of them are, he is slovenly. Camp cooks are a different breed. Their work is carried on under the critical inspection of sarcastic punchers, out in the open.

It was plain to be seen how this cook had been spending his time earlier in the evening so that he had to remain up late and peel boiled potatoes for the breakfast fry. A tablet and pencil lay on the table; near the lamp was a sealed envelope, fattened by many pages.

"Got too much edycation for to be a good cook," Red mused as he crept nearer with a hand out toward the screen door. "Cooks that read an' write are notion-ate an' talk back sassy. We'll see!"

As the screen door squeaked the cook lifted his eyes from the newspaper and looked up, startled. Then his mouth opened, his eyes widened, the pan of sliced potatoes slid down from the apron between his knees, and as the knife fell from his fingers he raised his hands.

"You're sure one intelligent feller—f'r a cook!" said Red with approval from across a leveled gun. "Now, don't squawk, an' maybe you'll die o' old age yet. These spuds you've spilled—hard-fry 'em, an' folks won't notice the dirt. I've had to cook a time 'r two when I was batchin', so I know all the kinks. Do we be peac'ble? Or do you feel sarcastic?"

The cook gasped soundlessly as a fish out of water, then finally stuttered, "Wh-what y-you w-want?"

"Which number is ol' Mister Jake Dunham's room? I got some special business, private, f'r to interest 'im."

"He was just down here—asked for ham an' egg sandwich!" said the cook quickly, as if hopeful of giving satisfactory information, and with jerk of the head indicated the frying pan on the stove. "I had to build up a fire."

"I don't think you hear well," Red answered in a tone of concern. "I didn't ask about his ham an' eggs. Where's his bed?"

"Right up to the top o' the stairs. Number Five, I think it is."

Red gruntcd. "I. ain't interested in no cook's thinks. What's the number o' his room?"

"Five," said the cook quickly.

"Now, listen, you. I got a mighty strong prejudice agin hurtin' cooks. I like to eat too well—an' hate havin' to clean up dishes afterwards. Even a bad cook is better'n doin' the work yoreself. So you've got my sympathies. But don't abuse 'em. I advise most friendly f'r you to set tight an' don't wiggle."

The cook's apron was not tied about his body. After the well known and not entirely dainty manner of cow-town cooks, it was stuffed down inside the waistband of his trousers.

Red plucked away the apron and, getting behind the cook so he would not be encouraged to make hasty motions at seeing Red put away the gun, tore the apron into strips.

"Now, put your hands down behind you with wrists crossed. An' don't try to play no jokes. I'm an awful peevish feller when I don't see the funny point to a joke. An' all cooks' jokes is bad—like their coffee. The proper way is to put

163

a half pound, 'r little more, o' coffee in a quart o' water an' let 'er boil till a bullet'll float. Then she's thick an' strong an' fit for to be drunk. This thing o' tryin' to pass dishwater off for coffee is what makes us punchers so bad tempered."

As Red talked he bound the cook's wrists, tying them fast to the chair. Then he tied the cook's ankles tight against the chair legs.

"Now, listen, feller. I never stole nothin' in my life, so me, I'm willin' to pay. An' have you got an extra shirt an' pair of pants? I'm all lobbed with mud like an Injun in mournin'—an' I don't feel like feelin' mournful."

Red drew some money temptingly from his pocket. "I'm in a hurry, but I'm sure hones'." He looked up, tempted toward the flannel shirt on a peg beside the chimney, then explained, "If you got funny, I might plug you, but I won't steal yore shirt an' pants."

Except that Red seemed entirely sober, the cook would have thought this a cowboy prank; but for all of his good-nature there was an earnestness about Red that was impressive. His eyes didn't look quite as friendly as his tone sounded.

"I—I got some pants in the n-next room there, where I bunk. An' a f-fresh-washed shirt," said the cook, wanting to be agreeable.

"An' I'll give you fifteen dollars, which is away yonder too much. But if I do live long enough after tonight to play some poker, I'm sure to lose it —I allus do!—so I'll be generous. An' my name, jus' in case folks ask who tied you up, it is Red Clark o' Tulluco, so—"

"Oh, my gosh, *you*—him!" the cook blurted, popping his eyes.

"I am. An' if you hear folks sayin' I ain't honest, you'll be a mighty low breed o' liar if you don't speak up an' conterdict 'em!"

"How did you dare come to town?" asked the cook, not asking a question so much as expressing astonishment.

Red grinned. "I come to hold some private conversation with a feller." He laid down two gold pieces, one twice the size of the other, and taking the lamp went into the little room off the kitchen where the cook bunked. He found the fresh-washed shirt and a nice, almost new, pair of hickory-cloth trousers.

With much haste, Red undressed and changed clothes. He knew that to sit in a saddle with wet and muddy trousers was conducive to much discomfort, including blisters. He, being a loose-jointed lanky young fellow, and the cook a fairly tall man and a bit skinny, the clothes were a good fit.

"Now," said Red, returning to the kitchen and putting the lamp on the table, "we come to where I got to act unfriendly. It grieves me some, 'cause so far you've been a purty nice feller. Where's your spuds? Uncooked uns?"

"Over there in the corner behind the flour barrel."

Red looked. He came first upon a box of onions and picked up a fairly small one, almost tempted into using it for a gag, but grinned as he tossed it back. He didn't want to torture the cook, and even an unpeeled onion might make the cook hysterical from being nearly choked.

So Red picked out a potato that seemed suitable. Then he washed off the dirt, explaining, "I bet this is more'n you sometimes do when you feed 'em to us fellers. Open yore mouth—away wide!"

The cook stared at the potato and firmly clamped his jaws.

"Good gosh! You act like a cayuse that ain't bridle broke. Open your mouth, feller!"

The cook stubbornly shook his head.

Red drew a gun, half raising it. "I don't wanta wollop you over the head. Hones'. I allus try to be friendly with cooks. They've sort o' got the edge on you when it comes to gettin' even. I knowed a cook onct that cooked up some prairie dogs an' called 'em cotton tails. He was buried with dishonor, but not till after the fellers had et. To this day if you mention prairie dog to a Cross Bar puncher he thinks maybe you are tryin' for to encourage him to shoot you. Awful sensitive, punchers is—'specially them as has et prairie dogs. Most near as bad-tempered as cooks. Come on, now. I've spoke my little piece."

The cook stubbornly shook his head. Red lifted the gun as if to smash down on the cook's head, and the cook's mouth popped wide in a straining yawn.

"Gee gosh, what a lot o' space you've got inside your face. Don't you go an' swaller my potater—'r bite my fingers!"

Red poked the potato, about the size of a lemon, into the cook's mouth, then with a strip of the apron tied it firmly. The most noise that the cook could make would be to gurgle about like a man under water.

Red looked about as if trying to recall what it was that he was forgetting, then, with a quick pounce, caught up the tablet and pencil. That was what he had meant to take with him.

He then helped himself to the cook's matches, reached out as if about to take the lamp, hesitated, and changed his mind. He would depend on matches. It might be easier to explain if he met anybody. With the lamplight in his face it might not be so easy to make folks think he was a lodger looking for his room.

"Now, feller," he said in parting, "if you go jerkin' an' buckin' yoreself around, you're liable to make a noise—an' me, bein' wide awake—'ll be first to hear an' come. If you don't think you'd like for me to come back all peevish, you just keep still an' meditate on the wisdom o' doin' what I tell you. As you can see—" Red pointed at the gold pieces—"I wanta do what's right. An' I'll shore think it right to bust yore head wide open if you make a commotion!"

Red went from the kitchen into the passageway that led to the washroom where there was a tin-lined trough in which were three or four basins to be filled from the water barrel. Red struck a match and found his way into the narrow hall. He struck another match and looked for a moment into the mirror where the pretty girl, standing at the head of the stairs, had seen and spoken to him. Jake Dunham's daughter. It was most amazing how a big fat heavy fellow like Dunham could have such a pretty girl. The magic of her beauty still lingered with fascinated memories in Red's thoughts.

"Doggone, Walt Rodman, he is a lucky man!" said Red to himself, feeling that all of young Rodman's troubles and dangers were trivial compared to the reward the gypsy-like girl offered him.

In thus coming into the hotel through the back way, Red had avoided passing near the saloon where idlers might be lingering, readily inquisitive, or the bartender, if alone, dozed over an old newspaper. He knew from the view he had had from the windmill that trade at the hotel bar had been slack tonight.

It was a late hour. He did not know just what time, but judged that it was close on to twelve. He felt that the later, the better for him, since he was less likely to meet meddlesome folks. He felt, too, that he was doing meddlesome folks a big favor in avoiding meeting them.

Red had stuck the pencil into his pocket and poked the tablet inside of his shirt so as to have both hands free. With cautious step he went up the dark stairs and the faint squeaks of the wood sounded alarmingly loud to his ears.

At the top he looked along the hall for any bright threads of light under the doors that would indicate some persons were wakeful. All were dark.

Red paused, hesitating. Dunham's room should be right here at the top of the stairs—if the cook hadn't lied. Supposing he had, and Red were to open the door of a room where there was a woman. She would be sure to yell—"An' then I'd have to scatter myself in some quick jumps!" He had the range-born timidity about scaring women. Blazing guns were just some Fourth o' July doin's compared to a woman's scream.

Red gingerly struck a match, then shook it out. He stood squarely before Number Five. But queer explosive noises came from the room. Yet in a way he was reassured. That was no woman's snore. It was the hoarse rumbling snort of a big-chested man.

"The rheumatism, it is troublin' his dreams," Red commented.

He stood, poised and thinking. If he opened that door, trying to slip in, Jake Dunham might wake up a moment too soon and have a gun handy. Nothing that he had heard about Dunham indicated that the coarse, burly old fellow was cowardly. It would be dark inside, and Dunham would have all the advantage. Red, holding his breath, carefully tried the door. It was not locked; that is, there was no chair propped against it.

"Got an easy conscience, like he was an honest man!" Red thought, with unwilling approval. "I gotta play honest too," he said, grinning in the dark.

He rapped gently on the door. No answer. He rapped again, wanting to awaken Dunham but not disturb anyone else. He didn't think there were many people in the hotel, but you couldn't tell who might have the next room—or how long his ears were. Red knocked again, not loudly. The queer explosive sizzling stopped. Red tapped insistently.

A deep, grumbling, half-awakened voice asked, "What is it? What'd you want?"

"Mister Dunham, that there Red Clark is here, an' I thought I'd come an' tell you—like you said to do if anything happened!"

"Heh? They got 'im? That's good! Now I can sleep better. An' Rodman? Did they catch 'im?"

Red, with gun in hand and three matches held as one in the other hand, opened the door slightly, saying:

"Not as I heard tell. But they's somethin' else I am to tell you—"

"All right, tell it!"

Red stepped inside, struck the matches, holding them over the leveled gun, and told it:

"The same bein' hands up! An' no talk!"

"Huh! Uh! Ugh!" said Dunham with three distinct and explosive grunts, startled and not quite understanding. But up went his hands. "Who are you?"

"I'll tell you in a minute. Don't you make no wiggle! This here is damn ser'us!"

Red, with quick, searching glance, noticed that Dunham's gun and belt were hanging on the back of a chair and not within easy reaching distance of the bed. Dunham surely did have an honest man's conscience.

The three matches filled the room with light, like a tiny torch. Red stepped back to the table and, holding the matches between thumb and forefinger, pulled off the lamp chimney with second and third finger of the same hand; with the other hand he kept the gun leveled. He touched the matches to the wick, replaced the chimney. A moment later the yellow flicker of the wick became a clear, bright light. Then Jake Dunham could see who it was that had come into his room.

171

Dunham didn't move. He sat up, huge and solid in the bed, gazing steadily at Red and expecting to be shot. He grunted heavily, just about as if unexpectedly poked in the belly, but said nothing.

Red went back to the door, closed it quietly, and, having removed the chair with gun and belt well beyond Dunham's wildest reach, spoke:

"Yes'r, Mister Dunham, that there Red Clark is here in town. Bein' an honest feller—as you're going to learn—I don't tell no lies. An' now you listen careful, Mr. Dunham. I don't want to be no more unfriendly with you than I can help. But I ain't goin' to be hung f'r no hoss stealin'. If I'm hung it'll be for killin' somebody as wears about yore size of pants. I reckon you know I must mean business for to come here to town like this just to have some private conversation with you."

Dunham's great full face grew reddishly dark as he listened, and his big body heaved with quick breathing. He was no doubt a little frightened, but he was mostly angry. Red's impudence astounded him. He was also astounded and indignant that his men and friends had seemed to be so careless and unwatchful as to allow the red-head, with a price on that head, to come into the town, into the hotel, into Dunham's own room and rouse him from sleep.

"Well, talk!" Dunham growled, glaring from under bristling brows.

"Y'see, Mr. Dunham, as we can't talk full an'

complete here," Red went on, "you git outa bed, git into yore duds, pronto! Move quick an' hurry, noiseless. If I've got to, I'll shore as hell kill you! But nex' to gettin' hung myself, that's what I don't wanta do. Yet, 'f you think I won't do it, you just try gettin' rambunctious!"

Dunham's eyes popped wider with a kind of blazing defiance. He had grown fat and heavy with the years; he had been spoiled by finding that he could bully folks; he was a rich man and the friend of rich men; he had been kowtowed to and so let his violent temper jump about with a free rein; but after all, he was Jake Dunham, an old-time fighting cowman and no coward. But there was no arguing with a man who had the drop—not when he was a lean-jawed lanky red-head who had flailed Tig Burns over the head with his own gun, stuck up a saloon full of quick-shooting cowmen, and ridden down Shale Butte—without breaking his neck.

Dunham would have liked Red immensely, as he liked all fighting harebrained dare-devils, if they hadn't bumped into each other, cross-wise, on sight. As it was, Dunham hated him with all the unforgiving stubbornness of the Dunham blood, which took a lot of pride in never forgiving. To him, this red-head was pretty much what a red rag is to a bull. But even a wild bull is almost respectful to the man who holds a ring in its nose and a pitchfork in his hand.

Dunham, in a way of speaking, was nose-ringed.

"What d'you want?" Dunham growled, furious.

"Now, Mister Dunham," said Red, earnest, "I want you for to notice I'm speakin' polite but firm. I ain't no heller, an' I ain't no killer, an' I never stole nothin'. Me ner Billy ner Tom Jones. We're just hard-workin' rowdy punchers. But you've got us plumb in bad. I don't wanta be no danged outlaw. But while you've got me postered as one, I'm shore goin' to be like I was a danged good one! An' if it's in the cards that I gotta go out shootin'—well, I can shoot! I ain't goin' to hurt no hair o' yore head if you don't get rambunctious—but call for a show-down, an' shore as hell ain't no place for a lady, you'll get it, prompt! Un'erstand?"

Dunham growled. He halfway thought perhaps this red-head was a little afraid of him and trying to be respectful so as not to make him too angry; and he also halfway felt that this red-head wasn't afraid of anything or anybody, and it puzzled Dunham that the fellow should be trying to seem respectful.

"What you want?" he growled again.

"Now, me, I got a plan all worked out. She's some elaborate. But when a feller's havin' for to fight to keep his neck out o' the knotted rope, he's liable to be some energetic, like me, now. My own neck an' that o' my two sidekicks, the which are just the same to me as some brothers,

174

is the most important thing in the world. So—"

"What you want?" Dunham repeated, not so much after information as to try Red's nerve by asking the same thing over and over. Dunham had been in tight places before. He had the range man's feeling that the enemy that did not shoot on sight—that is, the fellow who would stand talking about it—was likely to be a little afraid to shoot and might be bluffed or cajoled.

"Well, sir," said Red, "I want you to climb outa bed an' git in yore duds. We're goin' for a walk."

Dunham shook his head very slightly, just enough barely to indicate a refusal.

Red spoke earnestly: "You 'pear to be gittin' a wrong impression. Don't you go an' think 'cause I ain't cussin' an' makin' threats, I don't mean what I say. I don't never cuss a man as has his hands up. 'Tain't right. But now you come a-scramblin'. Just 'cause I won't cuss you ain't no reason f'r thinkin' I won't shoot you! Out o' that bed, *pronto*!"

Old Jake sat hesitant and blinking. There was a ring in Red's tone that gave a warning he clearly understood and couldn't ignore. He had no notion of refusing to do as told, but it was hard for him to realize that this was not a bad dream. He knew well enough it wasn't, and without showing any fear he decided it was wisest to do as told. He didn't at all guess that about the last thing in the world Red would be willing to do was to shoot an unarmed man.

With grunt and heaving twist of his big body he got to the edge of the bed and sat up, looking about the floor. Then he reached for his socks and with slow weariness pulled them on.

Red took Dunham's gun, put his own down within quick reach, and keeping his eyes on the ponderous old cattleman, began to prod out the shells. He knew that he would have to let Dunham carry his gun because, if by chance they met anybody, that anybody would think it plumb queer to see old Jake without his gun—most near as queer as if old Jake went walking around without his britches.

Having prodded out the shells, Red then took one of the thongs he had cut away from the saddle out of his pocket and tied the gun fast to the holster. He had not known just what he was going to do with the thongs when he cut them loose, but he knew that good stout strings often came in handy.

Dunham watched him cautiously, with some uneasiness and much understanding. He asked in a kind of level, sour growl:

"You goin' to try to take me off some'eres?"

"Yes'r. An' what's more, I'm goin' to do more'n try. I'm goin' to do it!"

Dunham made a sound something like "Hrnh-urr!" Then, "What if I refuse to go?"

"Smart feller like you c'n answer that question easy!"

"You shoot me," said Dunham, "an' it'd wake folks. You'd be caught."

"I reckon." Red nodded. "An' you'd be dead. Yore body'd sort o' be my breastworks!" He tried to look as if he held four aces.

"An' you've got it in mind, I reckon, to take me off some'eres—where nobody can hear the shot?" Dunham asked, watching intently.

"F'r a smart feller, you're bad at guessin'. Fact is, Mister Dunham, I don't want for to make you even any more uncomfortable 'n necessary. I ain't no feller to do things spiteful. I'm reason'ble. Also plumb ser'us an' earnest."

"All right. You win. So s'posin' we call it off," said Dunham.

"How you mean?"

"I'll call in them posters an' turn your friends loose 'f you-all will promise to leave the country."

"No, sir. I don't wanta be insultin', but I don't trust no man who makes me promises when I got the drop. Sorta makes me dubious. So you'd better hustle a little, an' don't be poky in dressin'. You got to un'erstand that if my plans fail you're goin' to be the first one to get hurt. So you'd better be mighty precautious in helpin' me along. Way o' speakin', you'd better chip in an' help me."

Dunham sighed heavily and went on dressing. He stamped into his boots, slipped into his vest, took up his hat, and breathing hard, put it on, then stood as if waiting further orders.

Red tossed the gun and belt to the bed. "Wear 'em."

Dunham fitted the belt about his waist. "You may think I'm lyin'," he growled, "but I got rheumatism bad in my left leg. So 'f I walk slow, I ain't pertendin'."

"I know you got rheumatism. I was layin' up on the windmill platform tonight an' heard you speak when—"

"You was doin' what?"

"I was layin' up there when you an' the sheriff rode in, with my sidekicks. I heard all that talk about hangin' 'em. Which is why you're havin' troubles now."

Dunham swore, sort of disgusted, as if thinking how pleasant it would have been to discover Red up there.

"Now, Mister Dunham," said Red, "I wanta say afore we light out that, personal, I think maybe you are an honest man who's got bad judgment about some things. Me, f'r instance, an' my friends. We ain't hoss thiefs. An' we ain't goin' to be hung as hoss thiefs. So now—" Red fished out the tablet and pencil—"you come here an' set down an' write like I say."

"Write? Write what for?"

"You'll savvy plenty as you write. Come along."

Dunham came slowly, reluctantly, mystified. He sat down with a furtive glance from the corner of his eye. Red saw the look and spoke:

"I hate to be like a danged parrot an' have to repeat myself. But onct more—an' no more—I'll say, listen clost. You jump me, 'r try it, and I'll kill you! You do like you're told, an' we'll get on peac'ble. Now write!"

Dunham opened the tablet and picked up the pencil. Red was squarely behind him, with gun leveled. Red dictated:

"Everybody in town, dear folks: Red Clark of Tulluco has come up here to my room and is taking me off somewheres. So whatever you do don't hang Tom Jones and Billy Haynes. He says the day you do he'll kill me. He says he knows you won't, so he won't have to kill me. He says when I come back to town I'm going for to be plumb sure and dead certain him and his friends is nice honest boys. Jake Dunham."

"Now," Red concluded, after peering over Dunham's shoulder, "you go ahead an' write whatever you want on yore own hook. I don't care what you put in."

Dunham eyed him, nibbled the end of the pencil, took a fresh sheet of paper, studied, then wrote:

"Dear Sheriff, you're a hell of a fine sheriff you are to let this fellow come into town like this and steal me like I was a calf. He was laying up on the windmill platform when we rode in. Your job is done. When I come back to town you'd better be gone. Damn your soul for a blind lazy goodfornothing pup. Yours truly, Jake Dunham. P.S. And I mean it."

Dunham threw down the pencil and stood up, his face full of red-hot blood; but his feelings were a little relieved. At least he had been able to cuss out somebody.

"Good gosh," said Red, having read the broad, firm scrawl, "maybe he'll not want you to come back!"

Dunham swore. "I don't care what he wants. I want him to know how I feel."

"Well, me, I'll be awful sorry, Mister Dunham, if he gets scairt and hangs them boys!"

"He won't. You don't need to do no worryin' about that. I ain't!"

"Then I reckon the sheriff'll do what worryin' is done." Red took up the lamp. "You walk on ahead, slow. Downstairs go back through the

180

washroom, then into the kitchen an' out back. If we meet folks, you just speak sour an' go on like it was none o' their business. The which it ain't. My face ain't very well knowed in this town, but if it's reckernized, put yore fingers to yore ears— if guns goin' off makes you jump!"

Dunham glowered at him with puzzled stare. He didn't know quite what to make of Red's easy way of speaking, as if he took matters pretty much as a joke yet also was dangerously in earnest.

They went out of the room, across the hall, down the stairs, through the washroom, and into the kitchen, where Dunham straightened up in surprise. The struggling cook had overturned his chair and lay as helpless as a turtle on its back.

"Stoop an' straighten 'im, Mister Dunham. I don't like for to see even a cook more unhappy than is necessary!"

Dunham said, "You're sort o' forethoughtful, ain't you?" and gazed at the overturned cook as if critically passing judgment on the way he was tied, perhaps seeing how well he might later expect Red to do the same kind of a job with him.

Dunham stooped with a kind of patient obedience and much grunting, then heaved the chair and cook upright.

The cook made a vague muffled blubbering noise, as if choking, and pleaded with his eyes; but Red shook his head. "Nope. I been as gentle with you as is safe. An' now, mister, jus' you look there on the table. Fifteen dollars I left for his shirt an' pants, the which I'm wearin'. I want for to point out ever' little thing I can for you to see it ain't my nature to steal nothin'." Red put down the lamp. "You an' me, I hope, is goin' to get purty well acquainted, soon. Now we're goin outdoors, down to the Stage Barn. Put yore hands down in yore pockets an' keep 'em there. I'll stay right 'long-side an' a little back o' you, watchin'. Awright. Le's mosey!"

CHAPTER X

"You Got the Swell Head!"

They went down the street without meeting anyone. Men were still stirring and would be stirring—that is, if they didn't overdrink and grow motionless—all night up at the Silver Dollar and places near by, close to the sheriff's office. The Stage Barn was down the other way.

As they came to the dark yawning doorway Red said, "This here is where we all first met and us boys got misunderstood by you. Now it's so plumb dark in here I can't see well. So you just put your hands behind you, wrists crossed, and I'll put my fingers there like I was a doctor takin' your pulse. That way I can catch any symptoms of restlessness as may appear. An' cure 'em, too—better'n most doctors. That's it. You're doin' fine. Now sing out for that barn boss. Tell 'im you want three fresh horses, two saddled. An' if he asks any questions, tell 'im to go to hell, emphatic."

Dunham called, not loudly.

"Oh, shucks, said Red, protesting. "Call like you meant it. Scare the pea-waddin' outa him. Be natural-like!"

"Hey-oh, Ghorly! Rise up!"

"Louder," Red urged. "With more feelin'.""

"Ghorly," Dunham boomed, "damn your soul! Hey-oh!"

A sleepy voice called in tones of protest from the grain room, where the man on night duty slept. When he realized that it was Jake Dunham who called, he came with a stumbling rush, dangling a lantern, and blinked up sleepily but eager to please.

"Three horses. Two saddled. Fresh ones."

"Why, Mister Dunham, whatever for, this time o' night?"

"Do as you're told!" Dunham shouted at him, being peevish anyhow, and just naturally roaring if anybody presumed to question him.

"I—I didn't mean nothin'. I was jus' askin'," said the barn boss humbly. He went out into the feed corral where the horses were kept and came back leading three. Dunham's saddle was already there, having been brought with the bunch of horses sent in after the men returned from the search on the range.

Red watched the saddling, keeping Dunham and himself well back in the shadows. When the work was done he spoke up:

"Ghorly, carry that lantern an' go back to your bunk in the grain room. Mister Dunham, walk along after him."

The barn boss gaped with mouth open in blank puzzlement because, from the way Red spoke up, he was taking charge and no doubt about it.

"Do as you're told," Dunham thundered. "Want us both to get shot, you damn fool?"

Ghorly, with something of the sound of a man poked unexpectedly in the stomach, stumbled ahead with neck so twisted that his face was backwards, almost hanging over his shoulder, and his mouth was open.

"Hang up that lantern," Red told him. Ghorly did. Red carried a rope he had taken from a saddle and deftly tossed it along the floor. "Now, Mister Dunham, you put a loop round his neck, a slipknot on his wrists drawed up behind, then lash his feet with a couple o' half hitches an' a hard knot."

"Whatever have I done?" the amazed Ghorly protested.

"You been born!" Red snapped. "An' are in the way!"

"Shut up!" Dunham added.

"We don't want him kickin' up no commotion," Red explained, "till we are well on our way. Might interfere with some plans you an' me has got!"

Ghorly's head was all in confusion. Dunham seemed to submit to being bossed, willingly. He lay unresisting while Dunham set about, with pretty much of a scowl, to tie him up. Red leaned in the doorway, critical. Dunham eyed him from time to time, not planning things he shouldn't so much as wondering at the red-head's calmness and almost good-nature. The fact that he wasn't fidgety very much impressed Jake Dunham.

"Don't make him suffer more'n necessary, Mister Dunham. 'Tain't his fault we're goin' off secret-like. When it's folks' fault I don't much care how bad they get hurt."

Dunham probably had not tied a steer in twenty years, but he went at Ghorly as if this was a steer and the timekeeper held a watch, handling him pretty roughly and no doubt wishing that it was Red he was tying instead of the inoffensive barn boss.

"There, damn you!" he said, straightening up and facing Red. "Now what?" He glowered as if moved by rash impulses.

"Le's just keep cool an' calm, Mister Dunham," Red advised. "If we start cussin' each other, my influence might be corruptin'. I'd teach you cuss words you never heard before!"

"I'd like to break your damn neck!" Dunham shouted.

"Sure. I don't blame you none. But you ain't goin' to do it. You're goin' to take up that lantern, go out there, take up the lead rope of the unsaddled hoss, climb on your saddle hoss, and then hang the lantern on a harness peg. After the which, ride out, headin' over across toward the blacksmith shop by the cottonwoods."

Dunham took the lantern and stumped out of the

186

grain room, forgetful of his rheumatism. He did as Red instructed, and they rode off with Red's horse right up against the flank of Dunham's. There was no danger of a man of Dunham's weight trying to ride off and leave Red and run the chance of being yanked from the saddle with a rope about his neck like a calf being dragged to the fire.

When they got to the cottonwoods where the hammerhead waited, Red said, "Now, me, I sure am sorry to be rude-like, but I got to ask you to drop yore reins an' raise yore hands. I don't want to do you no injustice by some suspicions, but I think maybe you'd get away from me if you could. After we get better acquainted I bet you won't feel thataway."

"I'd like it better if you didn't talk so damn much an' try to be funny!" said Dunham, raising his hands.

"Now, see how you don't un'erstand things!" Red grumbled plaintively. "I ain't funny. I'm ser'us. 'Cause I don't snort an' beller an' cuss you think—why dang it, you must think folks are only polite to other folks when they're scairt of 'em!"

As Red talked he kept a wary eye on Dunham's upraised arms, which were faintly silhouetted overhead, and at the same time went about tying the horse on which he had ridden from the Stage Company's barn. Then he mounted the hammerhead and told Dunham to reach for his reins.

"Now then, Mister Dunham, we are settin'

187

out. Just push forward on the lope, straight cross country—keep off roads—toward that place knowed as Robbers' Roost!"

"So that's where you've been!" said Dunham in the tone of a man bitterly disappointed that he hadn't guessed it before.

"Yeah?"

"It was that report about you been seen down south that threw us off some!"

"Yeah?" Red repeated questioningly.

"Yes, damn you!" Dunham shouted.

Red exasperated him, or so he felt, more than any man he had ever met in his life, and his life had been full of exasperation. There was, to Dunham's way of thinking, something utterly unnatural about Red's good-natured ease. Dunham would have felt more comfortable if Red had shown anxiety or even a brutal menace—those things would have seemed natural. But to act a little amused and not appear at all troubled was just too much for Dunham's understanding; and what he didn't understand made him mad.

They went on, now at a trot, now at a lope, now walking, now and then stopping for a few minutes to rest the horses. About every hour Red would ask Mister Dunham to change his saddle to the led horse. Dunham was a heavy man.

Red pushed the horses pretty hard, wanting to be clear away from the town, which would surely hum like a hornets' nest after it has been whanged by a club, when folks learned what had happened.

Of one thing Red was sure, and that gave him great contentment: Billy Haynes and Tom Jones would not be hanged for a while yet.

Dunham watched hour after hour for the chance to lay hands on Red, for Dunham was powerful and knew it, and he was willing enough to take a fighting chance. But he had no chance. Red had been only a kid in his teens when his father had pinned a deputy sheriff's badge on him and taken him along on man hunts, had had him by in handling prisoners; and Red knew to a nicety, and almost unconsciously, just how far to keep out of reach so that a desperate man would not be tempted to jump at him. Horses naturally gait themselves head to flank, and Red stayed on Dunham's flank nearly all the time. He was talkative and willing to be sociable, "even to a feller as was mad enough to bite!" but Dunham turned sullen. So Red smoked cigarettes, hummed to himself, and meditated.

He knew that it was hard going for Dunham. Big men tired in the saddle, and Dunham did have rheumatism; but there was not a whimper out of him. When he spoke he cursed but did not complain.

"Bet you was a nice feller twenty year or more ago," said Red, musing. "Then you got rich. Riches shore spoil a man. Now, me, I bet I won't ever be spoiled thataway—not unless I quit playin' poker."

"Shut up!" Dunham growled.

"Easier f'r you to poke yore fingers in yore ears than f'r me to not talk—when I feel like it!"

Shortly before dawn they stopped for Dunham to change his saddle again. Before remounting, he turned toward Red and asked with a growl, "Since you like to talk so much, tell me, how'd you come to throw in with Walt Rodman?"

"Well, sir, Mister Dunham, I don't know what you'll do with the facts if I give 'em to you. Probably won't believe 'em, the which is sure bad luck for folks. Facts allus orta be believed. Now, sir, Tom Jones, Billy Haynes, and me worked together f'r the J-R down in Tahzo, an' gettin' some weary of the same scenery we said, 'Let's go up to Martinez, blow our wages, an' hook up with the Double X.' "

"You played hell, didn't you!" Dunham grunted, with satisfaction.

"We shore did!" Red agreed amiably. "An' just f'r to show you how peac'ble we was, we waltzed to the marshal's office, give over our guns, an' started for the corral. That's where you met us. We didn't know you. Gosh A'mighty, if we'd knowed 'twas *you,* we'd been so danged polite you'd have thought we was shore nice boys! That's how we got misun'erstood. That's why now I'm havin' for to take this

190

here means to get ourselves better acquainted."

"Go on, where does Walt Rodman come in?"

"He's comin'. Jus' you keep listenin'. We went up to the hotel to eat. Me, bein' the last out o' the washroom, a pretty girl from up on the stairs there, right where yore room is, she looked down an' said, 'Shh-hh-hh!' She took one look at my face, an' bein' a better judge o' human nature than her Daddy, knowed right off that I was honest. She give me a letter to give to Walt Rodman. When I come to find out who he was an' what he'd done, I didn't see no chance for to follow instructions. Matter o' fact, I purt-near forgot about me havin' the letter.

"Then, up to the Silver Dollar, Tig Burns, he walks in, an' learnin' I'm the son o' Sheriff Clark of Tulluco, why, Tig, he—"

"Of who?" said Dunham, not quite sure he had heard aright. "Sheriff Dan Clark?"

"Yes'r, he was my Dad, an' a good one. F'r almost twenty year Sheriff Dan done things as oughta be done over in Tulluco. Me, I'm too short-legged f'r to follow in his footsteps, but there in the saloon when Tig, he—"

"So you are Dan Clark's boy?" Dunham growled in a slow, heavy voice, glowering as if a little puzzled at Red.

"Yes'r. An' I ain't done nothin' since I'm half so proud of as makin' him have to buy cigars an' drinks f'r friends by gettin' myself born!"

191

"Hurh!" said Dunham in a kind of queer, explosive way. "An' me, I was one as had a drink on him the day you was hatched. *Hurh!* He took us up to the house to show what he was so damned proud of. I thought then, though I never said it till now, that Dan Clark deserved somethin' that looked a little more human than what you did! Red little squirmin', squallin' worm, you looked!"

"Then you an' me in a sort of a way is old friends,"said Red, pleased. "An' ever'where I go I find folks like me better 'cause I was sensible enough to pick Sheriff Clark o' Tulluco f'r a Dad. Yes'r. Why, when I was workin' for old Powell over in Lelardo, folks—"

"Are you that damned Red Clark of Lelardo?" Dunham said in a new tone of surprised interest.

"I been in Lelardo, an' my name's Red Clark."

"Why, you raised more hell over there—"

"No more'n here. An' see here, Mister Dunham, if you'd heard o' me an' knowed my folks, then who the hell did you think I was when you postered me for bein' a horse thief?"

Dawn had begun to tremble over the mountains, flushing the sky.

Dunham answered slowly but without accents of apology:

"Reds are common as hosshair, an' Clark's a frequent name."

He peered as if trying to see something in Red's

192

appearance that would help him feel convinced that this was the son of Sheriff Dan Clark.

"Yeah, I know, but I allus am particular to say Red Clark o' *Tulluco*. That there is a sort o' brand-word on me."

"I don't mind as I heard it," said Dunham, a little reflectively. Then, emphatic: "An' probably wouldn't have give it no thought if I did. Good men, they have a lot o' worthless sons!"

"Not my Dad, he didn't. No, sir!" said Red promptly.

" 'Sides, they's a lot of Clarks, 'r used to be, over thataway."

"Yes'r. All relations o' mine, I reckon. But none so red-headed as me! An' they're all nice hard-workin' fellers. Now, ain't they?"

"Bore a pretty good name," Dunham admitted with reservation. "But good men's kids can go bad quick. Take Walt Rodman, f'r instance. He—"

"We're discussin' the Clark fam'ly, Mister Dunham! An' as I was tellin' you, there in the Silver Dollar, Tig, he comes up to me an' starts hankerin' for trouble by mentionin' my Dad an Maw unfavorable. So I—"

"You jerked a gun when he wasn't lookin' an' whanged 'im over the head!"

"You been listenin' to some danged poor liars, Mister Dunham. I never!"

"That's the way ever'body told me the story, anyhow."

"Prob'bly 'cause they was afraid o' what Tig would say to 'em later an' private. Why, Mister Dunham, Tig, he stood face to face an' willful deliberate he said some things as would make a horned toad come right up outa his hole an' chase a steer off the range. An' if I'd 'a' thought then what I suspicion now, Tig Burns would be nothin' but some bacon rind in the devil's skillet. Somethin' tells me 'twas him as shot my Dad— in the back!"

"I don't b'lieve that a-tall!"

"You don't have to. I believe it. Tig knowed too much about how it was done, an' he talked too jeerin'. Maybe you don't believe neither that Tig Burns uses split-nosed bullets in his guns?"

"I don't," said Dunham.

"Y'see, right there, you don't know what's goin' on! He does. I carried off his guns. My Dad was killed by dumdums. I ain't much good at figgers, but I can shore put two an' two together. Yet I can't see why the hell a man like *you* trusts a man like him. That's plumb amazin'."

The dawn had brightened until distant objects began to take on hazily their true outline, and a cool pearly glow filled the cloudless sky.

In the faint light Dunham stood with his back to the saddle and looked staringly at Red Clark. He spoke heavily, with weary exasperation, as if speaking of something that had long worried him:

194

"Who the hell am I to trust? Too much f'r one man. I got to go East frequent on business. My own daughter is a damn fool! Sometimes my nephew Wally ain't much better. Rustlers are runnin' off my cows. Nesters are a-crowdin' in up to the water. Me an' ol' Rodman, who was the one man I trusted more'n even myself—an' he never failed me!—had the ranch mortgaged, hair, hide, an' horns, right up to the hilt. We made wills leavin' it to each other, so there wouldn't be no split up an' foreclosures. I nearly pulled 'er out of the hole—then, just when I was ready for to act peaceful, hell starts poppin'."

"We was speakin' o' Tig Burns," said Red, trying to bring him back to that disagreeable subject.

"I know. I know, Tig ain't ever'thing I like f'r a man to be. But at least when Tig goes out an' talks to folks they listen! He gets things done. I'm too heavy in the saddle f'r to ride like I ort. And rustlers is stealin' me blind. Goddam it, all my life till recent years I had men about me as I could trust implicit! Now 'pears like nobody is much depend'ble no more. Take that Walt Rodman that I used to love like a son!"

Red inquired, mild and coaxing, "Just what you got agin him, Mister Dunham?"

"What have I got against *him?* Why, he killed the best friend I ever had—his own father! Ain't that enough to have against anybody?"

"I ain't arguin' f'r Walt Rodman, Mister

Dunham. My special job is to persuade you me an' Billy an' Tom Jones don't deserve hangin'! But—"

"An' you'd better not!" said Dunham, stubbornly angered. "You bein' Dan Clark's boy sort o' 'splains things to me a little. Sheriff Dan was allus cool as a cucumber. But that Walt—tryin' to get holt of the ranch, he is tryin' to marry my girl. Meant to marry her, then have me killed an' ever'thing would be his! He got drunk there in town an' said as much! Fellers heard 'im!"

"If the same fellers told you that as told you I whacked Tig Burns on the back of the head sneak-like, they are liars!"

"*Hurh!* You can lie just as quick as anybody else, can't you?"

"Nozir! I can't. I never had the proper bringin' up for to be a good liar. When my Dad paddled me, he took my britches down so I'd have some memories. An' now you listen to me, Mister Dunham. Whenever I do tell a lie, such times as is needful, I take particular pains for to get it believed. So, if you knowed me better, the fact you don't ever believe me would convince you as how I was tellin' the truth. Yes, sir! An' I'm goin' to tell you, like you asked, how we come to hook up with Walt Rodman."

Dunham grunted, scowling.

"Now, after we rode off on them horses you said we stole, an' down the Shale Butte—an' me, for one, I sure thought I was goin' to hell with some grease on my pants—but we was lucky—wc lit out for the mountains an' bumped into some folks as thought we was Double Xers lookin' for Rodman. But I had yore girl's letter—she's shore the purtiest girl I ever seen in my life—"

"An' the biggest fool!" said Dunham.

"Anyhow, after I give Rodman that letter, we sort o' become friends, our troubles with you bein' similar. Now, Mister Dunham, he says—"

"That I killed his father, 'r had him killed, for to steal the ranch!"

"He don't! He talks a heap respectful o' you, an'—"

"You're a liar!" Dunham shouted. "I know how he talked there in town when he was drunk!"

"You don't! You only know what some folks said he talked like. An' the world, it is full o' liars!"

"An' out in Californy," Dunham went on, "they had 'im in prison for some kind of a mine swindle. He knows this country so damn well I think it is him that is stealin' my cows in droves. He pertends to think he's got some rights to 'em!"

"My gosh, Mister Dunham!" said Red, sitting up in the saddle as if the breath had been knocked out of him. "He ain't no friend o' mine like Billy an' Tom Jones. An' I been mistook in fellers lots o' times. But if Walt Rodman ain't a square

197

feller—then you have to skin a man's face for to see what lays behind, same as you skin a cow to git at the hair brand!"

"He's pulled the wool over your eyes! That's what!" snapped Dunham.

"Don't reckon, do you, nobody could pull the wool over your eyes, huh?"

"You can't! I'd like for to wring your damn neck!"

"We ain't goin' to fuss about that now. Jus' as long as you don't try to do it. Who told you all that truck about Walt Rodman?"

"Plenty o' folks. I seen the letter that come from Californy. Wally sent out word f'r to make inquiry. That's what come back."

"Gee gosh!"

"An' now you stealin' me thisaway—like I was a damn scairt girl! I got business—troubles—I oughta be in a dozen different places right now, an' here I am—"

Dunham broke off in a storm of curses, his big face growing darkly red, apoplectically.

"I'm a heap sorry—in a way," said Red sympathetically. "But y' see, I got fam'ly troubles too. Billy an' Tom Jones is the same as brothers to me. An' there wasn't no other way to persuade you not to hang 'em. An', gosh dang it, Mister Dunham, you done wrong for to 'cuse us o' horse stealin'. You postered us as outlaws! Why, 'f I hadn't been in such a hair-flyin' hurry, I wouldn't a-swapped my Blackie horse f'r two hammerheads!"

"Yes, but I guessed right off that you were in with Walt Rodman! An' tryin' to get yourself a big name by jerkin' out Tig's gun an' lammin' him—"

"No wonder you're havin' troubles!" said Red angrily. "You deserve 'em! The truth's plumb useless to you. An' let me tell you somepin, big as you are! If you don't quit sayin' I sneaked Tig's gun an' cracked his head, right here I'll throw my guns away an' land on yore neck—jus' to show you plenty!"

Red's voice had the edge of a honed razor. And in the cool morning light his eyes were narrowed and his lean face was set with a look that Dunham knew for the warning of a man who had killed and would kill. He did not for a moment think that Red would throw away his guns and make a fight, or Dunham would have tormented him into doing it. He did think Red might lose his temper completely and shoot.

"You've got the drop, so I can't help myself," Dunham grunted.

"Then climb your horse an' let's go! You're harder for to reason with than a drunk Injun. I reckon it takes some stubbornness for to be a big man"—Red was talking as much to himself as to Dunham—"an' butt ever'body else off the road 'r walk over 'em. An' you been spoiled. You need

199

to have some o' the grease sizzled outa you. You got cross-eyed notions. You fly off the handle too quick, like there in the barn when we first met. A cowman that can't ride his range for himself is like a blind man playin' poker. Yes, sir. You been back East too much an' et out o' the fleshpots an' drunk from finger bowls. You got the swell head—same as too much bad whisky, an'—"

"Shut up!" Dunham bellowed, spurring his horse, yanking at the lead rope.

"All right, I will," Red replied good-naturedly, and keeping on Dunham's flank. "But I'm goin' to think of some more fittin' remarks, an' next stop we make, I'll recite 'em!"

Then, as he rode on, meditative but watchful, Red hummed to himself sort of mournful:

"Bad Bill he shot the sheriff, an' he shot
    the marshal, too,
He shot the town all up an' down, just
    like I'd like to do.
But they hung 'im, oh, they hung 'im, oh,
    they hung 'im, on a tree;
"An' he said, 'Folks, I don't make jokes,
    but this is one on me!
I allus thought I'd go head-down plumb
    into hell an' fry,
But that ain't so 'cause here I go toward
    heaven as I die!' "

CHAPTER XI

"Me, I Was Born Lucky!"

They went on and on. The day grew hot, the way rough. Red kept a twist in his neck, looking cross country, to each side, behind and ahead, too, being just a little uneasy lest they meet with some of the men who might have scattered during the night and ridden over this way on the chance of heading off Rodman and himself if they did try to get into the mountains after sunup.

Red was hungry and thirsty, but there was nothing to eat, and there would be no water until they got over these rough foothills. They were not making as good time of it as he had counted on, and at this gait would not get into the Roost before the middle of the afternoon.

"Well, sir," said Red, hooking a leg over the horn as Dunham, dripping sweat, dismounted to make a change of horses again, "I been thinkin' o' them fittin' remarks. An' these are them—this is harder on you than 'twould be on most folks. But you ain't squealed. Cussed some, as is natural—but no whines. You got grit an'—"

"Aw, go to hell!" Dunham growled savagely.

"Nozir, I won't. I'm an honest, truthful boy as earns what he spends an' don't hurt folks needless. 'Sides, I don't like the smell o' sulphur. Makes me sneeze. An' what's more—"

"Shut up!" Dunham bellowed.

"Me, I got a sens'tive nature. Such a tone o' voice hurts my feelin's. You got what's called a bear-toned voice. Now, I figger that yore troubles is—"

"Shut up, can't you!"

"Not easy, no. As I was sayin', I figger you are an honest man as has a weakness f'r listenin' to liars an'—"

Dunham swore furiously, bellowing.

"Awright, then. Awright!" said Red, waving a hand. "Let's jog!"

Twenty minutes later, dusty and hot, they came through a manzanita thicket where the trail lay open and level for almost a hundred yards before it turned sharply and coiled upward on a spiny hogback.

There before them rose up two men who had been lolling in the shade and restfully smoking cigarettes. One had used his saddle for a pillow, lying back with leg crossed over a crooked knee. The other squatted, cross-legged. Their hobbled horses cropped along the trail. They had evidently been there quite a while, or meant to stay for some time.

Dunham and Red instinctively drew rein, Dunham hopeful and Red alert, suspicious.

The men in the shade were too far off to be

identified, but Red guessed that they were Double Xers. If so, they were a long ways from home and perilously near to being on the trail to Robbers' Roost.

"Maybe we're in for somethin' that's goin' to look mighty like a dust storm—but have a different smell," said Red grimly. "Ride on an' set tight! An' remember, Mister Dunham, you'd better help me out, 'cause you're the first that'll get hurt. Bein' so big, you're easy hit. They mayn't know me. If not, tell 'em we're goin' on. If they do know me—then me, I'll do the talkin'. Step along, slow. Don't hurry. I got to have plenty o' time for to say some prayers!"

Red pulled down his hat firmly, rather furtively loosened his guns, feeling the handles, drew his toes to the edge of the stirrups, and began rolling a cigarette. When the cigarette was made he put it between his lips and took a match, but did not light it. Reaching back to strike a match on the seat of the britches is one way of getting a hand to a gun without the other fellow getting the notion at the same time.

On they rode at a walk. The men in their path stood waiting with cigarettes half lifted, watchfully.

Red mused hastily. He talked to himself silently, just about as he mused aloud or talked to other people. "I got me a suspicion as how I'm goin' to get my feet wet. I could cut an' run an' be gone before ever them fellers could top a horse. But I couldn't take Mr. Dunham along. Which'd be the worst luck I could have. He'd comb the country like I was a long-lost son, to get me an' hang me on the same tree with Billy an' Tom Jones. So that's out. But if we do get by these hombres, they are a-goin' to tell tales about the Old Man goin' on in comp'ny with a stranger—which folks from town'll un'erstand plenty. Then I won't know much where to hide Mr. Dunham. All of the which means I just naturally got to collect these here two fellers an' tote 'em along too. Make quite a procession!

"But, gosh darn it, if luck keeps on shovin' me into things I don't wanta do thisaway, ol' Jesse James'll get his name scratched off the list o' bold bad men, an' me—Red Clark—'ll be the model f'r all preachers' sons. Preachers is all right, maybe, but their young uns has funny notions."

Red heard one of the men exclaim in a high tone of surprise and relief:

"Why, it's the Old Man hisself!"

"Speak up!" said Red to Mr. Dunham firmly in an undertone.

Dunham called out in a dull, uninterested voice, " 'Lo, boys."

"Why, 'lo, Mr. Dunham," one answered in a sort of funny tone. "Why, where'd you come from—here?"

"Oh, I'm just ridin' around," said Dunham.

They had ridden up to within twenty yards of the Double Xers, and Red was tense and cool, keyed to alert watchfulness. He felt there was something just all wrong. These men didn't act much as if they were glad to see Jake Dunham. Red recognized them as the two men who had come into the Silver Dollar with Tig Burns and had paused for a moment, eying him, when they had asked Burns if he was getting himself a little raw meat to chew on. So Red was sure that they were going to recognize him any minute.

Jake Dunham rode on at a slow plodding walk, and Red followed closely with hat brim pulled low to hide as much of his face as he could. He rode with reins slack, both hands loose and dangling, judging the distance.

Then, just as Red thought it was about time to speak up, one of the men shouted in amazement, "Why, Pete! The Ol' Man's bringin' that red-headed—"

"Kill 'im!" Dunham bellowed with full blast of voice, a deep hoarse roar, and on the instant, even as he shouted, he jerked his head about toward Red and swung his foot from the stirrup. With heavy lunge, going into an almost headlong fall, Dunham dropped off, all in a heap, on the far side of his horse.

The thought, half commending, whizzed through Red's mind:

"I might've knowed he had the grit to try somethin' like that!"

As Dunham fell, Red dropped the reins, dropped the match he was carrying, and his hands swept toward his holsters.

Almost at once there was the flashing crack of the Double Xers' guns, two to a man, fired by the up-tilting jolt of the draw. Yet in their haste every shot missed, quite as if they were blanks.

Red was as quick witted as a boy who has grown up among gunmen could be. Though he drew with whiplike jerk of wrists he did not shoot at once, but rammed the spurs into the hammerhead with scraping, cutting jabs that tore the hide under the tender flanks.

The deep-breasted weary horse, stung with pain as if lashed with dull knives, threw all of its powerful strength into startled plunging bounds straight at the amazed men, not thirty feet ahead.

That this wild red-head would ride at them, close in, come point-blank, was as amazing to them as if he had flapped his arms and sailed skyward. It was the most unexpected of anything that Red could have done. The men jerked themselves back on high-heeled boots and long-shanked spurs with hasty, stumbling jumps to keep from being knocked down and trampled under the flying hoofs of the horse that came like a thunderbolt on legs.

Both were dead shots and knew it; but, startled

and overanxious, they fired with arms half frantically wavering in the lurch to catch their balance.

Red straightened up, leaning far back against the cantle and, with arms at full length, shot with cool rapidity to the right, then to the left, as he flashed by, rocking high in the air.

One man dropped his guns and with the wavering clutch of upflung hands groped wildly at nothing, straight overhead. Then he sprawled with a drunken flop, facedown in the dust, arms still out across the trail.

The other, hard hit in the breast, was knocked into a spinning stagger, and one gun dropped from his fingers. But he had the heart of a fighting man and, turning about, blazed away almost aimlessly with eyes half blinded by the shock of the bullet that had torn through his left shoulder. He was pointing vaguely toward where Red, a hundred feet away, having rammed his right gun into his holster, was having a struggle to turn his horse.

The hammerhead was not a cow pony and so was untrained in turning on a dime at full gallop. Besides, he had got the bit in his teeth and had a tough mouth. Tig Burns had been no gentle hand with the bit, so Red had to yank and jerk the frightened animal as all the while, with backward glances, he watched behind him.

The Double Xer, with clearing vision, emptied

one gun, threw it away, and taking the other into his right hand, straightened up, firing.

Red, with a long, left-handed reach, aiming behind him from a horse that hopped stubbornly, fighting the bit, shot once, carrying away the fellow's hat; twice, and almost cut his ear; a third time, and the man dropped as if struck with a heavy mallet.

Dunham had fallen from his horse; then, with the instinct of a range-born fighting man, had yanked at his gun. But it was tied fast to the holster, and also it was empty. With scrambling, ponderous heave of body Dunham got to his feet and ran with heavy lurch toward the guns of the first man that fell. Had he been less bulky, more active, he would have had the guns up and going. As it was, he had dropped to his knees to pick up a gun, and his hand was flat on it, when Red, on a snorting, angered horse, rode toward him with gun leveled.

" 'Tain't no use, Mister Dunham!" Red jeered. "You've et too many fleshpots an' finger bowls. Get yore hands up quick, 'cause if this fool horse changes sides on me I'll have to shoot!"

Dunham was breathing heavily. He made strange guttural, angered sounds, like a man who was being helplessly choked; but he heaved himself back on his bent knees, with hands up, glowering.

"No hard feelin's, I hope," said Red as he

swung from his horse, " 'cause I promised to shoot you if you tried any monkeyshines—then didn't!"

He pulled the knotted reins over the horse's head and dropped them. The hammerhead, after a plunging backward jerk, stopped, trembling, shifting its feet, but standing, hitched to the ground.

"You killed two o' my good men!" said Dunham, growling and furious.

"I never done no such thing! Which just goes to show *you* can't think straight. You started this here dust storm yoreself! They'd been alive an' well yet, but you rolled off yore horse, yellin' f'r 'em to get me. I ain't easy got—bein' born lucky!"

"You are that," Dunham agreed sourly.

"Some lucky yoreself, too," Red insisted. "A nervouser feller than me would have plugged you. But I got faith in your common sense. Get to your feet an' stand over there a little to one side till I sort o' collect myself."

Dunham sullenly obeyed.

"You got into action most surprisin' quick— f'r a fat man," said Red. "I got to be more precautious about you. When you warwhooped thataway I nearly fell off my hoss, an' that's a fact! Now, what d'you reckon these fellers was a-doin' here? Hunh? Was they here by accident, or waitin' for somebody? Acted like they was a-waitin'—yet anybody as would wait for Walt Rodman, or even me, with saddles off an' horses hobbled, ain't got proper notions about how to do such things—has they? Well, if you don't wanta be soc'ble, I can't make you."

Red picked up the fallen guns and put them into his saddlebags.

"I'm collectin' these things for to go with Tig Burns's. An' I wonder is they some sandwiches in their saddlebags?"

Red investigated and a moment later announced, "They ain't. But here is some carterges an' shells"—meaning by the former, loads for a rifle; by the latter, loads for a revolver. "An' they fit my guns. So we'll take 'em."

Red meditated, eying the hobbled horses, then announced: "Nope, I won't trade horses, 'cause then anybody that happened for to see them we leave would know we had passed thisaway."

Dunham's horse had stood almost in its tracks, the lead horse too, with the rope about the horn of Dunham's saddle. Guns going off did not make any of these horses do more than dodge a little, as if big flies were about.

"Onct more, Mister Dunham," said Red, "I got to ask you to change your saddle an' let's be on our way."

That being permission to drop his arms, Dunham slowly brushed at his clothes with haphazard slaps as he walked over slowly to transfer the saddle. He felt bitter and had been furiously disappointed. He had been sure his men could knock Red out of the saddle. A man on foot had a big edge over a man on horseback when it came to shooting. Dunham had no liking at all for Red, but some unwilling respect. He could not keep down a certain vague, half-angered admiration.

From boyhood Dunham had been a range man, and he knew good gun work when he saw it. With his saddle in his hands he turned and, as if the thought had just come to him, bellowed, "You been lucky! That's all. Lucky!"

Red grinned. "I told you so. I was born thataway."

"I never seen such damn luck!" Dunham growled as he placed the saddle. He was trying to deny the unwilling admiration that he felt for this red-head, and so loudly put it all to luck.

"But," said Red, "you oughta see me when I'm really right. Took me five shots to drop two fellers. That ain't no fancy shootin'. O' course, they was purty skinny fellers—"

"Are you tryin' to be funny? After killin' men!"

"No, I ain't. I'm tryin' to be agreeable an' make conversation. An' if you want to know, I'll tell you I don't give a whoop about folks I shoot when they're trying to shoot me. Neither would you!"

Dunham mounted and started up, with the lead horse.

"Whoa," said Red. "An' just wait a minute. Now that you're back on yore perch an' settin' quiet, I wanta 'pologize to ol' hammerhead here."

He gently pulled the horse's head between his hands. From the uneasy jerk with which the hammerhead always tossed up his head, anyone would have known what sort of man Tig Burns was. A horse that has never been hit over the head isn't afraid of being hit.

"I'm sorry, Son," said Red. "But it had to be, an' you done your share noble. Yes, sir. Only your edycation's been poor. Any little ol' scrub of a twenty-dollar cayuse'll set on his hind foot an' spin around prompt—too prompt sometimes. I know you don't love me no more. But you just wait. I'm nicer'n I look—as the ol' maid said to the widower!"

Dunham twisted about, looking, listening. His eyes fell on the bodies of the two men, both deadly gunmen, fellows that rode with Tig Burns. And this red-head neither bragged, strutted, nor tried to appear modest. He had the inconsequential manner of a varmint hunter that has knocked over a couple of coyotes. Dunham understood that Red had been through this sort of thing before, many times. His father, Sheriff Clark, had been a cool hand in danger; but the sheriff had a touch of grimness that was wholly absent in the son.

Somehow, and much against his will, Dunham began to feel that maybe he had not heard the exact truth about what happened to Tig Burns there in the Silver Dollar. He watched Red nuzzling the horse and talking to it almost as if to a girl. Hard to understand, that boy.

Red swung into the saddle with, "All right, Mister Dunham. Let's be movin'!"

They rode on, mile after mile, with Red meditatively humming without the slightest idea of what he was singing. He was still puzzled how those two men happened to be on the trail, so leisurely waiting.

At last they came to a little stream that ran with flutter of watery noises over the rocks. The horses drank.

"We ain't got no cups, Mister Dunham," said Red. "But you get down if you want and poke your face in the water. Me, I'm goin' to."

Dunham looked longingly at the water, moved a leg as if to dismount, then shook his head. A moment later he added slowly, "I'd like a drink. But I can't lay down on my belly an' hands like I could onct." Pause. He added bitterly, "You been right in some remarks you've made. My belly has got too big!"

"Toss me your hat, Mister Dunham," said Red.

Dunham took off his hat and tossed it. Red

stooped to a clear deep pool and filled the hat, then went near Dunham, and, watching him closely, offered the hat with a far arm's reach.

Dunham understood and grinned a little sourly as he put out his hands slowly and took the hat full of water. Red grinned back at him.

"Yes'r, I'm suspicious of you," said Red. "You c'n get off a hoss gosh-darned quick. An' if you was to come off on top o' me—hell, there ain't enough o' me to make a soft place to fall on! So I 'vise you not to try it!"

Dunham leaned from the saddle and poked his nose and lips deep into the hat, drinking, pausing to puff, drinking more. He threw out what was left of the water, swished the hat and put it back on his head.

"That tasted good," he said in the tone of a man who was determined not to say "Thanks" but nevertheless wanted to say something.

It was halfway beginning to seep through his stubbornness that, after all, Red had treated him from the first with something like respect. And after that little shake-up down below on the trail, Dunham, in a kind of dull, unconscious way, was beginning to realize that this boy was not in the least afraid of him or of anybody. He had felt that Red had been polite and unabusive simply to make a good impression and perhaps soften his (Dunham's) feelings, and had determined not to be softened in the least. Yet, broodingly, he realized that Red had said things to him nobody had ever dared to say. For one thing, called him "fat," spoken of his "belly," accused him of mismanaging his affairs. Dunham was troubled by the unwilling admiration he had to feel for this wild-headed youngster.

They rode in silence, mile after mile. Then Red spoke up:

"We ain't far now from where we're goin'. Then we'll eat. Good gosh, how we'll eat!"

"Red," said Dunham, twisting about heavily in the saddle, "how many notches you got on your guns? I'm curious."

"Nary a one!"

"You're a liar. Why, down in Lelardo alone I heard—"

"I ain't, gosh dang it! I ain't no killer for to go nick up some nice guns just 'cause some other feller was too pore a shot to hit me! Hell, I been in so much smoke that if I was a ham I'd 'a' been home-cured long ago. An' the only reason I ain't as full o' holes as a bacherlor's sock is 'cause— like all bacherlors—I'm lucky, like you said an' I agreed."

"Yes, but that's not all," said Dunham somberly. "You can shoot!"

"Shore. But, Mister Dunham, when guns are goin' off, some other things may help a little— like bein' able to shoot purty fast an' fairly straight—but there's just one thing that keeps you from gettin' hit, and that there is luck. Hell, if you ain't got luck you might just as well shoot yoreself—'cause some other feller'll do it for you, prompt.

"There was a little boy from 'way back
   East,
Nice little boy, but he got deceased—
Bought hisself a gun for to have some
   fun:
Said, 'I can't figger jus' why there's a
   trigger,
An jus' for to see what the thing can be,
I'll peek in the hole—pull it, an' '—
   whoopee!

"He didn't have no luck, that feller, all just because he was born back East."

CHAPTER XII

Jake Dunham Makes a Promise

As they went up the trail nearing the cabin, Red kept a sharp lookout for any of the men who were likely to be on guard. He knew their dislike, and fear, of Dunham, and so was a little uneasy that they might misunderstand the situation and take a pop at Dunham on sight.

Red fidgeted a little. He knew from his own experience that these guards had the inclination to shoot first, then hold some conversation. He said:

"Mister Dunham, if you don't mind, you'd better stop an' let me go ahead for a piece. Then you foller, slow. An' don't go knockin' up your horse by turnin' tail an' tryin' to lope down that trail. If you fall off an' break a leg, you're too big for me to heave back in the saddle."

Red took the lead, but kept a sharp lookout back at Dunham, who rode with hands on saddle horn, plodding on quite as if willingly. Red sang out, "Hi—oh—oh!" His voice rang with wavering echoes as if somebody far off was mocking him, but there was no other answer to his shouts. "Plumb funny! Gosh darn it, heretofore, a chipmunk couldn't come a-sneakin' along up here without bein' told to halt an' state his business!"

"Maybe," said Jake Dunham, "my boys have been here a'ready an' cleaned out this nest o' scoundrels!"

"You can't guess worth a damn! First place, they ain't scoundrels. Nex' place, if what you hope was a-happenin', you'd be hearin' guns a-goin' off."

At last they came into the clearing before the cabin. Again Red sang out and paused, waiting. No answer. He looked all about, vaguely suspicious; yet the fact that every horse was out of the corral indicated that the men had ridden off.

"Well, we'll stop the night here, anyhow. Pile off, Mister Dunham. An' if you'll just unbuckle that belt an' let her fall, I won't be nearly so nervous about what you might do if I don't keep watchin' to see."

Dunham at once unbuckled the belt, letting it fall.

"Fine. Now you just put your horses up. I'll get out the feed." Red drew the rifle from its scabbard and, tapping it, said, "An' if I was you, Mister Dunham, I wouldn't try for to run nowhere. The fact is, I'm an awful poor shot with one o' these things, an' 'twould break my heart for not to be able to stop you. An' you don't want to break my heart—it's just my neck, ain't it?"

Red grinned, good-natured, just joshing, not at

all menacing. Dunham stared at him with a kind of slow, sour smile. He hated this red-head, but halfway had begun to wish that he didn't. There was something about Red that made Dunham remember the wild, heedless, rough companions of his own boyhood: fellows that didn't have a lick of meanness in them, yet were dangerous as dynamite and good-naturedly full of the devil. Dunham had learned on the long ride that Red was not as impudent as he sounded, but talkative as a magpie. It had kind of eased his tense rage to be called "Mister Dunham" every time he was spoken to, when Red, if he had had a streak of meanness, might have called him any abusive names and made threats. "Mister Dunham" had come so naturally that it had the sound of genuine respectfulness. Dunham knew that killers were sour, nasty men, said little except in a menacing, spiteful way, and hadn't a particle of good-nature about them. He believed Red was a killer, yet the boy seemed just as happy-go-lucky as any puncher on the range.

"You shore like to talk, don't you!" said Dunham critically.

"Yes'r. It's the easiest way I know of to put in the time an' keep yoreself from gettin' lonesome."

Dunham grunted, not approving.

It was late in the afternoon. They went up to the cabin together, Red keeping well beyond any sudden reach of Dunham's powerful arms.

"You been up here before, Mister Dunham?"

"No. Never. Rodman and some of the boys come up that time we cleaned out them outlaws. I was over to the other side of the range."

"Well, sir, you see how she's built. Like a piece o' pie. Them danged outlaws knowed how to make things difficult f'r honest folks as had the laudable intentions of dustin' 'em off."

Dunham stood in the center of the three-cornered cabin, turning about slowly with a look of understanding. It was a strong little fort, this cabin. There was not much of any way to attack it. The rough-hewn logs were daubed over with mud. The roof was covered with shakes and these ended flush with the walls so there was no overhang to interfere with the marksmanship from the loopholes. There had been good woodsmen among the outlaws.

"Well, Mister Dunham, before I c'n start cookin' I got to be rude to you again. See there—" Red pointed to the guns he had thrown on a top bunk—"I can't leave you runnin' loose while I'm over the stove. You might get yoreself into mischief. An' I'm hungry. Ain't you?"

Dunham, almost a head taller than Red, broad shouldered as an ox and as heavy, looked down steadily. Every minute they had been together, excepting once, Red had kept well beyond any jumping reach that Dunham might make. That once was on the trail when Red had passed him

220

to go on ahead and do the hallooing. Then he had ridden past with a drawn gun—cautious but not nervous.

"What you mean?" Dunham asked, but in a tone that showed he knew.

"I got to tie you up, Mister Dunham."

Dunham frowned thoughtfully, then spoke:

"See here. Are you willin' to take my word?"

"Are you willin' to give it?"

"Yes."

"That you won't wiggle if I don't tie you up?"

"Yes."

Red pushed back his hat and scratched at the cowlick, eying him.

"Some folks," said Red, meditative, thinking aloud, "has queer notions about what's funny. An' honest. I mind a feller onct I tried to be nice to because he promised pretty. 'N' he got the jump on me an' laughed. He said 'cause I was a fool wasn't no reason for his bein' one. But he was, anyhow. He couldn't shoot worth a damn. No man oughta break his word 'less he can shoot good! Down back there on the trail you was awful anxious for to show me how well you c'n shoot. I got a supperstition that it is purty blame good, too!"

"I hadn't give you my word then," said Dunham calmly.

"That's right. But see here, Mister Dunham. I won't tie you up painful. Just enough to keep you nice an' quiet so my mind'll be easier while I'm cookin'. I c'n cook a lot better if I don't have to be jumpin' about sudden ever' half second to see what you're doin'. I'd be awful skittish. That'd be bad on both our nerves, wouldn't it, now?"

"Anybody ever tell you that Jake Dunham ever broke his word?"

"No, sir. But," Red added, grinning, "I shore hope you do, onct. I got me a sort o' memory as how you promised to break my neck!"

"We can settle that later. Now, here, I'm willin' to give a promise."

"For the time bein', you mean?"

Dunham nodded.

Red scratched his forehead and spoke hesitatingly. "But, you see, if you did break yore word here an' now, I wouldn't be left alive for to tell people you'd done it, at least just this onct!"

"I'd be alive to remember I'd done it," said Dunham quietly.

"Maybe so. Maybe not, too. Bein' skinny, I ain't easy hit. Skinny an' lucky."

"I'll give you my word," Dunham repeated with firmness and an air of patience that did not seem quite characteristic.

"Gee gosh, you sort o' make me feel bad. 'Cause I do wanta do you all the favors I can, Mister Dunham, without hurtin' myself. Maybe you've noticed—I'm awful selfish about not

222

gettin' myself hurt. Why you so set agin a little thing like bein' tied up gentle?"

Dunham looked at him steadily and made no answer.

Red went on, talking more to himself than to Dunham. "The only time I don't get overhet at bein' fooled is in poker. An' right now you're wearin' a bear-cat of a poker face. Still, when us boys was a-leavin' the J-R, ol' Joe Richards he come out to tell us good-bye, an' he said, 'You worthless scamps'll learn yoreselves some manners up there on the Double X 'r Jake Dunham'll kick hell outa you. He won't stand for no monkeyshines like a poor ol' man like me!'

"You know what sort o' poor or hell-fire-eater 'ol Richards is! Yeah. About as mild when he's riled as a sore-tailed bear. 'Jake,' he says to us, shakin' hands, 'is a good man to tie to—if you come up on his blind side.' Which we shore didn't! You an' us had an argyment before we'd even been interduced. The which was bad manners on yore part. But does she really mean somethin' to you not to be tied up?"

"Yes."

Red flung his hat clear away and scratched his head with both hands; then, suspicious:

"But you got somethin' up yore sleeve. You look it!"

"I'll keep my word."

"I'm scairt, Mister Dunham. But bein' scairt

223

ain't no new feelin' for me. An' the fact is that, while I don't ever hope as how we'll be friends, I'd like to persuade you I ain't such a bad feller. But, hell afire, if my Dad bought you a drink when I was born, you an' me, in a way of speakin', is old acquaintances! All right, Mister Dunham. Sure, you just set down an' make yoreself to home!"

Dunham stared at him for a long time, then in silence put out his hand. Red started to take the hand, shake on the bargain, then he shied off, grinning.

"Whoa-up here! Just a minute," he said. "That promise was you wouldn't wiggle out of a chair. It don't cover breakin' my neck if you can get a hand on me before you set down! I knowed you held a joker—like a lawyer does."

"I've give my word," said Dunham calmly. "It does, settin' or standin'."

"An' you wanta shake on it?"

"Yes."

Red cocked his head, pulled at an ear, and eyed Dunham with a grin and much distrust. "But you got a joker—now, ain't you?"

"I'm playin' square."

"Plumb dead square? Honest Injun?"

"Yes."

"Awright sir, then, here goes!"

Red stepped up and put out his hand. Dunham took it, pressed it, dropped it, all with a kind of glum matter-of-factness, binding the bargain between them. He didn't seem even much pleased at having his own way about it, but turned away and, pulling a chair about near the center of the room, sat down, stretched out his legs, and began rubbing his left knee.

"Gee gosh," said Red, apologetically, "I plumb forgot about that rheumatism. An' you not squallin' none kept me from rememberin'. Now, listen, Mister Dunham. Our bargain goes, settin', standin', or layin'. So you pile over there on a bunk an' rest yoreself right."

Dunham looked up at Red, glanced over toward the bunk, then, with, "I believe I will," got up and went to the nearest bunk as if it was something that he very much wanted to do. Red knew that he must be a very tired man and in pain.

Then Red, with much bustling and whistling and humming, started the fire and meditated joyfully:

"I don't know what done it, but he ain't goin' to hang nobody now! Nozir. Somehow he's beginning for to think we ain't such bad fellers. Yes'r. And just for to show I'm 'preciative, I'll kick up a good fillin' supper, with some real ol' 'lasses-like round-up coffee. Him bein' an old-timer, he'll like the sort o' coffee you have to chew on to drink. Now I wish I'd brung along that cook I left tied up back there in the hotel. Maybe he'll enjoy me singin' him to sleep!"

So Red sang. But Dunham did not sleep. He lay on his side with a hand under his cheek, eyes wide open, and watched Red with a kind of saturnine blankness.

An hour later, Red, looking flustered and hot and happy, with floury imprint on the seat of his pants, and more flour sprinkled about on his shirt, piled a heap of fried potatoes, deer steaks, warmed-over beans, and stewed dried apples on the table. Then he fished biscuits from the hot oven bucket and carried the half gallon pot of black, almost solid, coffee to the table.

"Awright, Mister Dunham. Let's us eat!"

Dunham arose slowly and at the first few steps limped slightly. He moved his hands, looked at them, and asked, "Can I wash up?"

"Sure thing. Water barrel right outside behind here. Only be careful you don't step too far. Sort o' short cut to hell back there. I'll hold the lamp."

Dunham walked out slowly and stood for a time gazing down into the darkness of the sunken valley, but made no comment beyond, "I've heard of it."

He splashed about in the tin basin, then came indoors, rubbing at his hands and face with the clean flour sack given him for a towel. Red replaced the lamp on the table.

Dunham came up slowly and, pulling back a chair, paused, staring fixedly at nothing. Then he turned to Red:

"All right now, Red. Any time you are ready to start back for town it will be all right. I made me a mistake about you boys. I done wrong to fly off the handle that way there in the barn that day. But I was riled by other things. I know I got a bad temper. An' it's hard for me to change my mind. An' I had suspicions all along that you *was* in with Walt Rodman—an' just lyin' about it. Carryin' me off thisaway, I didn't know what you-all might be up to. But after you let me set here free thataway, I knowed you was truthful in sayin' all you wanted was to persuade me you boys was honest. I know now you didn't bring me up here for to turn me over to Walt Rodman. That was my joker you kept talkin' about. I wanted for to make sure."

"Good gosh!"

"Yes," said Dunham calmly, with steady look. "If you'd been up to any devilment, 'r was in with Walt Rodman, you'd never a-let me loose. An' the way you kept singin' an' hopped about cookin'— I knowed you'd been truthful with me. An' I reckon damn few men are these days, with me!"

"Gosh dang, but it makes me feel good as a rainstorm in hell!" said Red, jubilant, swinging his arm over the table to shake hands.

Dunham took his hand, without friendliness but without sullenness, and added grimly:

"Yes, an' you was some truthful too in them remarks you made about my belly, an' the fact that I don't know my own business like I ought. Course," he said deliberately, "it helped some in your favor because it's hard for to believe that Sheriff Dan could hatch a bad egg. But you are damn near one, boy. Since we are speakin' some truths, I'll tell a few. You are reckless in makin' use of other folks' property, an' you don't much mind shootin'. Them is bad signs."

"I won't fuss none, Mister Dunham. I sort o' think maybe you don't un'erstand me complete, yet. Howsomever, I'm feelin' good by what you've said. An' we'll light out back to town first thing in the mornin'!"

They ate. Dunham began as if he were not hungry, but his appetite increased. He was a big man and liked good food; lots of it. He ate heavily, but remained unsociable beyond sniffing the coffee, sipping it critically, then saying, "This here is all right."

Red chewed and chattered, singing the praise of Tom Jones and especially Billy Haynes.

"Nobody, Mister Dunham, ain't ever balked at payin' me my wages 'cause my work wasn't up to snuff, but them boys—Billy with his short legs like a crooked peanut, he can ride anything as wears hide f'r clothes. An' Tom Jones, he—"

Dunham did not listen. He had troubles, range troubles, family troubles, was unhappy and dissatisfied. He had halfway forgiven Red for having dragged him out of bed, dragged him

228

a day and a half cross country, but he did not feel friendly at all. Dunham had tamed his own bucking violent temper enough to admit that he had made a mistake, but the jolting struggle of doing so had left him in no more of a mood to be agreeable than a wild bronco is in a mood to be friendly after being ridden.

After the supper Red said, "You go lay down again, Mister Dunham. I got water on for these here dishes an' 'll do 'em prompt. My Dad, he used to snort at folks as let dirty dishes stand. Said they was slovenly an' not f'r to be much trusted. In my whole life I've never felt stronger temptations than not to wash up dishes when my belly's full. Nozir! Whisky an' poker ain't a circumstance to dodgin' greasy dishes that want their faces wiped!"

So Dunham lay down again, and Red, with a cigarette between his lips, scraped, splashed, and splattered, making a great rattle. The water was hot and burned his fingers, the steamy suds made him sweat, his belly was full and made him sluggish, and having been long without sleep he thought of all the snoozing he was going to do this night.

"Red!" Dunham called with the rising tone of a man who had spoken before and been unheard.

"Yeah?"

Dunham was sitting up, alert, listening. "Somebody's out there—hailed the house!"

Only some pots and pans remained to be cleaned. Red, wiping his hands on the dishcloth, tossed it at the table and went to the door. He heard a faint call and answered, "Hi-oh!" A shout came back vaguely.

"That there is Walt Rodman comin' in," said Red. "Sounds sort o' peaked. I'll jus' go out an' meet 'im!"

Dunham was up and stood resolute. "I don't trust him. I won't trust him! Let me have a gun, Red!"

"No, sir, Mister Dunham. But see here, in a sort o' way o' speakin' you belong to me. I'm in charge. Walt Rodman ain't got no hankerin' to hurt you, but if they was ten Walt Rodmans as did, I'd see they didn't. That goes! Both ways from the Jack an' on all four feet! Think I'm goin' to let anything happen to you—*now?* Not this side o' hell!"

"But he mustn't know I'm here, I tell you!" said Dunham with rising temper.

"An' I'll be plumb glad for him not knowin' myself—till you are willin'. But I know just as well as I know anything that ain't proved yet that you've made a mistake about him too. You got to hear how he talks about you! Listen. He's comin', and we got to be quick. Here—"

Red looked overhead at the wide, heavy platform laid across the rafters, still used as a sort of storeroom.

"You climb up there an'—"

"I won't!" said Dunham.

"Now, listen to me. My word's just as good as yours ever was when I promise somethin'. And I promise this here: An hour from now, after you've listened to how Walt Rodman talks an' you still don't trust 'im, you tap on them boards, an' I'll take his guns off 'im an' stand him in a corner!"

"You promise that?" Dunham showed interest and hope.

"I shore as hell do. But un'erstand, I ain't goin' to let you take 'im into town as no prisoner. No, sir-ee! I won't ever help you catch him, but I'll see as how he don't catch you—'r me—'cause I'm ridin' into town with you! Now, I mean 'er. Ever' word. I play square with all hands. Come along an' start climbin'!"

Red took the lamp from the table, setting it on a wall shelf; then he dragged the table close to the wall where pieces of the saplings had been let into the wall logs as a sort of peg-like ladder. He put a chair by the table.

"That'll help you climb easy. An' my gosh, Mister Dunham, ain't we got well 'nough acquainted yet for you to trust me? Hurry up!"

"I feel like a fool," said Dunham stubbornly, but weakening.

"You got no call to!"

"When I tap?"

Niobrara County Library
Lusk, WY 82225

"After about an hour. Give him time to talk free an' easy. I'll bring yore name up."

"You promise, honest?"

"I promise, cross my heart, hope to die!"

"I'll risk it, but—"

"Ain't no 'buts' to it!"

Dunham stepped on the bottom of the chair, then on the table. He had to stoop to keep his head below the rafters. Then he stood at the wide opening and looked about over the dark, dusty platform where he was to stay.

With struggling heave and groping of toes for the pegs, with Red boosting as hard as he could, he wriggled up.

Red quickly moved the table back into the center of the room and replaced the lamp. From overhead came Dunham's grumbling mutter:

"If I ain't a damn fool I miss my guess!"

CHAPTER XIII

The Guns of Tiger Burns

Red felt a little uncomfortable about not going out to meet Rodman, but he knew that Dunham was peering through a crack suspiciously, and listening. He would surely smell a put-up job if Red tried to have anything like a private word with Rodman, so he stood in the doorway, waiting.

"You all right, Walt?" he sang out.

"Better'n I might be," Rodman answered wearily. He had not stopped at the corral, but rode at a slow walk right up to the door and said, "Give me a lift down, will you, Red?"

"Sure! Whatever is wrong?"

"I got nipped last night."

"Bad hurt? That shore is hell! We all had to do some scatterin'—"

Red talked loud and fast for the minute or two that he was out of the house beside Rodman's horse, for he wanted Dunham to feel sure that he was overhearing everything that was said.

Rodman, leaning heavily on Red, came in, weary and pretty frayed. He sat down with a heavy sigh, very like a groan. He was almost covered with blood and seemed a little dazed.

"Which way you come, Walt?"

" 'Way round and across the Gorgione Ridge. It was losing blood that weakened me. I shook them off in no time last night, but I was afraid to come over the trail. Where are the other boys?"

"They had some bad luck, but I figger they are plumb all right now. Safe an' snug. Yes'r. Tom broke a leg, an' Billy's stoppin' with him. But where's all yore friends? They's nobody on the trail, watchin'."

"Isn't there?" Rodman asked without interest, sipping at the lukewarm coffee Red had brought. "I don't know. But I guess they left Hollar to watch an' went back over to their diggin's to see how things were getting on. Then Hollar lit out. He's all right, but not to be trusted."

Red was beginning to work at the rough sort of bandages, or rather wadding, that Rodman had made to check the blood.

"Bullet come clear through, Red. Rifle. Numbed me some. But it's the bleeding that got me. Seem awful chilled. It's not really cold, is it?"

"Not so I can notice, it ain't."

"I feel like a stuck pig. And look it, too. Losing blood makes you cold, I guess."

"Want something to eat?"

"No, but I'd like some whisky. Is there any?"

"Yeah, you bet. There's that bottle we took off Hollar an' hid."

"I'm glad you boys got off all right. I'd feel bad if you got hurt mixing up in my bad luck."

"Shucks," said Red. "We was all in the same boat with Mister Dunham steppin' on our tails. For all you knowed, we was danged bad outlaws. 'Course, you asked me private an' earnest if we was, an' said you couldn't throw in with us—but outlaws can lie, can't they?"

"Hell," said Rodman wearily. "I have been made an outlaw. The worst kind. Accused of killing my own father. Accused of wanting to marry Clara and kill Jake so I can get the ranch. Bah, life is sure tough, Red."

Red brought the pint of whisky from behind the sack of onions, and a cup. He poured a drink, gave it to Rodman, and set the bottle near the lamp.

"I reckon," Red suggested, "you feel peevisher than ever toward ol' Jake, now, hunh?"

"Yes, damn him. I'm wondering if he's really been fooled by what other folks have said of me, or if he is trying to fool other folks. Maybe *he* hired them men to say I got drunk and talked. They lied, and men don't lie like that without a reason. Usually the reason is, somebody pays them. It isn't like what I've always thought of Jake. You can't ever tell about people. My God, but I am weak! I thought I'd never get here. Who you going to trust in this world? Dod Wilson sold out on us—or me, rather. He always put up to be my friend. You been back long, Red?"

"Yeah, I rolled in this afternoon. Sort o' got lost

a time 'r two on the road and had to stop. But say, Walt. But why would Mister Dunham want to make up any stories like them? You ain't got no claim on the ranch nohow."

"It's Clara, I suppose. To influence her. Quick as this shoulder gets straightened out, I'm going back East and find her."

"Without takin' no what you call revenge on Jake Dunham, hunh?"

"To hell with him. If we ever meet I'll kill— no, I won't, either, if I can help it. Clara would never have any use for the man that shot her father. She's what I care about. I was a fool ever to come back to this country. But having money, and thinking maybe I could talk face to face with old Jake—*What's that?*"

"What's what?" Red asked, turning from the bunk that he was making up carefully for Rodman.

"Thought I heard something out back."

Red listened a moment, glancing overhead, and thinking Rodman must have heard Dunham stir. "You're a little feverish. Take some more whisky. I'll have you layin' down in a minute."

"Gosh, but I am weak! Oh—ho—Red! Look out—*Tig Burns!*"

Red was standing with his back to Rodman, and both arms out and up on the corners of a lifted blanket that he was trying to fold evenly. Now with twisting stretch of neck he looked backwards, letting the heavy blanket simply fall from his fingers, and so stood with hands up and back turned to the guns of the dark chunky man who half crouched in the back doorway, with eyes agleam.

"Got yuh!" Burns snarled grimly. "Smart hombre, you!" This with many oaths. "Smart hombre to have your hands up when you smell me comin'! Huh! Keep that other arm up, you!" Burns yelled at Rodman.

"I can't. Shoulder's busted. I didn't know I could lift it at all."

"Stand up!" More curses. Rodman stood up. "Unbuckle your belt—move slow! This is my party. I'm goin' talk, an' you fellers are goin' to listen. Ha-ha-ha!" Burns seemed really amused.

Rodman slowly unbuckled his belts, letting them fall about his feet.

"Turn round slow, you—" He yapped curses at Red.

Red turned slowly. He knew that he did not have a chance of any kind. Tig Burns was a fast dead shot. Before Red, swift as he was, could get a hand to a gun butt he would be full of holes. But he was planning that, when Burns told him to unbuckle his guns, he would put his hands down slowly, then jump sidewise with a limber dodging weave of body and draw. Would be hit—no doubt about that; but many a man that is hit first isn't the one that is buried.

"Now *you*"—Burns was talking to Rodman—"go over there to that red—" Foul names followed. "Git down on yore knees before 'im. Reach up an' unbuckle his gun belts!"

Burns was not taking chances. The wonder was that he had not killed both of them instantly.

As Rodman came near him, Red was tempted to snatch at his guns, but that would be suicide—nothing less.

Then, with sudden hopefulness and for the first time, having had all his thoughts scattered by the fight of helplessly facing Burns's level guns, Red recalled that Jake Dunham was up there, listening. Mister Dunham would be in no hurry to interfere since Burns had said he was going to talk. One word from Dunham, and they would be—perhaps not free, but at least not murdered. Perhaps, unexpected help having come, Dunham would now think himself absolved from the bargain he had made with Red; but somehow Red didn't feel that old Jake would. He might hold Walt Rodman a prisoner, but he wouldn't go back on his bargain with the boys. At least, Red thought so.

Rodman, kneeling as told, loosened the belts. They fell, with the guns spilling from the holsters. Red wore his holsters tied with thongs to his legs so that if the guns, by riding, were ever jolted down halfway tight, the holster would not swing and give when he had to jerk to free the guns. Rodman untied the thongs.

"Crawl off to one side on yer knees an' git up!" Burns told Rodman.

As Rodman arose, Burns laughed, sneeringly, pleased, as if really amused.

"This here is a good joke," he said. "A hell of a lot better joke than you lousy coyotes know. Too good f'r to keep. I got to tell it! First, I got to get you fellers placed like I want you. Come around left o' the table—an' walk wide o' that lamp! Even look like you wanta knock 'er over an' you'll die some ten minutes 'fore I'm through talkin'!"

As they came, Burns edged the other direction, keeping lamp and table between them. Burns was in his stocking feet, and so had crept in upon them, soft as a cat. He showed his white, small, cat-like teeth in a wide grin.

He made them stand back up against the wall, well away from the back door. Burns, laying one gun on the table, drew table and all farther away. He pushed the lamp a little to one side so as to have a better view, sat down, and poured himself a drink of whisky. Then he pushed his hat back and laughed.

"Dead men, both of you. Dead men tell no tales. You won't! An' this here is too good to keep!" He laughed, really amused. It was not a hearty laugh, but the cackle of a cold, merciless fellow who was pleased by the sort of thing that made other people shudder. "Huh. Me, I killed both your dads an' now I'm goin' to kill a couple o' calves as is called sons!"

He peered at them, enjoying the shock and grinning with cat-like teeth.

"M-my father! You? Why?" Rodman gasped, astounded, dazed.

"Huh! Same reason I do ever'thing. Paid for it!"

"Did Jake Dunham pay you to k-kill—"

"Hell, no!" said Burns, emphatic.

His hand moved out as if for the other gun that was lying on the table, but his groping hand touched the cup, then moved on to the bottle of whisky. He poured the drink without watching what he did, keeping his eyes on them, but taking care to give himself a suitably big drink.

He drank, keeping his eyes level. He smacked his lips, wiped his mouth on the back of his hand, and chuckled jeeringly.

"You bein' dead men, 'twon't do no harm for to whisper in yore ears. Wally Dunham an' me figgered things out. We got 'em figgered farther, too. Ol' Jake's goin' to die mysterious, too. Then Wally an' the girl gits the ranch. After the which he gives me the half of it. An' after that there," said Burns with frank evilness, grinning, "I'll take precautious pains f'r to git it all. Then me, Tig Burns, will be sole owner o' the old Double X. Too bad you lousy coyotes won't be alive for to see! Wally's clever an' careful—someways. Got a feller in Californy to swipe some sheriff stationery and write out to us here how you'd been in prison, Rodman. You ain't nothin' but what's called a pup-pet! So's Wally, only he don't know it—yit awhile. But I'll learn 'im. Same as I'm learnin' you—" He cursed them.

Then to Red: "Yes, I killed yore damned old Dad. Plumb too meddlesome. I used to be on the dodge. Don't mind tellin' you—" he chuckled— "dead men! I used to be up here with the boys. I come up that rock wall from the sunken valley tonight. That's another thing I had agin ol' Rodman. He run us outa here. Then me an' some fellers went down to Tulluco. I laid f'r that sheriff. Soaked him with lead—plumb full. Yesterday, after the talk I had there in town with Dod Wilson, I guessed you fellers had hid out up here in my old Roost. I come into the sunken valley down there today an' waited—somebody brought a light right out back tonight for to tell me plain, folks was home. So I started comin'. Las' night I couldn't get even in rifle shot of none of you coyotes. Now I got you both! An'—just one more little drink to make me enjoy myself more, an'—"

"Then," said Red, with a squeak in his throat, he was that tense and helpless, "it's you an' Wally as has—"

"Been stealin' the Ol' Man's cows while bein'

241

hired to catch rustlers? Shore! Easy. An' we had to cook up somethin' nice on Walt here because the Ol' Man was gettin' some pious notions that now the ranch was out o' debt he maybe ought to whack with the son o' his dead pardner. In a way o' speakin', the whole damn ranch is mine, an' I don't want it whacked with nobody. So I seen to it that we spoiled any such notions as them!"

Burns poured more whisky. He was not, and was not to be, in the least drunk. It took hours of steady drinking to make him wobbly. But the hot liquor warmed his tongue, gave boastful zest to his pleasure, made him want to talk.

"Well, now I got to git it over with, I reckon. An' I sort o' hate to. Ain't so enjoyed myself in ages. An' it's just so much pleasure to meet you, you red-headed skunk, after the trick you played me! But I got to git it over with, I s'pose. Wally an' the other boys was to come up over the reg'lar trail late tonight. We planned on sort o' havin' a little round-up. We guessed if you got through you'd be here."

Then Red understood why those two Double Xers had been on the trail. That, perhaps, had been selected as a sort of meeting place after they had scoured the country.

Red also understood why Jake Dunham did not dare make a sound. That would be suicide for him. Burns would kill him, have to kill him, now and at once.

"I been sort o' listenin'," said Burns, picking up the second gun. "Me, I got good ears. An' I hear hosses comin' far off. So we gotta have this over with pronto. Six thousand dollars, me, I'll git for doin' something as is shore a pleasure!" He grinned at them with lips drawn back and a glittering light in his black eyes. "Dead 'r alive! Yeah. An' I'd shore lose six thousand dollars rather than 'prive myself o' this here pleasure!"

He stood up, kicking back the chair, listening.

Red too could now hear the faint, muffled, far-off sounds of ironshod hoofs that occasionally struck rock. The click carried far through the still night.

Burns, with the slow movement of a man sucking in every drop of this delightful revenge, began to bring the guns into a level aim, almost shoulder high, with neck drawn in, staring hard and grinning with his teeth.

"One word, Burns," said Red hoarsely, with effort. "Then to hell with you. It's all right f'r us to go out"—Red was carrying his message to Jake Dunham, helpless, overhead. "That's part o' the range game. You win. But shore as there is a God in heaven—an' He's got mighty big ears, too!—you're goin' to get what's comin' to you, right! Knowin' that me, I c'n die peaceful! So shoot, you goddam lousy buzzard, an' see if I care!"

"Bluff talk!" Burns snarled, angered that

Red was not showing terror, thus spoiling his pleasure. "If the boys wasn't comin' I'd entertain myself shootin' off yore long nose an inch at a time—the which I c'n do, damn you!"

"You're a liar!" said Red. "Bet you can't!"

"Goddamn you, shut up!" Burns snarled, peevish. It hurt his fun to find Red defiant. The proper sweetness in revenge, his kind, was to have a man whimper and beg.

And so, half in hope of breaking Red's nerve, he leveled the guns again, crouching, hands close together, and hesitated, the better to make Red and Rodman squirm as he peered at them over the gun barrels.

The night wind stirred the pines with gentle sighing, and the sound of many horses drew nearer, running.

Rodman gasped with mouth open. Red, as tense and heart-hurt as any man that ever stood on the gallows' drop with a knotted rope to his neck, pulled himself together with head up, straining every nerve and every muscle to cheat this murderer of what satisfaction there might be in seeing a victim cringe.

Then a voice, jubilant, reached them. Off in the darkness some man had seen through the lighted doorway and bawled, "Hey, Wally, shore as hell ol' Tig's got 'em covered an'—"

Burns, with wrists loose, tight squeeze of thumbs and slow pressure of trigger fingers, fired. It pleased him to aim at the dead center of both foreheads—give the boys that would see the corpses something to talk about. He would say, of course, that they had tried to make a break, tried to bolt.

And so he fired—he who could cut a string and smash the falling bottle. The explosive boom of the guns was such as few men have ever heard from forty-fives. It was a crashing roar, terrific. In the confined space of the cabin the report had the sound of cannon rather than small arms. And as if the invisible hand of God had swept at them, the guns seemed jerked from Tig Burns's fingers and fell as if thrown, striking the table with chattering thud, then bounced, skittering to the dirt floor.

For one amazed and panic-stricken speechless moment Tig Burns, with bulging black eyes and jaw loosely gaping, stared at his outstretched and empty hands and was stunned by the mystery of what had happened. With nervous twitching jerks of head he glanced about fearfully, as if wanting to see, yet afraid to look at whoever or whatever had disarmed him. There was nothing to see— nothing but the low swirl of gun smoke about him. With hands not yet quite lowered he stepped back, dazed.

At that moment Red, who had been as much amazed as Burns and almost deafened by the explosive roar of the guns, came to life with a yelp of, "Now, damn yore soul!" Red flung himself headlong in a scrambling snatch for the nearest guns—Rodman's—that lay on the floor where they had been dropped. He leaped like a wild-cat pouncing, skittering with hand out in eager snatch for the gun, yelping, "You're the dead man now!"

Burns, in terror and mystification, staggered back with arm upthrown as if to guard his face, then turned and with a shout as if he had seen devils snatch at him, plunged through the doorway; and he made a lucky jump aside into the darkness as Red, not yet on his feet, but flat to ground like a wounded man, shot rapidly, emptying the gun.

Men out in the darkness and near the doorway yelled surprise and warning one to another, spurring their horses to one side, cursing and calling to Burns, yelping, "My God! What's happened?"—"Tig! Oh, Tig!" Some of them, half doubtfully, because it seemed the thing to do, shot.

Red snatched up another gun, then, with a whoop that he afterwards described as like that of an Injun chief drunk at his own wedding, jumped to the door, swung it shut, lifted the heavy crossbar. Instantly, with the scampering haste of a man gone mad, he turned about, got to the back door, stepped outside, and with the strength of one suddenly possessed, began to roll the half-filled water barrel inside, sloshing the water all over his waist and legs.

As soon as it was in the house he slammed shut the back door, threw over the crossbar, and squawked like a fellow out of his head, "Don't tell me there ain't no God!"

Then he laughed, a little hysterically. He had no piety. He hardly knew what he was saying. But he just naturally felt that way about it. Down deep in his honest range-bred heart he just couldn't believe that there wasn't something about honesty and truth and square-dealing that kept a man from harm.

With head thrown back toward the platform on the rafters he yelled in a way that made Rodman sure Red had simply gone mad:

"Hi, up there! Now, what d'you think! Huh! I reckon you'd better come down here an' kiss me—an' Walt! I sure need somethin' for to brace me up! Oh, golly glory! I don't know what happened, but did you see them guns jump right out o' Tig's hand like they simply wouldn't shoot nice boys like us!"

And Walt Rodman dropped back against the wall as if falling when he heard the heavy booming voice of Jake Dunham, as if from heaven, answer:

"Damn their souls—the pack of 'em! You boys—I can't ever do enough of what's right for you boys!"

Rodman shook his head, dazed, sure that he was out of his mind and hearing things, seeing things, for there was a big pair of booted legs dangling from the platform and kicking with groping impatience at the ladder pegs.

"Red! Red!" Rodman begged. "I must be—my mind! Look there! Do you—"

Red was busily slamming the window shutters into place and barring them.

"Shucks," he called. "We had comp'ny. I invited him for to come up an' get acquainted with us fellers." He had fastened the last window. "Now we're all set f'r some entertainment. Better be a good show 'cause I'm a heap critical!"

He ran to Dunham's feet and guided his toes to the pegs.

Dunham, with hat gone and shirt half pulled out by the scrape of the wood on his belly as he let himself down, stood dusty and sweaty, solemnly staring at the astounded Rodman. Then he crossed the cabin with a long stride and hand out.

"Boy, they've fed me loco weed!" said Dunham. "I don't know as how we'll get outa here—any of us. But if I do, near everything I own is yours! Girl, cows, land. While me, I'm going to some lunatic place an' be took care of!"

They shook hands with a kind of dazed solemnness, Rodman not speaking. He just couldn't.

Amazement and emotion were choking. He tried to smile, but seemed a little afraid, as if not yet quite sure this wasn't the delusion of a man out of his head.

Dunham's big arm held Rodman in an unaccustomed effort at gentleness as he helped the young man to a chair, stood over him, and gazed down into Rodman's upturned eyes that swam dizzily. The shock of his wound and loss of blood, the frightful strain of Tig Burns's menace, and Dunham's coming down off the rafters, were just too much for Rodman's feverish brain. It did not seem real.

Dunham patted his shoulder and turned to where Red, frowning in puzzlement, was examining Tig Burns's guns in the lamplight.

"Whatever happened, Red?" Dunham asked. "I couldn't see nothing where Tig was standing—an' was afraid to move. But I never heard so much noise from guns!"

"Me neither, Mister Dunham. But there was shore a good reason for Tig thinkin' the devil had 'im! I don't know what could've happened, but the muzzle o' one is split an' the other'n bulged. Like the bullets was oversized 'r somethin'. Maybe the devil did poke his fingers in 'em! That made 'em kick like Tig had holt of a couple o' real hog legs—you know how a hog can kick! An' it's only fellers as can't shoot good as grips a gun like 'twas somethin' as might try to get away

249

from 'em. So they simply jumped right outa Tig's hands."

"Sure the nearest thing to a mir'cle I ever heard of!" said Dunham solemnly. "Tig, he simply can't miss!"

"He shore as hell did, anyhow." Red turned the guns over and over, then his eyes took on a far-away stare and a slight grin quivered on his mouth. He laughed suddenly, dropped the gun, slapped his leg. "Ho ho, my gosh, my gosh, my gosh!" He began to stamp about like an Indian doing a war dance, rocking with laughter.

"Whatever the hell has got into you?" Dunham asked, almost uneasy, Red acted so crazy.

"Ow, Mr. Dunham! Ol' drunken crazy Hollar done it! He shore done it! An' now me, I got to buy him peanuts, whisky, an' such-like luxuries the rest o' his life—an' I hope he lives a thousand year!—for to pay him back!"

"What you talkin' about?"

"Me, I'm talkin' of Hollar, bless his danged old hide! He's cuckoo an' batty, an' he caught Tig drunk an' asleep, an' instead of killin' him, like he oughta, he soaped his guns! He come up here drunk an' gigglin' and a-talkin' queer. I thought he meant he'd made 'em slick. But Hollar has got more brains 'n we give him credit! He rammed soap up the barrel. It dried tighter 'n cowhide in hell—bless his idjit soul! No wonder he giggled! Tig ain't used ner had to clean his guns since, an'—no wonder he was scairt! His guns simply blew up in his hands. If my guns was to act like his did, I'd know spooks was a-ridin' me. Oh, my gosh! Now, whenever I'm lonesome an' need me some entertainment, I'll just think of the look on Tig's face when his guns jumped!" Red added, grinning, "Bet my face too looked funny! I had my mouth all set for to say, 'Hello, Mr. Satan!' an' poke out my hand for to try to make friends!"

Dunham grunted, half chuckling in spite of his somber scowl:

"I bet you'd purt-near done it, too!"

CHAPTER XIV

"Crazy, Reckless, Careless, but—"

Someone was beating at the door with the butt of a gun, and Red sang out, his voice jubilant and mocking, "Come a-walkin' right in, feller!"

Wally Dunham's voice answered with an impatient shout:

"Hey, you fellows in there! You're all through an'—"

"Glad f'r to be tol', 'cause we didn't know it!"

"—you'd better open up an' come out! I'm deputy sheriff, you know. This here is legal. Hear me?"

Red grinned at Dunham who, with gathering cloud of explosive anger on his face, strode forward to roar his answer; and Red pulled at his arm, whispering hastily, "Gee, my gosh, don't! They don't know yet what's happened to 'em! They don't know you're here. Let's listen awhile. Wait, an' we'll give 'em some surprise as'll make their whiskers curl!"

"Hey, you in there! Hear me!" Wally called again.

"We hear a lot better'n you think, feller! Go ask Tig—I mean *Kitty* Burns if we ain't good listeners. An' for dead men we mean to talk a lot! You go tell 'im!"

"What you talkin' about?" Wally asked, mystified.

"Tig—I mean *Kitty*'ll understand plenty. Hey! Hey, there!"

"What is it?"

Red grinned widely and lifted his voice in a shout:

"Go tell that singed-tail Kitty that the whisky he drunk—it was *poisoned!* You tell 'im an' see what he says. He's dyin', sure!"

"Poisoned? What'd you mean? Some whisky?"

"Sure! Don't he act funny? Go ask 'im!"

There was a hasty babble of conversation outside. His friends had seen that Tig was acting peculiar, sort of depressed and unwell, talking to himself mostly with cuss words, sorrowfully.

There was more pounding on the door. Wally Dunham's voice rose again in a kind of argumentative shout:

"Come outa there! We'll not hurt you, an'—"

"I know gosh danged well you ain't goin' to hurt us!"

"Where's my uncle Jake? Word come out to me from town about what you done! You killed him, damn your soul! An' them boys down there on the trail—snuck up on them!"

"Yore a liar—as usual!" said Red.

"Where's my uncle Jake?"

"I hid 'im."

"You killed 'im!"

"No, Wally, I take a heap o' pains not to do nothing to please you. I don't like the shape o' your nose. You got a skunk-like smell. Besides, you want to marry my friend's girl—"

"Shut up tryin' to be smart! Come on outa there. There's eight of us, all ready to open up! You can't get away! You killed old Jake an'—"

"Good gosh, Wally! You don't sound 'preciative a-tall!"

"What do you mean?" said Wally in stressed tones of indignation.

"What makes you think we killed Mr. Dunham?" Red, Yankee fashion, answered with a question.

"You carried him off from town. We know all about that! His horse an' saddle is here, but he ain't! So where is he? You killed him!"

"How you know he ain't here, hunh?"

"Tig would have seen him an' got him loose!"

"Ti—I mean *Kitty* couldn't see straight! He was poisoned an'—"

"I'm not going to waste more time!" said Wally, talking big. "Come on out, 'r we'll dig you out!"

"Go ahead! Dig some nice holes that we can use f'r yore graves. That's the only thing I'd hate about shootin' you—would have to get up a sweat diggin' a hole to poke you in!"

Wally cursed, exasperated. "Are you coming out alive, or do we—"

"Wally, you go set down a while an' rest yoreself. We want to talk it over, me an' Walt. An' you'd better hurry an' give somethin' to Kitty Burns to make him vomit. That whisky was shore poisoned. Ain't he begun to feel pains in his belly yet? He will right soon!"

"Poisoned—you mean really poisoned?"

"Go ask 'im! Ask 'im if he don't feel all queer an' colicky! An' tell him from us, thanks f'r the little speech he made. We're a lot smarter'n we was before he learnt us. He'll un'erstand—plenty!"

"What the hell are you talking about?" Wally bawled, puzzled and a little uneasy.

"Go ask Tig! I know he's a sick man, but coax 'im gentle!"

"You goddamned smart aleck! If you don't come out o' there—"

"If that's the way you're goin' f'r to talk, get away from our front door! Go on, get away, plumb away! You hurt my feelin's, actin' cross thataway! Hey, an' ain't Tig told you they is loopholes for to plug ary man that comes near this here house? Git! An' when you come back to talk to us some more, you come a-waltzin' under a white flag! If you don't *git,* I'll show you somethin'!"

Red dimmed the lamp, stood on a bunk, peered

255

through a loophole, caught a vague, shadowy glimpse of men hovering there close to the door, like terriers waiting at a rat hole. Red shot quickly.

There was a howl of surprise, much startled jumping and scurrying.

Tig might have told them that no one could approach, or stand near, the three-cornered cabin without putting themselves in range of the loopholes; but Tig's thoughts were busy with other troubles.

Some of the men out there opened fire on the cabin, but they might as well have been shooting at any other pile of logs.

"Now, Mister Dunham," said Red, "out o' all them eight fellers out there, I reckon there's some that wouldn't stand for to see you killed, but—"

"I'm not so sure, not so sure, Red," Dunham answered with gruff bitterness.

"Yes," Red agreed, "I reckon you've got reasons for to be some doubtful. Likely enough all them fellers has been in with Wally an' Tig in the cow stealin'. 'R most of 'em. Gosh, I bet it makes 'im itch all over, like cactus stickers in his pants, for to be called 'Kitty'! The which is why I do it!"

"I'm near bustin' with longin' to tell 'em what I think!" Dunham growled.

"If you step out an' cuss and 'cuse Wally an' Tig, somebody's most sure to plug you. The which'll be Tig, for a certainty. He will anyhow, first chance. It's dead certain Tig ain't goin' to confess to nobody out there how he blabbed to us 'dead men'! But when he learns you was in here—he'll have a fit. Reg'lar cat fit, Me, personal, I guess that as soon as we open the door we'll all be dead men. An' they'll tell in town that me an' Walt killed you."

"That's about right," said Dunham thoughtfully.

"Tig thinks jus' 'cause he didn't see you that you ain't here—but 'pearances are deceivin', as the feller said after he married the widder lady. She wore bought hair an' store teeth. Least, that's what the song about it says. Me an' widder ladies ain't much acquainted."

"Red, don't you ever act serious?" Dunham asked, curious, not reproachful.

"Hell afire, Mister Dunham. Gruntin' an' groanin' don't help a feller think. I'm doggone ser'us right now. I could weep for wishin' my back hadn't been turned when Burns walked in on us."

"It worked out luckier as 'twas, Red. He'd 'a' shot on sight, then."

"An' what the hell do you think I'd 'a' been a-doin'? Sayin', 'Please, Mr. Burns, don't hurt me'?"

Dunham shook his head, not answering. Red didn't seem in a mood for good advice. Dunham glanced about, remarked, "We've got plenty of guns an' shells, anyhow!"

"More guns than shells, a'most! We got grub an' water. It's a sort o' instink with me for to think o' water when I hole up. You see, I was just a little shaver onct when, ridin' out with my Dad, some folks come along unexpected, an' we holed up in a 'dobe—one room. An' it didn't have no roof. An' no water! Then I learnt what folks mean in speakin' about not havin' ice water in hell! I loaded for my Dad, an' them fellers got awful sorry they had found us. He could shoot, my Dad could!" Red nodded, meditative.

Dunham, in an attitude of strained listening, remarked, "They 'pear to be talkin' things over out there. Mighty quiet. What you reckon they'll be up to?"

"I can't waste time tryin' to guess what notions the devil'll put in their noodles. But us, now I figger we got a choice of three ways for to act. Not tell 'em you're in here, an' let 'em think me an' Walt is alone, an' him bad hurt—the which'll maybe encourage 'em to come a-sneakin' up clost to the loopholes an' get shot! Or maybe they'll try to bring up a fire an' smoke us out. Which won't be so easy done as wished for. Or we can tell 'em we got you here—a pris'ner. An' let you speak up to sort o' prove it. That'll make Tig near bite hisself! I'd shore hate to be as big a fool as he's goin' to feel when he knows. He thinks hisself a purty big one as 'tis—his 'dead men' not bein' yet in a shape to bury. Or we can tell 'em you've throwed in with us to stick it out—and why! The which'll mean they just naturally feel they've got to wipe us out. They'll stick for days, till they do. However way we figger, it comes back to the same thing—we got to set tight an' whittle 'em down. The which ain't easy. They've sort o' got the advantage there, like Walt's Dad and the boys that drove out the outlaws. They just what you call focus their guns on a loophole an' when the time comes pour in the lead. But all the trees an' stumps near by havin' been cleared off makes it harder for 'em."

Walt Rodman spoke up. "Harry and Cliff and Pete ought to be coming back down this way tonight or early in the morning."

"Who're they?" Dunham asked.

"Friends o' Walt's," Red explained. "Ol' fellers up here tryin' to mine, ranch a bit, hunt an' fish a lot. Walt thinks maybe they went off to feed their chickens 'r something, leavin' old Hollar on guard while us boys rode to Dod Wilson's place. If they do come up an' start bushwhackin' this bunch, it'll be a good show. Them boys is plumb accurate with rifles. But most likely they'll come nosin' in and ask, 'What's the matter?' an' get buried without ever knowin' the facts."

"If my shoulder wasn't busted," said Walt holding the cup of water Red had brought him,

"I could climb down the rock wall back there—Burns's horse is there, hobbled—and so get to town and bring back people. But—"

"*My* shoulder ain't busted!" said Red.

"Nor mine!" Dunham added.

"You couldn't make it, Mister Dunham," Red explained. "That trail's just a place cut in the rocks for to fall down off of head first if you ain't careful. Takes a skinny feller."

"And I don't think you could find the trail out, Red," said Walt.

"Huh. I got a nose for ways out like a dogy's for water. Hell, I c'n climb, crawl, swim, an' walk—also, if bad scairt, fly a little too. You don't know what a lot of 'complishments I got! But can you two hold down the fort?"

"They're shoutin' somethin' out there now!" said Dunham.

"They wanta talk. All right. We'll listen." Red got near a loophole, but did not poke his head up, and shouted: "What you-all bellyachin' about? Don't you suppose me an' Walt wants to sleep tonight?"

The yell came back from where Wally and some of the others had taken cover in the corral: "You fellows comin' out?"

"Sure! How's Tig feelin' by now? Dead yet?"

"Well, come on out, then!"

"Sure!" Red bawled at the top of his voice, wanting to make sure everybody heard: "Just as soon—as we get through—talkin' over—what Tig told us!"

"What'd he tell you?" someone asked.

"Ask Tig—I mean Kitty!" Red shouted. "It was plenty enter-tainin'!"

"What'd you tell 'em, Tig?" a voice called.

"I never told 'em nothin'—'cept I'd like to chew 'em to death!" Burns called savagely.

"Oh, what a whopper!" Red bellowed reproachfully. "Who killed ol' Rodman—an' why! Who's been stealin' cows an'—"

Oaths broke out, and a splatter of bullets. Wally squawked, "Shoot! Shoot 'em!" Tig yelled, like a wild animal screaming, and opened fire. Red laughed, jeering. Then he caught up a rifle, jumped to another loophole, fired twice, rapidly, jumped on the bunk before still another, and fired again. Shots thumped the logs, replying. Voices rose, strained and angry, in a kind of snarling quarrel.

"I told 'em nothin', I tell you!" Tig shouted in fury. "They're just guessin'. Keep blazin' away! We got to bury them skunks! Hit that Red an' they'll both be down. Rodman can't use his arm, an'—"

"Yeah, Kitty Burns!" Red shouted, "you go bite yoreself—an' die, as if a rattler done it!"

"Kill him, boys!" Wally urged frantically. "Kill 'im!"

Red jumped from the bunk, grinning. "He

wants 'em to keep shootin' so I can't talk! We make Tig mad enough, an' he'll shoot hisself just for the pleasure o' hurtin' somebody! I bet he thinks I'm a Jonah. He'll be plumb convinced if ever we meet—but, Mister Dunham, I reckon I was lucky to have had my hands full when he snuck in! Otherwise it's right he wouldn't have had so much time for to talk. But I'm going to kill him, plumb face to face, just so he'll feel bad at havin' been beat fair an' square on the draw all the time he's wigglin' in the devil's stew pot!"

"Don't try it, Red," Walt urged. "Ever!"

"Don't try it, son," said Dunham, serious. "Tig don't do no sort o' work but practise drawin'!"

"Don't try it," Walt repeated. "If we get out of here we'll hunt him down like any other varmint. But he can't be beat on the draw. Like Mr. Dunham says, he keeps a-practisin'!"

"Hell," said Red. "Shot my Dad—in the back!"

"Mine, too, Red!"

"Not in the back! I'm goin' to kill 'im if I ever get the chanct, face to face! And with these same guns I took off him—an' split-nosed bullets!"

"But, Red—"

"Don't argy with me! That's personal business I got with him—if ever I get the chanst. An' I'll sure as hell get it, because that yellow-hearted killer is goin' to keep hisself tucked behind a log out there an' sneak off about the time we get the bunch whittled down to our size! I know his breed. An' if I was scairt o' them or him I'd go off an' hide!"

Red's eyes blazed. Dunham and Walt exchanged looks. Both shook their heads, but neither spoke.

Two hours went by. The men outside did not seem to know just what to do besides shoot now and then, and now and then yell for Red and Walt to come out. "The which," as Red said, "was plumb silly." From time to time Red, just to keep them stirred up and unhappy, answered jeeringly, calling upon Tig, "Hey, you tame cat, you! Tig-ee, Tig-ee, Tig-ee!"

Presently a voice answered, "What you want now?"

"Where's the skunk miscalled a Tiger? Hey, you mouse catcher!"

"Tig ain't here!" the voice answered.

"You're a liar," said Red.

"I ain't!" the fellow shouted back, indignant. "Tig's gone."

"Awright, I'll talk to Wally. Wally?" Red called. "Hey, you wall-eyed deputy sher'ff, you!"

"Go to hell!" Wally's voice answered.

"Yeah? Listen, Wally. I want to ask a ser'us question!"

"What is it?" Wally shouted, interested, almost hopeful Red was willing to bargain.

"How much—did you pay—for that letter—from Californy—about Walt—"

A blaze of oaths crackled in Wally's mouth. It was as if Red's words were blows that slapped his ears. No two ways about it now: Tig, thinking the fellows in the cabin were as near dead as men that dangle with broken necks at ropes' ends, had blabbed.

Then, suddenly, Wally began urging the men to stop shooting: "Be quiet, you fellows! I want to talk to him! What-all did Tig tell you?"

"Ask 'im!" Red bawled.

"He was just lying to fool you!" Wally squawked.

"He sure did—fool us—if he was lyin'—'cause we believe 'im! But folks has seen that letter. How much did you pay for it?"

"What else did Tig tell you?" Wally cried.

"Plenty!" Then Red turned to Dunham and commented hopefully, "Maybe now him an' Tig'll have a fuss an' Tig'll shoot 'im."

"Hey you! You, Red Clark!" Wally called.

Red didn't answer him. He was talking to Dunham, saying: "Tig ain't out there. That's certain. He'd have spoke up an' called me a liar. Wonder where he's gone? Bet he's run away already!"

"Hey, Red Clark!" Wally was calling, and others too, wanting to talk. "You come out and tell me what lies Tig told—and I'll see you don't get hurt!"

Red would not answer. "Let 'em worry,

anxious. I like for folks that are tryin' to kill me to worry some. An' Tig would sure have had some more fits if he had heard Wally cussin' him thataway. I wonder, now, did Tig climb back down the cliff—"

"He wouldn't—not in the dark—I don't think," said Walt. "He must have borrowed boots, or spurs, anyhow, and took one of the horses out there."

Old Jake Dunham said nothing, but he glowered, his big face swollen in explosive anger, glowered straight at the log wall as if staring through, trying to look his treacherous, petted, murderous nephew right in the face. For the first time in many years, if not indeed in his whole life, Jake Dunham felt almost humble, because he knew, without any chance at all of mental evasion, that he had been a fool, had blundered, been hoodwinked, had misjudged men blindly.

"I'd like for to tell him I'm here!" said Dunham. "Let him know what I know an' see what he says!"

"Huh! He'll say, 'Dear Uncle Jake, come out to my welcomin' arms—them fellers has all lied about me! You know I'm an hones' lovin' nephew. Don't—' "

"I'm goin' to tell 'im!" said Dunham, and moved as if to get to a loophole and shout.

"I wouldn't, Mister Dunham. Honest! He's goin' to find out soon enough. You tell 'im now, he'll do one o' two things. Either cut an' run, lope clear outa the country an' never come back, which is the most likely. 'R he'll buck them fellers out there up to feel they just got to kill us, which'll be bad if they start doin' things that'll keep us from sleepin'. We all need some sleep. Me, right now I got to start makin' some coffee—I'm that dead f'r sleep."

"I don't want him to get outa the country!" Dunham growled, meditative.

"Then we'll have to treat 'im coaxin'—like I been doin'! Make him wanta stay an' get shot!"

With that Red set about making the fire and filled the coffee pot.

The smoke and sparks pouring from the chimney gave Wally an idea. He hailed the cabin with:

"You fellows! Hey, you fellows in there! Come on out—now! We'll smoke you out! Burn you—alive!"

Red grinned, not answering. Dunham, glumly in a chair by the table, scowled and swelled up, wanting to rise and say things, but did not stir. Walt Rodman, wearily lying on a bunk, moved slightly, the better to listen.

"You hear?" Wally called in a screaming shout. "Rodman's down—*you,* Clark, you can't keep us from settin' fire to the house!"

Red shouted, "You start playin' with fire—

you—you'll get your nice cord'roy suit—all scorched!"

"Come on out—now—an' we won't hurt you!" Wally was trying to coax, as much as a man can when he shouts at the top of his voice.

"Won't you—hones'?" Red answered.

"No! Honest! Come on out! I want to talk!"

"Sure you won't hurt us?"

"Sure! Honest! I promise!" Wally yelled.

"Hones' Injun?" Red bawled—and so for a long time tormented Wally by pretending to be considering the advantages of surrender, bargaining. Then concluded by asking: "When you—an' Tig—get the Double X—will you give me—a job—as foreman, huh?"

That made Wally foam, splutter, curse.

Red's coffee was boiling. He could not pause to talk longer, but turned to the stove, and Dunham's look followed him staringly. Dunham said, half approving but a little mystified, "You are a funny boy, Red. Crazy, reckless, careless, but I sort o' think you're smarter than folks that ain't!"

"Me, I allus try to have some fun," said Red, dipping into the flour bin. "Little jokes make me feel as good as a drink o' whisky. 'F I had a bigger funny bone I wouldn't never need no whisky." He wiped his hands free of flour, poured some coffee, held out the cup to Mister Dunham. "Here. This'll plug up the cracks in our bellies.

267

Awful monot'nous, bein' cooped up thisaway. Me, I'm a man o' the Open Spaces. Yeah. Woman from the East onct waltzed up to me, an' she said, 'You are a man o' the Open Spaces, ain't you?' An' me, sir, I started feelin' round nervous-like for to see what buttons was open. Yes'r, that's how funny them Eastern folks talk!"

Having made the coffee, Red decided they all needed some flapjacks, too, so he poured water into the flour.

Dunham chuckled faintly at the Eastern woman's remark, then arose sluggishly, heaved himself up on a bunk's edge, and peered out from a darkened loophole. He noticed dim shapes gathering brush, bringing it from over in the timber. He told Red what was up.

"That crack about the Californy letter's made 'im desp'rate," said Red. "That an' him an' Tig ownin' the ranch. Plenty o' brush out there—but who's goin' to bring it up to the house?"

Several armfuls of dried wood and brush were gathered and carried into the shelter of the corral. There, Wally and his men held a long powwow. Setting fire to the cabin seemed the one way to get Red and Walt out and have it over quickly. The dangerous thing would be in trying to sneak the wood up to the house. But there were six thousand dollars on those fellows' heads. And Wally, knowing that they must not on any conditions be allowed to live long if he himself were to stay alive, promised rewards recklessly.

"Let's play possum, Mister Dunham," Red suggested. "Draw 'em into the open. Up close. Then we'll wake Walt here up—"

"I am awake," Walt answered. "An' one arm, it is still good."

"Yore whole dang body is still good!" said Red. "We'll just dim this lamp a little more. I wisht they'd hurry. My flapjacks'll spoil. Can't cook an' have yore thoughts on somethin' else."

Presently Red said softly, "All right, Walt," and pressed a loaded revolver into his hand. "You stand up here on this side till I give the word. They're gettin' ready for to try it."

Dunham and Walt stood watching from one side of the wall, Red on the other.

"I bet," Red mused, "they drawed straws for to see who was goin' to have the pleasure o' committin' suicide. An' bet Wally he helt the straws—an' didn't run no risk o' gettin' stuck! They think maybe Walt is dead, or the same thing. That me, I'm restin'. They think I couldn't watch both sides to onct, nohow. So most likely I'm the only one in here to shoot at 'em. An' they ain't got a proper respect f'r my shootin' abilities—like I hope to make 'em have! Life, it is just like poker—if you ain't seen the other fellers' cards you ain't no business thinkin' too firmly. Here they come! Goin' to make a double-barreled try at it!"

Two dim shapes, scarcely looking like men in the shadows, because they crouched low and each carried an armful of wood, detached themselves from the darkness of the corral and began with a kind of stealthy slowness to edge along in half circles, making for each side of the triangular cabin. There was a vague stirring movement among the other shapes that stayed behind. They were ranging themselves to open fire if protesting shots came at the wood carriers.

These fellows who were coming held the wood in one arm, a drawn gun in the other, being very uneasy about their venture.

"Bankin' on me bein' busy eatin'—or asleep. Well, I am, nearly," said Red. He now could see only one man; the other had passed out of sight on the other side of the cabin. The fellow that Red was watching came on with slow, uneasy caution.

"That ain't no way for to do it, feller!" Red commented critically. "Slower you come, the longer it takes you, an' the more chances you've got o' bein' seen. If you moved fast, you'd been here by now!"

The fellow who was coming up on the other side must have come with a quicker step, else Jake Dunham did not have Red's patience. Dunham fired once, twice, three times. Rodman shot at the same man, who was already dead and falling.

Then Red shot once. The bullet must have struck into the armful of wood, for the man fell over, dropping his wood, but the next moment he was on his feet, running, but with backward fling of arm fired where he had seen Red's gun flash. A storm of rifle bullets was flying at the loopholes. Red shot again, and the wood carrier went down, this time not having an armful of wood for a breastplate. A moment later Red could see the man crawling off. Red let him go, not out of mercy, but because, as he explained later, a wounded feller makes sounds that discourages his friends from goin' and doin' likewise!

"But me," he grumbled, "I'm gettin' to be a pore shooter. Just nicked 'im a little. Now, my Dad could have took off his eyebrows so neat the feller wouldn't even have winked!"

"You know, Red," said Dunham as he stepped down, turning to help Rodman from the bunk as Red fussed with the lamp, making it brighter, "there are times when I begin to suspicion that you exaggerate a wee mite about some things!"

Red grinned. "Most talk'tive fellers do. Ain't you noticed?"

"Now," said Dunham, with emphasis, heaving a deep sigh, "I feel better. It's been hard to set by an' take no part in your own fight."

The rifles had stopped. The exasperated men out there were holding more powwow.

"Now, me, I'm goin' to finish my flapjacks," said Red, and turned to the stove.

Dunham watched him, half wondering yet somehow not at all believing there was much show-off about Red's nonchalance. He had the most amazing indifference to gun play that Dunham had ever seen.

"You must've sucked in your milk through a gun barrel," said Dunham.

"Who, me?" Red straightened up with flapjack turner in hand and brandished it by way of gesture. "My Maw died before I was a weaner. Dad got a cow an' an ol' Mexican to nurse me. Feed time, old José'd drag me out by the scruff o' my neck, squeeze a tit and shoot 'er at my mouth. One an' same time, thataway, he filled my belly an' washed my face. José was powerful inventive at labor savin'. You like plenty o' 'lasses with yore flapjacks, don't you? All good cowmen do!"

Dunham turned from where he had been peering. "Go ahead. Eat yourn first."

Rodman would take nothing but a little coffee. Red sat down to eat, but before he had chewed a mouthful Wally Dunham began to call at him.

"Yeah—now what?" Red bawled. "Want to tell me how bad it is for you to play with fire?"

"You can't get—away! We'll starve you out! Stay here till hell freezes!"

"Awright, stay till hell freezes. See 'f I care!"

"Hey, listen, Clark! You *can't* get away!"

272

"Who wants to get away? We're comfort'ble!"

"Listen. Clark! Tell me something. Will you?"

"Tell you what I think o' you—'f that's what you wanta know! You are a lousy, yeller-bellied, flea-bit, wind-broke, hoof-rotted son of—"

Wally cussed some too, then bellowed: "You'd better tell me. Did you kill Jake?"

" 'F I say *yes*," Red squawked, "will you pay me—what you promised for to pay Tig?"

Wally cussed some more, called Tig a liar, made remarks about Red's ancestors, promised again to stay till hell froze, but all with an exasperated fretfulness that amused Red.

Wally went into consultation with his men, and Red returned to his flapjacks. Jake Dunham said, "Boy, why don't we just waltz out there an' shoo off these coyotes?"

"F'r two reasons, Mister Dunham. One of 'em is they are liable to kill you, the which'd make Wally rejoice more'n is rightful he should. Other'n is that he might light out an' leave the country. An' I've got a plumb strong hankerin' for to attend Wally's funeral—without havin' to ride around over a couple o' states to get to it!"

"I guess you're right," Dunham agreed reluctantly and sat down.

Pretty soon Wally bellowed with a new sound in his voice: "Hey, you! I'm goin' to send—word to town—hang your friends!" Then, but with a suggestion of afterthought: "Tig's gone in to do it!"

273

Red meditated and spoke aloud. "He's a liar. But he might send in word. Fellers that ain't honest can shore think o' the gosh-danged worst things to do! 'F Tom an' Billy is hanged—be just like Wally to do that! Listen, Mister Dunham. You can hold down this fort. I'm goin'! Tig's horse is sure to be down in the sunken meadow, hobbled. I'm goin'. I'm goin' right now!"

"In the dark, Red?" Walt protested. "You'll fall! And can't get out—"

"I'm goin'! Be just like that buzzard out there to send word to town sayin' he's rescued Mister Dunham here, an' Mister Dunham says to hang my friends. I'm goin', I tell you!"

"But," said Jake Dunham, "you'll be shot there in town the minute anybody lays eyes on you!"

"I won't! Anyhow, I gotta go! Here, you—" Red clawed about the shelves over the stove for the piece of pencil used to make out the grocery list—"write me a letter for the sheriff." Red pawed about for paper and found nothing but a bag. "Write 'er on that. Somethin' like, *Dear Sheriff, I take back all I said. Get you a big posse an' come with Red a-whoopin'. 'Fectionately, Jake.* I'm goin', I tell you. An' what's more, I'm comin' back!"

While Dunham bit the end of the pencil, scowling, trying to think how to word his note, Walt Rodman tried to give Red directions, such as, "As soon as it's sunup, go over to the white rock, then turn left till you come to the spring and a little beyond, then—"

Red listened carefully, coffee cup in hand. His flapjacks, forgotten, lay cold on the table.

"It's quite evident," Walt was saying, "they don't know about the trail down the rock wall. Few people do. And Tig only because he was in with the outlaws that time. He didn't tell anybody how he meant to sneak up here, and he was too much knocked out to talk after you run him out of the cabin! But don't you fall, Red. Take off your boots. Tie them around your neck. Let 'em hang back. Be sure to go down backwards, too. Have plenty of matches handy."

Red took off his boots, then rammed the guns he had taken off Tig Burns in the Silver Dollar down into the boots, one in each boot to help the balance.

"Just in case I happen for to bump into him along the line some'eres," he explained.

"You stay plumb away from Tig!" said Dunham, with a sound of old-time authority. "I don't want you hurt!"

" 'F I meet Tig I'll shore take it as a sign o' favor from Prov'dence an'—"

" 'Twill be a sign," Dunham growled, "that his father the devil is still tryin' to help 'im!"

"Prov'dence can lick the devil any ol' time!" said Red cheerfully.

"If Tig's horse isn't down there, Red," Walt

275

explained, "there is a little buckskin that will let you catch him."

"That there horse o' Tig's'll be there." Red spoke with assurance. "He didn't walk into the valley down there. He didn't climb back down—not him, bein' so plumb nerv'us as he was after talkin' so fluent an' open to us boys!"

"Here," said Dunham, handing over the note. "That ought to do it—if you can get to the sheriff. We'll be all right here, Red. I've stayed awake seventy hours at a stretch, lots of times. An' it's easy to keep a lookout. Besides, now they are some whittled down. Tig's gone. One's dead. Other'n bad hurt. Was eight. Now it's five."

"I'll have to give 'em a partin' word," Red explained, "so they won't be wonderin' why they don't hear my voice no more. Hey, you gazooks out there! Listen to me! All this yellin' I been doin'—it is bad f'r my throat. I'm done talkin'. From now on—guns—they talk! Un'erstand!"

Curses came back at him, and threats. "All of which," said Red, "never broke no bones."

"You fall," Walt began, "and all your bones will be—"

"Fall? Me? Hell! I'm lucky, allus." Red was busy tying the boots firmly across his back, Dunham helping. "Outside o' poker," he went on, chattering, "luck's allus done ever'thing possible—'cept make me handsomer'n I wanta be. I got me a good wide mouth—suit'ble f'r

276

food! Never yet missed a piece o' steak that come near it. Some eyes as ain't near-sighted—an' allus spots the biggest pertater in the pot, prompt! A nose f'r to smell an' enjoy what's in the skillet. An' I got ears that poke out like they was on tiptoes, allus, for to hear, 'Come an' git, Wolves!' Yes'r, if you're too good-lookin', like I ain't"—Red was knotting the string before his breast—"it gives fellers that are bigger'n you a jealous hankerin' for to work your face over, the which is annoyin'—partickular if they do it. So me, I'm satisfied. Good-bye, Walt, old kid! I'm goin' to get drunk at yore weddin', shore! She's the purtiest girl I ever seen in my life, an' I admire her judgment in pickin' me for an honest feller. She's the one that really started things that has set us all straight an' square again!"

"That's right, Red," Walt agreed.

"Good-bye, Mister Dunham. My virtues is not many, but not lyin' is one of 'em. An' I said that when you an' me got better 'quainted you'd sort o' halfway think I was a nice boy!"

"You are a smart boy, Red," said Dunham, taking his hand, holding, pressing hard, "but there's one thing you don't know an' I bet couldn't guess!"

"Yeah?"

"Yeah."

"Meanin' what?"

"Meanin'," said Dunham, looking pleased,

"that you are now the range foreman of the Double X. To hire an' fire, complete! It's in that letter you just stuck in yore shirt!"

"Holy gosh! Me? Then, to be honest by you, I'd better fire myself quick. I'm shore incomp'tent!"

Dunham shook his ponderous head. "I never seen a man, no man—much less one crazy, reckless, careless—as had so much good sense as you an' come allus nearer doin' right!"

CHAPTER XV

On the Road to Town

Red stepped out of the back door cautiously, pushed it to, but it was held open by Dunham, who stood watching. "Careful, now, Son," he growled.

Red crawled to the edge of the rock wall, lay down, turned round on his belly, and pushed himself slowly backwards, with feet groping for the narrow ledge just below.

There was one good thing about this trail, so he thought: Since you couldn't see behind you anyhow, it was just about as easy going down at night as in the day.

" 'Bye, Mister Dunham," Red whispered. "Don't do no worryin' about me—I c'n do plenty f'r myself!"

Then he edged down out of sight. "Nothin' to this at all but goin' slow," he told himself.

And he went slowly. It was just about like creeping down a very narrow steep stairway that had no banisters on one side.

The outlaws, of which Tig Burns had been one, thinking of ways of escape and wanting the use of the sunken valley, had made or improved the trail.

"Where Tig Burns can climb up, me, I c'n shore

279

climb down," Red told himself reassuringly. "I wonder why," he questioned himself, "that you can mark off a strip six inches wide on level ground an' walk her straight an' never wiggle? But if you've got a three-foot trail along the edge of a cliff an' a sure-footed hoss, still you get sort o' queazy. Anyhow, that darkness out there looks solid enough to hold me up!"

About halfway down there was a place where, though he lay cautiously, with bare feet groping, he could not feel any bottom.

"What's happened to this gosh-danged trail!" he grumbled. He could feel the side wall, but below him there was nothing to rest his toes on. "Hunh! I got to wiggle around somehow an' have me a look."

The night was brightly starlit, but this rock wall was banked in dense shadows.

"Hell," Red muttered after some cautious wiggling. "I can't turn round. An' my neck ain't long enough for to bend back an' see."

He struck a match, but the glare was too close to his eyes, and besides was between him and the place where he wanted to look. "Nice pickle!" he muttered. If he raised the match high enough to be out of his eyes, its light would not be strong enough to carry below him. He tried three or four matches but could not clearly glimpse anything. And empty space lay right out alongside his left hand.

"Gosh ding dang dong!" he grumbled, and meditated. "Well, sir," he decided, "Tig, he come up here in his sock feet—so he couldn't have kicked no big hole for me to drop in! Yet she shore feels like ever'thing ended right here b'low this half-grown ledge. Be a nice place, wouldn't it, for to meet a rattler all coiled up an' waitin'! I'd better think o' somethin' more cheerful if I'm goin' to keep happy. Now, if I wiggle down much farther tryin' to feel with my feet, I won't be able to hold my balance. Will just have to go on down. An' she's a long, long, *long* way to the bottom! Yet if she was much of a drop Tig couldn't have climbed up, could he? All right, then, you fraidy! Say your prayers an' let's go!"

So, pushing cautiously, Red wiggled back and back, groping downward with outstretched leg and reaching nothing but the side wall. And there was nothing but smooth rock for his hands to hold to. He had to hold with palms-down pressure as well as he could.

"Whoap! Another inch an' I can't crawl back. Already my heart has stopped beatin'—just holdin' its breath! An' my pore feet don't feel nothin' but some cool night air. Well, I know one thing. Tig Burns never used no wings to come up here. I'm goin' down—if I fall a mile!"

He pushed himself farther, so that he lay with his short-ribs right on the edge of what seemed the "jumping-off place." And now that he could

281

not crawl up again because there was nothing for his fingers to fasten on and pull, he knew he had to go on down. But being in that position his feet could now swing down almost vertically; and his groping toes, fairly crinkled by the strain of apparently dangling in space, found a step about three feet below the ledge on which he was lying.

Red stood on it and lay belly-down against the ledge, resting.

"See, I told you there *had* to be some way to get down! What you want to go scarin' me for?"

He moved slowly, hands on the ledge, one foot still on the step below him, feeling out with the other foot, which readily found support. He cautiously got down on his stomach and crept along backwards.

From then on it was, or so Red felt, easy going. When he reached the bottom he sighed in great relief as he looked up at the sheer wall of rock.

"Yes'r, I'll have me some nice long gray whiskers an' need a cane before I ever try that again. Bet my head's full of gray hairs now."

He looked about and saw the dim shadow-shape of a horse close by. At almost the first step he stumbled against something soft that clinked faintly, and striking a match he saw Tig's boots. Tig had taken them off right at the foot of the trail before starting up. The glint of the silver spurs took Red's eye. He grinned and at once began putting them on his own boots. Tig's were showy and expensive, long of shank, big of wheel, with ornamental stampcd leather.

"Gosh darn, he pervides me with guns, spurs, horses, an' information!"

Red put on his own boots with their new spurs, stuffed Tig's guns down inside his belt, and walked toward the horse. It was not only hobbled but picketed too. A hobbled horse can go quite a ways, and Tig had not wanted to have to walk far. That the horse might have died without water, or starved after the grass was cleaned within range of its rope, apparently had not occurred to Tig when he rode off up there from the cabin. That sort of cruelty made Red mad.

"Not only with guns, horses, an' spurs, but with good reasons for wantin' to kill him!" said Red.

He searched about with lighted matches and found the saddle and bridle.

"Yes, sir," he agreed, patting the horse's neck, "Tig shore does get himself good critters, for the which I rejoice a heap."

As he saddled he went on talking to the horse. "Son, you look sensible. I suspicion you know the way outa here better'n I do. So you just sort o' take the slack reins an' light out for home. Will you? I hope you don't mind overmuch, but I'm goin' to ride you purty hard, Son, 'cause I'm in a hurry—but, gosh dang yore hide, you oughta swell up with pride. You're carryin' the range foreman of the biggest cow outfit in the state—ten states!"

The saddle carried no bags but a rifle. Red took the rifle out of the scabbard; stood it up against a rock. "Never could hit nothin' with one o' them things, nohow."

He poked Tig's guns firmly down in the scabbard.

Red mounted, starting off slowly, letting the horse walk easily, and so warmed him up for the long, hard, nearly pauseless push that was to come later. He knew the direction toward the White Rock, for that had been previously pointed out to him from the rock rim; and just as soon as he saw that the horse seemed to know all about which way he was going, Red let the reins dangle. "Go to it, Son. I may be smart, but I never did pertend to have horse sense!"

When they came to White Rock, Red dangled the reins loosely, shaking them without the least guidance, and clucked, but he kept spurs away from the horse's side, thereby letting it know that it was expected to choose its own way. The horse put forward its ears, put out its nose, interested, and with no hesitation at all—having come in over the trail but a few hours before—turned left, climbed, twisted, and ten minutes later stopped at the spring to drink.

"Yes'r," said Red, patting the neck, "me, I'm a smart feller, hoss. I got me the good judgment to let you use yourn. Now I reckon we climb through some brush."

The horse, unchecked by rein, untouched by spur, went on, pushing through brush and under limbs that nearly raked the sleepy Red from out the saddle. On they went, climbing slowly, at a walk, with Red lying forward in the saddle, not dozing so much as trying to, and rather hazily reviewing the happenings of the last few days, which already seemed much like a confused dream or rather nightmare.

"Me, range foreman of the old Double X! Gosh A'mighty, luck is shore queer! I guess my boss'll be Walt Rodman. Le's see. Me, a foreman, I'll get between sixty and eighty a month—and a lot o' cussin's. An' foremans have to be silent, watchful fellers. They don't have much fun."

At dawn Red stared about at unfamiliar landmarks and wondered where the devil he was.

"Hoss, I don't know where the hell we are. But you do. So keep goin', Son. Keep goin'! But dang yore soul if you dare take me out to the ranch instead of to town!"

The horse did keep going. Red sat fretfully in the saddle. He was afraid to lope, because a loping horse might not follow its own sense of direction.

They went on, on and on. Red felt almost drunk from lack of sleep and rubbed a little tobacco in the corners of his eyes. It hurt and made him cuss, and for a while his eyes watered, but it helped him keep awake. Keeping awake on a slow horse when a fellow is sleepy is pretty hard work. He smoked gloomily, staring at the country, all unknown to him; and he wondered how Mister Dunham and Walt were making out, and half regretted that he had left them.

Then, looking down, he saw tracks. He had looked down before but had not noticed tracks. He piled off the horse with a bound, comparing the hoof prints, and was reassured when he knew that the horse was doubling back on its own tracks.

Red put his cheek against the horse's velvet nose. This horse, too, was suspicious, nervously jerky, about any move near its head.

"Don't worry, Son. Tig Burns ain't goin' to wallop many more horses over the head. No, ner no other damn man while I got somethin' to say about running the Double X. A man as will hit a hoss will hit a woman, an' a feller that'll hit a woman oughta be drugged by the heels over all the cactus patches 'tween here an' hell." Red gently rubbed the horse's cheeks. "Son, I'm goin' to have me some praises sung by fellers for findin' my way out in the dark an' bee-linin' for town—an' all you'll get is some extra oats. Pervidin' you keep your mouth shut an' don't let on to folks as it was you done it!"

He mounted, feeling greatly refreshed and

eager. Gently he put the horse into a trot, then a canter, then let it walk, trotted again, cantered, then a harder lope. And on and on, on. Red dozed a little, awakened startled, looked about, meditated, and presently entertained himself with reflections and comments.

"Tig Burns, he was onct a baby, an' I bet looked cute suckin' on his big toe!—If he'd died young, folks maybe 'ud allus 'a' thought Wally was a nice boy—which shows the advantage of dyin' young f'r some people!—Gosh, what will Billy an' Tom Jones say to find out they got to come to *me* to get hired for the Double X!—An' maybe I'll get to kiss the bride at Walt Rodman's weddin'! But to be real hones' with myself, I bet I'm scairt to—she's so gosh-blame purty! I don't get scairt at all when a girl ain't purty—I wonder why that is?"

Before noon Red saw familiar, or at least remembered, landmarks.

Then he began to ride hard, yet not hard enough to punish the horse. He even paused and two or three times, unsaddled, letting the horse breathe freely before he refolded the sweaty blanket.

It was near sundown when Red sighted Martinez in the distance.

"We been a long time, Son. 'Tain't your fault. I don't think you've quite got the speed of the hammerhead, but you shore have got stayin' power."

He rode fast, pushing the horse hard, apologizing with, "You c'n go to the barn, get fed, and sleep—but me, I'll have to climb another hoss an' start right off back. Now what's comin'?"

He saw dust flying above a low gray ridge on ahead of him. Men were coming. How many? Red looked about and quickly pulled off the road, watching. Two riders topped the ridge, riding hard.

Red mounted again and got back on the road, going slowly at an easy trot. The hazy shadows of twilight had begun to fall in the distance, and the far-off mountains lay banked in deep purplish darkness.

"I wonder, am I in for some ruckus? No, I ain't!" he answered himself firmly. "I'm tired o' ruckuses. Peace an' some quiet, that's my natural desires."

Red strained his eyes in the gathering darkness to see if he could recognize either of these men. He could not, but he did not feel that either of them was Burns. They seemed too tall in the saddle, not chunky enough. Red pulled his own hat low. They were coming at a gallop. He went on at a trot.

As they flung up their hands, drawing rein sharply to stop their galloping horses, Red tugged slightly, stopping the horse. Plainly they did not know him, since they did not act suspicious; but Red, not wanting trouble, drew both guns.

"Poke some holes in the sky—'r try to! Up with 'em!"

The men in amazement lifted their arms, glaring surlily.

"'S all right," he reassured them. "I'm just takin' a little precaution to have no trouble with you boys. I got a little piece to speak, an' I don't want no excitement. Now, me, I'm Red Clark o' Tulluco an'—"

"You got through!" one blurted in simple astonishment.

"An' a-comin' to town!" the other gasped.

"Was you-all thinkin' some of ridin' back up there?" Red inquired carelessly.

They did not answer, but frowned stubbornly.

"My good gosh!" Red spoke wearily. "You fellers got bad manners not to talk back when you're spoke to! Now, I don't like tellin' folks what I'm goin' do. Sort o' gives 'em the 'vantage. But I'll tell you somethin', both o' you. I'm a heap li'ble to spill you outa them saddles sudden—me bein' nervous—if you don't answer questions."

They seemed to think that he meant it. Red went on:

"Now, who are you?"

"Double X men," said one.

"Where was you goin'?"

"Word come Wally had you an' Rodman cornered up yonder," said the other.

"Who brought it?" Red asked. These men were

wearing only one gun apiece. Tig Burns's bunch rode with two.

"Tig Burns."

"I 'spicioned that. But why only you two ridin'? Where's other folks?"

"Everybody as could climb a horse is out lookin' for you!"

"F'r Mister Dunham's body, too!" said the other.

"For *what?*" Red shouted.

"Folks figgered you took 'im off an' killed 'im. Then was pullin' out o' the country!"

"Folks is bad at figgerin'," said Red, disgusted. "You mean there ain't nobody there in town now?"

"Nobody much when we rode out. Tig's there, waitin' for folks. When we rode in just now he told us to make a start."

Red reflected that if Tig thought Dunham was dead, he was also sure that Wally and the bunch would wipe out Red and Walt—therefore, him and Wally just naturally already owned the Double X!

"Are you boys some special friends o' Tig's?" Red inquired mildly.

"No, we ain't!" one answered quickly.

"But we're some special friends o' Mister Dunham!" said the other with firmness.

"Was either o' you in the Silver Dollar that night when I interduced myself to folks?"

"Nope. But we heard."

"Heard how I yanked Tig's guns out when he wasn't lookin' an' walloped 'im? That it?" Red asked.

"We heard, yes."

"Well, I never done no such thing! But I reckon Tig must've said he'd kill anybody as told I took his guns when he *was* lookin'! I could tell you a lot more truth, but it wouldn't do you any good, 'cause you wouldn't believe it. F'r instance, what'd you say if I told you men me an' Mister Dunham was friends, an' I'd sort o' helped him find out who was stealin' his cows and was up to some other meannesses? What'd you say, hunh?"

They did not answer, put peered distrustfully.

"The same bein' one Tig Burns an' Wally Dunham themselves!" Red added.

The two punchers looked at each other, but said nothing.

"Maybe you've had some suspicions similar, hunh?" Red suggested encouragingly.

No answer.

"Wally, he hired a feller in Californy to steal some sheriff letter paper an' write that letter about Rodman," Red explained.

"Ain't above 'im!" said one.

"We don't like Wally," said the other. "Never did. Most folks don't."

"Listen," Red continued. "You an' me are strangers, an' I don't blame you boys f'r bein' mighty suspicious of me. I'd be too in your places. I got to talk fast, 'cause it's beginnin' to get dark. But here's some facts—"

Red told the story, cutting the corners on detail and talking fast.

When he finished he asked hopefully, "You believe me?"

"Sort o' halfway, yes," said one.

"We don't put nothin' much above Tig," said the other.

"Ner Wally," the first added.

"Then listen to me. I suspicion you boys wanta do what's right. Well, me, I do too. I guess maybe you don't wanta trust me—much. But I'm a heap anxious for to trust you. The way you spoke up sort o' pointed about bein' special friends o' Mister Dunham when you didn't know my feelin's makes me right willin' to wanta like you, both of you. Now, me, I don't guess wrong often on a man or horse bein' good leather—though I'm a heap more acc'rate on horses than men. They ain't got so much natural cussedness in 'em. Now, lookee here, you boys—" Red was feeling about for the paper bag on which Dunham had written—"I'm goin' let you read this here."

Red rode up to one of the men and held it out, keeping one gun in his hand but not leveled. Both his eyes, however, were carefully peeled for any flicker of suspicious movement from either man.

He felt, in fact, he knew, that no man or any two men could draw and shoot more quickly than he, with gun already out, could shoot; and for all that he was trying to be fair, plausible, peaceful, he was dangerously on edge, pretty frazzled from excitement and fatigue, with nerves strained to near the snapping point.

"It's gettin' a little dark," Red went on. "Strike yourself some matches, if you can't see—but be sure to take yore matches out o' your vest pocket! Don't go reachin' for 'em—an' don't try to strike 'em on the seat o' yore britches!"

The man did not use matches. He had good clear eyes and held the paper up and a little to one side to catch the fading light. After a moment his eyes got the focus and he read aloud, slowly, stumbling a bit over Jake Dunham's handwriting, but making out the words all right:

"Dear Sheriff, Just so you'll know I'm writing this of my own free will, I'll say something only you and me knows about, the same being when is white chips worth more than blue? Everything is all right between you and me again. As big a fool as I've been I can't much blame you for being sometimes one too. Just so you'll know how much my feelings about things is changed, I am telling you that I am making Red Clark my range foreman. I

293

find he is the son of my old friend Dan Clark of Tulluco. He will give you facts. You'd better believe 'em or I'll raise hell. Don't you dare try to explain to me afterwards that you thought Red was lyin'. You believe what he tells you no matter how crazy it sounds. Your friend, Jake."

"Sounds a little like Jake awright," said the man who had listened.

"Some," said the other, handing the note back to Red.

"Now, will you boys promise to ride in with me to town?" Red asked. "If you've got the sense God give a goose you'll see I'm honest to be a-doin' it—when I could plug you, here an' now, if I wasn't! I wanta meet Tig an' then wait for the sheriff an' folks to come, myself. You ain't takin' no chanct on me, but I am willin' for to take a hell of a big one on *you!*"

"Sure!" said the man who had read the letter.

"You bet!" said the other. "Nothin' could be fairer than that."

"Come on, then." Red was tired, dead tired, and his head did not feel very clear. One notion was crowding his thoughts hard: Tig Burns was right there in town, and he was going in and settle things. These seemed honest boys; they were friendly to Mister Dunham, which was about all

Red asked of any man just then. He thrust his gun into his holster.

"Pardner, you jus' dropped your letter, there," said the man who had read it.

Red looked down, leaned from the saddle, peering.

"Put 'em up, feller!" came the sharp order from the man who had just lied about the letter having fallen. "I halfway think you may be truthful, but me, I don't take no chances on *you!* We'll ride right along back an' let you talk to Tig!"

Red, stung into full wariness, saw all in a flash that only the one man had drawn. The other, having given his word, apparently had not thought of breaking it. Red was always stubborn about putting his hands up. He knew that to be taken in for a talk with Tig was just the same as being put before a firing squad. He answered deceptively:

"Sure thing!"

He slowly lifted his arms and at the same time drew both toe-tips from the stirrups.

"Now, come a-ridin' along in front o' me!" the man commanded.

Red, with a sudden backward fling, went right out of the saddle in a practised somersault, one hand pulling at his gun in the air. An astonished oath was shortened by the sound of the shot as the man with the drop fired and missed at ten feet.

Red struck the ground on his feet, but the jolt of landing and the instinct to crouch sent him forward, knees-down, with one gun uptilted and the other coming clear of its holster. Bullets crossed with smoky red spurts gleaming in the gathering dusk. Red jerked his head sidewise as if slapped—the lead seemed that close to his ear. But the man was half knocked from the saddle, and in falling jerked at his horse with involuntary upward fling of his left arm; then he reeled forward and slid off slowly, head first, and lay motionless at the feet of his horse.

Red peered up at the second man, who sat motionless, with hands up, looking down at the two leveled guns.

"What's the matter with you?" Red's voice was waspish, almost a savage jeer. "Don't you wanta take no part in the doin's?"

"I give you my word, feller!" He spoke firmly, not explaining, just stating how he felt. "I'm s'prised Joe Johnson broke his thataway!"

Red, alert with distrust, eyed the man. "Well, I ain't!" he snapped. "Chance f'r to make himself a repytation was just a little too much for what honesty he had. 'Tis with most men. Gosh darn, old Jake was right! Who the hell is to be trusted in this here world? What's yore name?"

"Slim Ford."

"All right. Get off an' look at yore pardner. I hope he ain't quite dead, but I ain't got much hope."

"He's no pardner o' mine. I ain't knowed him long. But I never thought he'd brcak his word when he could see you was playin' square."

"How you know I was playin' square? Maybe I'm clever'n I look an' was lyin'? Maybe I got some aces up my sleeves, hunh?"

"If you'd wanted to plug us there wasn't nothin' holdin' you back. An' besides, me, f'r one, when I promise somethin' I stick. I promised to go back with you to town. I'd rather be laughed at for a fool than knowed f'r a liar!"

"All right, Slim. Your wages is raised! Me, bein' foreman for a spell, good men ain't goin' be underpaid. An' you ain't goin' to be laughed at— not on my account. Get off an' take a look—" Red gestured.

Slim got off, went up to Johnson, knelt down, then straightened up, dusting at his knees. "He's dead." Slim began to roll a cigarette and spoke meditatively. "I reckon he thought maybe—I don't know what the damn fool thought!—but maybe he figgered you was lyin' an' Tig there in town would pat him on the back. He sort o' bootlicks Tig."

"Yeah. I reckon Tig's boots, they have bcen pretty well shined thataway?"

"Some. Me, I like old Jake. Me an' him allus get on. He's got his faults, an' I got mine. Jake's honest. By God, you c'n stand for a lot o' faults when a man's that! I wouldn't give ten cents a carload lot for fellers like Wally. No good on earth 'cept to cut up f'r cat-meat—an' I don't like cats!"

Red grinned wearily.

"As f'r you," Slim added, taking a match from his vest pocket and lighting it on his sleeve as he looked straight at Red, "any fool c'd see as how a man that made a bargain like you offered us just had to be playin' square."

"I hoped so," said Red. "That's how I figgered. Usual, I'm not so bad at figgerin', either. But how come I ain't met nobody—if ever'body's ridin' out f'r me?"

"Mostly they've been pokin' about f'r Jake's body, sure you killed 'im. They didn't figger you could travel fast enough to suit yore hurry if you had to lug Jake along. An' that there friend o' yourn, Billy, he sort o' whispered confidential-like in the sheriff's ear that you was sure to be headin' down Tulluco way. An' that there Tom Jones he acted outa his head an' talked too, some way. I guess them friends o' yourn an' a fox was raised off the same tit."

"Slim, I bet you are sort o' goin' to like them boys. Climb yore hoss. We're on our way."

"How about him?" Slim gestured toward the body there in the dust.

"He can stay there till I get some personal affairs straightened out. He done what made him have to get shot. If he was alive—but he ain't. Come on."

CHAPTER XVI

"Damned Ol' Angel in Disguise"

It was about three miles to town.

Red rode along in silence, and Slim Ford was not talkative. As they drew near they looked ahead and saw the main street crowded with horses and the shadows of men moving about and in and out of saloon doorways.

"The sheriff an' them musta just rode in," Slim guessed.

"Listen," said Red. "We're goin' stop here at one of these Mexican's houses. 'N I'm goin' to send word to the sheriff f'r to come an' see a fellow as can give him news. To come alone. That there is purt-near the plan I had all along. I got to persuade 'im first, then—"

"I'll go myself an' bring 'im," Slim offered.

Red eyed him broodingly, then nodded. "I'll risk it. But don't you tell him who ner what. Un'erstand? An' bring him alone. I may have some trouble arguin' with him, but I'll offer him a bargain he can't refuse. I'll agree to ride right along back up to the mountains with him an' his men. He *can't* turn that down, now, can he?"

"I'll be glad to help you persuade 'im he can't," said Slim. "Nothin' could be fairer than that."

Slim put spurs to horse and galloped off.

Red turned into the lighted doorway of a small adobe and called out in Spanish. A small old man came to the door, followed by the family.

"Señor," said Red, "may I stop here until a friend comes for a talk with me?"

The little old man gazed up at Red, bowed politely, swept his hand with the gesture of a prince offering entrance to his castle.

"Yes, señor," the old man replied. "God sends the traveller! And you, señor, you are not Spanish?"

"No, but I learned it before English," said Red.

The Mexicans eyed him apprehensively as they saw him draw two other revolvers from the rifle scabbard.

"Don't get scairt," said Red in English. "These here are just keepsakes that I pack around for good luck! Here—" he took money from his pocket and offered it to a boy—"please, my friend"—Spanish again—"take my horse around back of the house, let him drink, and loosen the saddle."

Red went into the house. It was a one-room adobe, and not clean. Supper was steaming on the fire with a strong smell of chili in the air. Red sat down wearily, stiff, tired, exhausted, but not hungry. Fatigue kept his stomach from remembering that it had not been fed. He drank lukewarm water.

The Mexicans eyed the guns that he had called "keepsakes," not knowing what the word meant, but reassured by the tone. Guns that wouldn't shoot, perhaps.

They had given Red the only chair in the house. The others used stools and boxes. They invited him to the table. He explained with his best effort at courtesy that he must wait for his friend, at which the children exchanged glances of alarm, having in mind that the pot had not been filled for guests.

The sheriff came, excited and curious, walking brusquely through the door, offering no word of greeting to the household.

At the sight of Red he stopped as if knocked under the chin, jerking up his head, gazed for one incredulous moment, then both hands automatically swung toward his hips.

Slim Ford, entering behind the sheriff, caught at his arm as Red, sitting, lifted one of Tig Burns's guns from the floor where he had laid them and arose.

The Mexicans shifted backwards with startled squeaks, and the sheriff dropped his hands, then in silence began to lift his arms over his shoulders as he said with a reproachful oath, "Slim Ford, I never thought it o' you!"

"Wait an' listen!" said Slim laconically.

"Nobody's told you to put yore hands up, sheriff," said Red with weary patience. "But you try to take my guns off me, an' there'll be a new sheriff in hell—where he's needed most bad, from all reports! Now, here—" he offered the note written on the paper bag—"you read this. Then try to figger if I look fool enough to come to town thisaway 'less I'm playin' square!"

The sheriff, in pretty much of a daze, read. He looked up at Red with a stare of blank amazement. He looked down at the paper again and turned it over.

"I reckon," he began doubtfully, "there's somethin'—*somethin'* to this. Old Jake has made me see he's wrote of his own free will. That there joke has to do with votes. Some folks in this here county as think themselves blue chips was sort of against me. Jake he said, 'White chips beat blues if they's enough of 'em.' Now what's what? Where is Jake an'—"

Red told him. The sheriff stood amazed, not wanting to believe, yet somehow convinced against his will. He had Jake Dunham's note and its warning that he had better believe whatever Red said.

Slim Ford, from the doorway, looked on, listening, had Jake Dunham's note and its warning that he had guessed right in playing Red for a square fellow.

"God—Tig an' Wally!" said the sheriff. "Tig Burns!" He seemed shuddering just a little at the thought that it was, or was soon to be, his duty to arrest Tig. "Many folks ain't goin' to believe this here"—he shook the piece of paper bag thoughtfully. "We got to go slow an'—"

"We're goin' fast!" Red retorted. "I ain't had no sleep since the devil was a yearlin', seems like; but we're ridin' tonight an' startin' now!"

"Men are tired, an' fresh horses scarce, but I'll see what—"

There was the sudden sound of hoofs on the road, and a lone rider came plunging toward town from the same direction that Red and Slim had ridden in.

"Can that be Johnson come to life?" Slim exclaimed. "Must be!"

"Go stop 'im an' scc!" said Red. "See who 'tis!"

Slim jumped to his horse, rode into the road, and stood there, barring the way with hand up, waving.

"Hey you, Joe?" he called as if half thinking he was shouting at a ghost. "Joe Johnson?"

"I ain't no Joe Johnson by a hell of a sight!" the horseman shouted, reining up. "He's dead back there in the road. An' ol' Jake's comin'—comin'—not ten mile behind. Mad as a hornet an'—"

"My gosh!" Red squeaked. "That's Hollar's voice—crazy—blessed—" Then from the doorway he called, "Hey, you damned ol' angel in disguise! Ride up here an' drop off! Go buy yoreself some skirts—I'll marry you! That's how I feel how much I owe you!"

"I'll be hornswoggled an' gosh dinged if it ain't Red! Ol' Jake's scairt plumb into a wild temper that somepin happen to you! An' the sheriff—Jake sent me on ahead f'r to see *you!*"

Hollar slid from his horse and shook Red's hands with both of his, pumping as if at a cistern with the house on fire. He simply blubbered incoherent fragments of sentences in the explosive eagerness to tell all his news at once; and, not being very intelligent at any time, was now hopelessly rattlebrained.

They all crowded into the one-room adobe with the Mexicans wide-eyed in uneasy amazement; for, though it is very well known among Spanish-speaking people that all gringoes are mad, yet the lanky Red, who had seemed a little different, and the imposing sheriff, too, now acted as crazy as the others in snapping questions at Hollar, in pulling and tugging at him.

After he got his speech into something like coherence, Hollar told them:

"Right after you got away, Red, Wally kep' bawlin' at you, wantin' for to talk. Ol' Jake, he couldn't stand it no longer. So he bellered back. He told it all—with the trimmin's. Well, sir, Wally was so scairt he—well, you know what some fellers do when they get plumb bad scairt, sudden! Then they was hell a-poppin' right.

Them fellers knowed they just had to kill the Old Man! An' they started in tryin'. Jake's shore hard to kill. He had his dander up an' enjoyed his self proper! You bet! Ol' Jake's awright. I jus' misunderstood 'im all these here years. He says that me, I can have anything—"

"To hell with all that!" said the sheriff. "What happened?"

"Uh? Oh. Why, y'see, when Red here an' Walt an' them boys come to town yesterday—'r whenever it was—you know what I mean? So much has happened I can't quite remember straight. But, anyhow, when the boys rode over to Dod Wilson's, the fellers up there at the cabin, they went back over to their diggin's—all of us went along 'spectin' to be back 'fore sundown— but, gee gosh! you never seen such a mess! Harry's burros was in the house like bride an' groom—settin' up housekeepin' 'r wreckin'! Chickens was out—mostly et up! An' wors' of all—"

"Tell us *what happened!*" the sheriff thundered, almost frantic.

"Well, ain't I, dammit! fast as I kin! Now—"

"Get back to old Jake!" said Red.

"Oh, him. Well, we was late startin' back from Harry's, but after we begun to hear shootin' we hustled, an' we come down on them fellers without askin' nary a question! No, sir! Jus' figgered our friends was in the cabin an'—"

"Never mind what you figgered! Get on, get on!" Red coaxed.

"Them that could still set a saddle, they jumped fork-legged. Wally lit out lickety-split down the trail—we found 'im with his head busted wide open on a rock where his horse fell. He's so damn dead he won't even wake up Judgment Day, I bet! Them other fellers—I don't know—I found Joe Johnson back yonder a piece on the road, but I don't know what happened to—"

"Stick to old Jake!" Red begged.

"Oh, say! When he opened the cabin door an' says, 'Howdy, boys!' you could 'a' knocked me over with a feather—pinfeather—outa wren bird! We all jus' stood an' acted like we had lockjaw, with our mouths open! Walt he was purt-near all in, but he talked, an' us fellers—old Jake said to us fellers he'd been a damn fool but was plumb cured, permanent! Nothin' 'ud do Jake but to make a start. He's back there apiece, an' I come on. He's powerful worried about you, Red. Gosh ding, he thinks you are the greatest boy that ever—"

"He's just had bad luck in not knowin' many nice folks. Got his ears twisted by listenin' to Wally an' Tig."

"Well, I guess we'd better ride out an' meet Jake, hadn't we?" the sheriff suggested.

"The first ridin' you do is up to wherever you've got my sidekicks," Red snapped. "Turn 'em loose. Ask 'em to 'cept yore 'pologies—kiss

306

their big toes 'r somepin! An' me—where is Tig Burns? What place? Silver Dollar, ain't he?"

"We'll sure round Tig up!" said the sheriff. "He was up to the Dollar, an' I'll—"

"You go turn my friends loose. Get a mattress 'r somepin an' have Tom carried over to the nicest room in the hotel, an' get a couple o' folks to wait on 'im till I come. I got business up the street apiece. Slim, you an' Hollar here, who is shore my mascot, can go along with me, if you want!"

"We'll all go up together!" said the sheriff. "An' I'll—"

"All right, then, but listen first. I'm goin' up to the Silver Dollar an' kill Tig Burns. With his own guns. Wearin' his own spurs. Ridin' his own horse. Usin' his own bullets. He shot my Dad—an' Walt Rodman's!"

"No!" exclaimed the sheriff incredulously.

"Did, too! Admitted it. So'f you've got any sheriffied notions about stoppin' me, speak up now!"

"Don't try it, Red! I'm askin' you like a—like a friend. If ol' Jake knowed—when he learns I ever let you try that, he'd—we'd have a fallin' out shore! So—"

"Listen," Red commanded. "Don't argy with me. 'F I don't do it—or try—I'll never have grit enough to meet a lookin' glass face to face again. No, sir! I'm goin'. Some things has got to be done, an' them kind I up and do!"

Red prodded the shells from Burns's gun, one by one, examining them. There were five shells in one, six in the other. Dumdums. Burns, like many gunmen, and like Red himself—though Red would not admit that he was a gunman—carried the chambers full. The half cock was protection enough against accidents.

With a quizzical glance at Hollar, Red then peered through the muzzle of each gun—making sure it wasn't plugged up. "Hollar," he said, "you are shore my lucky piece! From now on, 'f anybody ever steps on yore toes, it's me that'll yell *ouch!* That's how I feel about you!"

And Hollar, used to being bullied and teased and insulted by men, beamed and wriggled with pleasure. Red was the tophole man in the country right now. Old Jake had made it plain that no long-lost son would have meant as much to him as Red Clark; and poor old Hollar, who hadn't had a real friend in years, felt as proud as if the Governor had invited him to dinner.

Red handed over his own guns to Hollar, saying, "Take care of 'em for me. They are *honest* guns, an' I'll want 'em back when the smoke clears away."

One by one he then rammed Tig Burns's guns into his holsters, pulling each out and thrusting it back three or four times, getting the feel, seeing how they sat.

Then Red, hat in hand, approached the old

Mexican, who stood with his timid children behind him.

"Señor, my friends ask me to thank you," he lied, "and your lovely daughter"—the daughter was fat, looked forty, and had a half-dozen children—"for the use of your convenient home in holding our conference. The señor sheriff considers himself in your debt"—the sheriff understood Spanish and gasped—"and will always be pleased to show you favor if any of your friends should ever have the misfortune to be misunderstood. And as for myself, Red Clark, range foreman of the Double X, count on me as your friend. Now, if the young señor will bring our horses, we shall say good-bye."

The sheriff, half grinning, said aside to Red, "What a lie!"

" 'Tain't," Red answered instantly. " 'Tain't never a lie if you say something you oughta say."

They left the house in the midst of bows and blessings, with all the Mexican youngsters clutching pieces of silver, which the elders would soon more or less forcibly appropriate.

Some people in various parts of the cow country wondered why it was that when Red rode, shot, or roped in any of the contests, that scores of Mexicans went broke if he didn't win—and mad when he did.

CHAPTER XVII

Tiger Burns

"I think," said the sheriff, meditative and solemn, with the bridle in one hand and a piece of chewing tobacco that he eyed as if critically in the other, "that me, I'd better find me some business elsewhere. I hate to see you do it, Son. You're a smart boy, but Tig is lightnin' an' trickier than hell! I ain't argyin'! I'm jus' explainin'. An' come to think, if I'm anywhere near present, ol' Jake is liable f'r to misunderstand an' think me, I oughta've stopped you." He took the chew, clamped down with his teeth, twisted and jerked, then spit. "I ain't meddlesome 'nough to interfere judicial. Ary man as packs a gun an' is shot square deserves it. But you're shore crowdin' yore good luck."

"Don't b'lieve 'im, Red!" said Hollar, with an air of proprietary friendship. "I know what you c'n do! I seen you do it!"

Red answered neither of them. The sheriff wanted to stand and talk some more, less hopeful, perhaps, of being persuasive than of delaying Red until Jake Dunham, known to be not far from town, could come along the road.

Red swung into the saddle. Slim Ford was

already waiting. Hollar, with fumbling haste and a yell of "Hey, wait!" scrambled onto his horse.

They rode fast. For some reason cowboys always rode fast in town. They come at a jog trot and walk for twenty miles to end in a burst of frantic speed.

As they neared the windmill Red lifted his eyes and grinned a little. He poked Tig Burns's horse with Tig Burns's silver spurs; then, with sidelong glance, gave the Chinese restaurant a shadowy grin. His face sobered as he touched first one then the other of Tig Burns's guns, just making sure they were still there.

The hitch rack before the Silver Dollar was crowded.

Red rode near the sidewalk and flung away the reins. Men were there, talking excitedly, some wondering what had become of the sheriff.

As Red stepped onto the sidewalk someone recognized him:

"My gosh—there! That's *him!*"

Red paused, settling back on his heels, running his eyes over their amazed and uncertain faces.

Slim Ford pushed in before Red, facing the men. "Out o' the way, hombres! This is a man's game! This boy's in the clear—an' me, I say so!"

Old Hollar, with a shambling rush, came up, blubbering news. Men heard, not understanding, and gazed incredulous. But they did understand Slim Ford. He was laconic and not sociable. But a man to be trusted. He pushed at them with a sweeping arm, and they gave way, staring.

Then one blurted as he saw Red make for the door, "Great God! Tig's in there an'—"

"He knows it!" Hollar yelped. "That's why he's goin' in!"

The Silver Dollar was well filled with men who had ridden hard all that day and were thirsty. Voices rang in a babbling clatter.

Nearly all were grouped at the long bar, with ten to a dozen or more huddled in one bunch, listening to Tig Burns.

Two bartenders with sweat on their faces busily shoved bottles, jerked away glasses, dipping them in buckets of stale water, and sent them scooting again. Spurs jingled as men shifted their feet restlessly. A thin gray mist of tobacco smoke floated about overhead.

As he entered, Red, without a pause, pushed his hat well up, back on his head. He took two long strides, raking the heavy spurs over the floor, then stopped abruptly, standing still, waiting.

Men with hurried tiptoe-sidling rushes came in behind him and moved quickly to the far side of the room or paused near tables and stood with knees half bent, ready to duck low.

A sort of feeling of hush began to settle over the men near the doorway—the kind of uneasy stillness that makes folk wonder and think of a coming storm.

The men at the bar began to look about, vaguely nervous and wondering. Even those who had never seen Red before took one staring glance at him, then jerked themselves up and went with skittering stride for corners, walls, and the end of the long bar. It was on his face, in his attitude, in the way he waited, just as plainly as if he had shouted that he had come there to kill or be killed.

Some of the men recognized him and seemed dumbfounded, or with a kind of blurting gasp mumbled half-spoken things, mystified.

"Why, what—what—*here!*"

"My God, it's *him!*"

"—doin' *here?*"

"Tig—kill 'im sure!"

"Outa my way—I want a corner!"

"That shore as hell is *him!*"

Red's eyes did not move from where he knew Tig Burns was standing.

Splutters of amazement reached Tig as peering faces and heads on far-twisted necks in a second's gaze recognized Red and instantly knew by the look of him what was up.

Men flung themselves aside hastily, for when other fellows are killing snakes it is no loss of dignity to get out of the way fast.

Both bartenders got up near the doorway end of the bar; and though one went on nervously rubbing at a clean glass with a wet towel, the other got down low, just peering over. He had no respect at all for the range tradition that a proper bartender never ducks.

One fellow, perhaps a little drunk, gaped at Red and started to reach for a gun, but Slim Ford struck his arm, pushed him, said, "Keep outa this! He's in the clear!" Slim Ford's eyes roved challenging as he added, "Me, I say so!"

And so Tig Burns, dark of face and muscularly chunky, with straight black hair hanging low on his cheeks, was left standing alone, elbow on the bar, and a glass of whisky between his fingers. His left arm dangled loose, palm back. His black eyes gleamed in a steady stare, and a sort of pin-prick of surprise was on his face. But the only visible move he made was to lean a little toward the bar and, without lifting his elbow, halfway casually push up his hat, setting it back on his coal-black head. But all the while his left hand with imperceptible slowness—slow as the crawl of a snail—moved back and back, sneaking the draw.

He knew, for he knew all of the tricks, had studied them as a gambler studies cards, that Red could not notice such delicate long-drawn stealth while Red's eyes met his own in an unwavering challenging stare. And if Red's eyes wavered, he, in half a second, would be a dead man.

Tig grinned, forced the grin, bluffing. It was his feeling that the boy was scared. Tig was used to having men scared when they stood before him. Also he was used to scaring them more by letting the seconds tick as he eyed them, or spoke with sneering insolence. He knew it was the way of some folks to break down and nervously claw at their guns, all in a panicky hurry. Others stood frozen with mouths dry and could not speak. Tig knew all about folks that had bucked up courage to face him; and he was a tricky actor. A gunman, no more than a gambler, ever wins every time without having much art to help him along; and if Tig was fast as the best, he was also more cunning than the worst.

So Tig, having moved his hat to help keep attention away from the creeping stealth of his left hand's sneaky movement, dropped his right hand lightly to the bar, again fingering the whisky. Then, with lips drawn back much as a cat does when it snarls, he asked:

"Well, feller? What you doin' here? Want somethin'? Hunh?"

Red stood motionless with left foot slightly out, both arms hanging loose, head up and shoulders back. He knew this game, for he was gun-raised among old-timers. He knew why Tig dawdled, wanting to make him nervous, rattled, so it would be easy to sneak the jump. He knew that Tig's hand had moved with the slithering slowness of a dead thing's shadow. But Red had sworn to himself that the first break must come from Tig

Burns himself; had sworn to give Tig the jump—and then kill him. Such was Red's downright, honest range-bred faith, not in himself so much as in the belief that when you were in the right you were bound to win.

"Yes," Red answered. "I'm waitin' f'r you to start drawin'!"

"Yeah?" Burns inquired, trying to sound skeptical and contemptuous.

"You killed my Dad!" Red said it and stopped, waiting.

The words rang clear in the hushed barn-like saloon. There were challenge, threat, and vengeance promised in the tone. Motionless men, watching with fascinated intentness from the places that seemed safest, felt a tingling chill: The boy was not afraid!

Tig eyed him, eyed him with sinister patience. Tig had been through this sort of thing before—and had never lost. Killing was an art with him. Instinct helped, and a long study of gunplay. He knew when and how to wait with insolent poise until nervousness jerked the other fellow's nerves to tatters; and a watchfulness, very like instinct, made him know when to draw just a split second before the other fellow.

Yet Tig was a little puzzled. He didn't like it that Red, who seemed scarcely more than a kid, could be so tense yet seem so cool, speak clearly without nervous tightening of the throat.

He did not for an instant think that Red could beat him even fairly to the draw, and he knew no man living was a straighter shot than he; but somehow this boy had been a sort of Jonah, and Tig was hell-bent on making doubly sure this time.

"Speak up!" Tig jeered. "I c'n hardly hear your voice. Sort o' weak-like an' squeaky. I'll move up a little closter. Hear better."

He moved with cat-like stealth, keeping an elbow on the bar, the whisky in his fingers.

"Now what was it you got to say?" Tig sneered.

"You killed ol' Rodman too!"

No answer from Tig. Just the hot steady look from glittering black eyes.

"You an' Wally had a liar write from Californy—"

Pause. No answer.

"—sayin' Walt Rodman'd been in prison."

Tig did not speak nor move.

"Said you an' Wally meant to kill old Jake—get the ranch!"

Burns took even all that as if untroubled, and waited. What Red said would mean nothing when Red lay dead. Tig could sweep all that aside with one word, "Liar!"

But at that moment, to Tig's utter astonishment, Red grinned with a wry down-twisted half sneer of lips, adding:

"An' old Jake Dunham, he was up overhead

on the rafters there in the cabin an' heard ever' word! He's comin' now!"

That hit and hurt, but Tig took it with only a startled flinch of eyelids; but he knew now was the time to kill—then cut and run. He wanted no more words out of this boy.

Tig, the tricky, who at such a close distance could not have missed even if blindfolded, turned his head a little and called across the room, "Hey, fellers, you hear this bleatin' f'r—"

Then it happened. Speaking with face slightly averted to deflect Red's attention, Tig, with outward-lunging swing of his right hand, threw whisky, glass and all, at Red; then, at the same time with a twitching upward pull of his left wrist, swung his gun out of the holster—and died before its hammer fell.

As the whisky came at him, Red threw back his head and, with one motion, rose to his tiptoes and swayed backwards. Every nerve and muscle flashed its strength in the quick pull to snap those sight-filed gun muzzles clear of their holsters. They came with a blaze in their mouths—both of them. They roared as one gun, explosively.

And Tig Burns, the deadly, shot through the heart with his own split-nosed slugs, dropped dead. His legs simply crumpled under him, and he sank as wet canvas falls, and lay in a huddle.

No word was spoken. Men held their breath, peering through powder smoke that with slow waverings drifted upward, languidly. They had seen but could not believe. This boy, face to face at four paces, had taken every trick that Tig Burns knew, had given him the jump—and killed him.

Red stood as if amazed and still suspicious. His smoking guns with uptilted butts hung as if watchful of the dead man—as though this downward-crumpling slump of body with gun unfired might be but another trick.

Then Red stirred. He lifted one gun slightly, gazing at it, looking at the undercut file notches of the barrel. One of them perhaps stood for his own father. With light toss of hand he dropped the gun near Burns's body. The other gun followed, clattering on the bare floor. Red had kept his oath and was through with the killer's guns.

Then, with rapid jangle of spurs and a thumping stride, like the stamp of a stallion, a great, ponderous, shadow-dimmed shape crossed the doorway sidewalk and bulked motionless in the wide doorway.

Red spun about, facing Jake Dunham.

"What—what—I told you—where is *he?*" Dunham bellowed, his anxiety taking on the full-throated sound of rage. "I told you not to try it!"

Red stepped aside and pointed. He said nothing, but grinned a little nervously, like a youngster caught at something forbidden.

| Books are produced in the United States using U.S.-based materials | Books are printed using a revolutionary new process called THINKtech™ that lowers energy usage by 70% and increases overall quality | Books are durable and flexible because of smythe-sewing | Paper is sourced using environmentally responsible foresting methods and the paper is acid-free |

Center Point Large Print

600 Brooks Road / PO Box 1
Thorndike, ME 04986-0001 USA

(207) 568-3717

US & Canada:
1 800 929-9108
www.centerpointlargeprint.com